D0431082

NO END TO
TROUBLE

Previously published Worldwide Mystery titles by
MARIANNA HEUSLER

MURDER AT ST. POLYCARP
CAPPUCCINO AT THE CRYPT

NO END TO TROUBLE

TROUBLE

MARIANNA HEUSLER

WORLDWIDE®

TORONTO • NEW YORK • LONDON
AMSTERDAM • PARIS • SYDNEY • HAMBURG
STOCKHOLM • ATHENS • TOKYO • MILAN
MADRID • WARSAW • BUDAPEST • AUCKLAND

Dedicated to my dear friend Amy Bowllan

Amy and I have taught side by side for twenty years and, although we haven't solved any murders—yet—we've had our share of adventures and more than our share of fun!

Recycling programs
for this product may
not exist in your area.

No End to Trouble

A Worldwide Mystery/April 2017

First published by Hilliard Harris

ISBN-13: 978-0-373-28403-0

Copyright © 2015 by Marianna Heusler

Printed in U.S.A.

ONE

IT WAS BITTER cold and the parking lot was deserted. He thrust his hands into his pockets and he shivered. He couldn't wait to get home, to plop in front of the TV, to rip open a bag of kettle chips, to chill out.

He was unusually tired.

That wasn't a good sign. Every terminal ailment he Googled warned that the first symptom of a serious illness was being weary for no reason at all. Maybe he should take his daughter's advice and go for a complete check-up. But he knew if doctors were looking, they would always find something.

He smiled to himself as he thought of his daughter, so beautiful, so sweet. And too good for that loser boyfriend she had been seeing. He told her straight out that the guy was no good, the first argument he had with his daughter in a long time, but it was a battle worth fighting.

He heard footsteps behind him.

He stopped and saw the shadow of someone dressed in black.

He opened his mouth to ask if the person needed help, but he never uttered a word.

Instead he saw the flash of a metal object come flying towards him and hit his skull with a massive force.

He heard something crack and he tasted hot blood, as it poured into his eyes and his nose.

Then he hit the pavement.

TWO

"I CAN'T BELIEVE that Father Felix is gone," Julia Hopwood moaned to her best friend, Amelia Johnson over the phone.

Mrs. Johnston quickly agreed. "Well, it's not as if he's dead. Although it was ridiculous to send him to Rome to help out in the Vatican. What does he know about working in an office?"

"Have you heard anything about the new principal?" Mrs. Hopwood was almost afraid to ask the question, because she knew that Mrs. Johnson possessed a wealth of information, and would present it in the worst possible light.

"Her name is Mrs. Logan. She was the principal at St. Jude's before the school closed. And she's bringing her own secretary, Miss Turnipseed."

"The kids will have a great time with the name."

"I hear that she's very conservative."

"Who? Mrs. Logan or Miss Turnipseed?"

"Both of them."

Mrs. Hopwood didn't respond. Sometimes, she knew that conservative was another way of saying judgmental. Mrs. Hopwood did not like to be judged, especially where her teaching ability was concerned.

"I also heard," Mrs. Johnson paused for emphasis, "that she is looking to bring some of her own teachers with her which means…"

"Which means," Mrs. Hopwood finished the sentence, "she is looking to get rid of some of us."

"She can't get rid of us," Mrs. Johnson said firmly. "You and I are the backbone of that school. After all, we solved two murders, one at St. Polycarp and one in Sicily."

"Which might be impressive, if we were detectives."

"She'll love us," Mrs. Johnson said. "Everyone loves us."

Mrs. Hopwood didn't think this was a good time to remind her friend of the long list of enemies they had made since teaming up as teachers at St. Polycarp.

THREE

To: JuliaHopwood13@gmail.com
From: AJohnson333@aol.com
Re: New Information

Found out a few things through the grapevine...

Mrs. Logan decided to raise the tuition. She wants St. Polycarp to be the most expensive Catholic School in town. That's all fine and dandy, but what about the families who can't afford it?

She is going to be calling us on the phone to arrange for a one to one meeting before school starts in September. If I were you, I wouldn't wear your neon green dress with your hot pink spike heels. You know the outfit I mean? The one you wore to Edith Edleman's funeral. And all that Jennifer Lopez jewelry you've been collecting from Kohls? Not for the interview.

And just so you know—

She is banning all chocolate, so you can forget bribing your students with Hershey Kisses. I know that they don't have nuts in them, but she is going to argue that even chocolate that has no nuts is made on the premises with machines that come in contact with nuts. Actually all candy and sweets are frowned upon and we're not supposed to feed the students at all.

There is going to be a hair code. So you can wear your hair curly, but make sure it's in a ponytail. Head lice.

We have to be very careful of FaceBooking or twittering, or pinning, because I understand she will check all that.

Now on the interview, we both have to emphasize that we love children and want what's best for them.

We shouldn't talk too much about our personal lives. Maybe you shouldn't talk much at all. You are liable to say the wrong thing. Evidently, she has a strong moral code, doesn't approve of living together or having affairs. Luckily, for us we are clear on that front—darn it.

So just dress in black, nod your head a lot, smile, but not too much—she might think you're an idiot—and repeat over and over that you were born to be a teacher.

I will let you know when I have more details.

FOUR

To: AJohnson333@aol.com
From: JuliaHopwood13@gmail.com

She's trying to get rid of us.

FIVE

MRS. HOPWOOD WAS not looking forward to her one on one meeting with Mrs. Logan. It didn't happen often but now and then her paths crossed with women who didn't like her. Perhaps they didn't take her seriously because she wore high heels and lots of jewelry and brightly colored clothes and, sometimes—not a lot— parents would claim that Mrs. Hopwood's overstated outfits were distracting.

On the other hand, most people liked Mrs. Johnson. Well, maybe they didn't like her exactly. It was more that they were frightened of her. She was a large African-American woman, who always felt that God was on her side. She believed that firmly and so did everyone else—including the parents.

Father Felix didn't care what parents thought, and he was always on the side of the teachers.

Maybe that was why he was now in Rome.

The moment Mrs. Hopwood walked into the small school, she noticed the changes. The hall bulletin boards had been replaced with butcher block paper and the scent of musk and vanilla filled the air.

A woman wearing a navy blue pants suit with a red printed scarf was seated at the front desk, gazing at a computer, with a grave expression on her face. She didn't look up when Mrs. Hopwood stood in front of her.

So Mrs. Hopwood introduced herself and stated that she had an appointment with Mrs. Logan.

"I guess you're Miss Turnipseed." Mrs. Hopwood managed to smile.

The woman didn't return the friendly greeting. Instead she stared at Mrs. Hopwood apprehensively. Mrs. Hopwood realized then that Miss Turnipseed didn't care one iota whether or not the teachers liked her.

"I'll tell Mrs. Logan you're here," she said in a deadpan voice. She rose and disappeared into the office behind her.

Mrs. Hopwood sat in a chair in the hall. That was another thing that had been replaced. Benches used to be lined up outside the principal's office.

Mrs. Hopwood thought that this was going to be more difficult than she had ever imagined because Mrs. Hopwood really, really liked Father Felix. He had been a good friend, and advocate for both her and Amelia Johnson. Even though he was firm, he was always fair, he had a great sense of humor and being with him, even in the direst of circumstances, was always fun.

And now, everything was going to be different.

"Mrs. Logan will you see you now. Right this way."

As though she had to lead the way, as though Mrs. Hopwood hadn't taught at this school for seven years and wasn't as comfortable in Father Felix's office as she was in her second grade classroom.

Only it wasn't Father Felix's office anymore.

His mahogany desk—which had always been messy—had been replaced by a white plastic table. Except for the computer, the only thing on the desk was a bouquet of red roses. A white file cabinet stood on the side. Nothing was out of place.

"Have a seat."

Mrs. Hopwood sat down on the hard chair and kept her back as straight as a pin. She rested her heart-shaped purse on her lap. She knew by the way that Mrs. Logan stared at it that she should have brought her simple black clutch. But wasn't it enough that she was wearing her only black dress?

She studied Mrs. Logan behind the desk. She saw a middle-aged, slightly overweight woman, sporting a blonde hairdo—short and curly—that hadn't been seen since Jessica Fletcher left *Murder She Wrote*. She wore bright red lipstick, which had stained her yellowed teeth, and a non-descript brown vest over a non-descript brown and green plaid blouse.

"You don't have a resume, do you?" Mrs. Logan asked suddenly.

"A resume?" Mrs. Hopwood repeated blankly. "No. I've been teaching second grade here at St. Polycarp for seven years."

"You don't have a Masters?" Mrs. Logan asked suddenly.

"No, I don't, but I'm thinking of getting one," Mrs. Hopwood added.

Mrs. Logan stared at her with cold, blue eyes and Mrs. Hopwood knew that her lie probably destroyed all credibility.

"And you have only taught in Catholic schools?"

"Well, I practice taught at Hadley Academy in Hadley, Massachusetts."

Mrs. Logan frowned. She had evidently not heard of Hadley Academy. "Let me tell you a little bit about my plans for St. Polycarp. One of the reasons that the Bishop gave me this position was because, in the last five years, the enrollment here has really dipped. Unless we can set ourselves apart from the other Catholic Schools in the area, and the other private schools as well, St. Polycarp is in danger of closing."

Mrs. Hopwood had heard that rumor year after year.

"I intend to turn this school around, to make it more elite. The teachers are going to use cooperative and project based learning. All of our subjects will be integrated. Nothing will be taught in a vacuum. We will be teaching the writing workshop model and doing F and Ps on all of the children. This year we will be using Singapore Math. I believe firmly that we are preparing our students for the twenty-first century. Our students will go on to become movers and leaders and shakers. There will be no slacking off. I won't allow it."

Mrs. Hopwood felt as though a speech like that deserved a clap. Instead she just nodded.

"Here is your curriculum." Mrs. Logan reached inside her drawer and pulled out a beige folder.

Mrs. Hopwood opened it up slowly. Evidently, she was going to have to teach a lot of new things, invent some teacher created material, and she wasn't going to be able to resurrect her year after year lesson plans. She got no further than the first line.

"I think there is a mistake," Mrs. Hopwood said with a sharp intake of breath. "It says here that this is for the fifth grade. I teach second grade."

"Not anymore."

"But my contract…"

"Your contract states that you will be employed at St. Polycarp as a teacher for the upcoming year. It does not specify a grade level. I already hired a very competent second grade teacher and, as you know, Mrs.

Otter decided not to return to fifth grade. That's where I had an opening."

Mrs. Hopwood knew nothing about fifth grade students and, when she met them in the lunch room, she was rather afraid of them.

"Do you have any questions?"

Mrs. Hopwood could barely shake her head.

"So, I will see you then on August 28th. We will have a week of professional development meetings, before school actually opens. Of course, you are free to come in at any time to get your room ready. In the folder, you will find the perameters of how your space should look. Only student driven material should be on the walls, everything should be neat and laminated, no personal items on the desk, certainly no coffee or water. And absolutely no cell phones in the classroom. But no worries, I will be inspecting each classroom before the students arrive."

Mrs. Hopwood stood and mumbled thank you, which only elicited a nod from Mrs. Logan. Miss Turnipseed didn't even bother to look up from her computer, when Mrs. Hopwood staggered by.

"Oh one more thing," Mrs. Logan stuck her face out of the office door. "You need to know that I will be conducting a Corey Search on all of my staff. I think in this day and age, when social media has gotten out of hand, and students are at risk for predators, it's the only right thing to do."

Mrs. Hopwood mumbled that it was fine, for what else could she say? She wasn't a criminal, at least she didn't think that there would be anything incriminating in that file. One could never tell, though.

What she was thinking was that maybe, just maybe,

it was time to look for another job. Was there something else she could do?

Because clearly teaching under Mrs. Logan would not be an option.

SIX

IT WAS MRS. JOHNSON'S favorite time of the day. Her husband was working late, she had just threatened her twin boys for the tenth time, so now they were quietly tucked inside their bunk beds. She was sitting in front of the television, sipping her nightly glass of red wine.

The phone rang. Of course, it was Mrs. Hopwood, who had called her earlier in the day with instructions to phone back as soon as possible. But Mrs. Johnson wasn't able to do so. She had to take her boys to the doctor for an annual school physical then reward them by treating them to pizza, which they used as weapons, hitting each other with the crusts. So when she finally arrived home, she had to bathe them and wash their new tee-shirts.

But Mrs. Hopwood didn't understand any of this because her own boy, Alexander, was off to college and, if he had been a terror at six, she had conveniently forgotten all about it.

Nevertheless, Mrs. Johnson was very curious about Mrs. Hopwood's meeting with Mrs. Logan.

Mrs. Hopwood didn't even bother to say hello.

"Horrid. She is horrid. And she doesn't like me. I can tell. She kept staring at my handbag—"

"You didn't bring the one shaped like a toilet bowl?"

"Of course not. Besides, that's hardly the point. She brought up the fact that I don't have a Masters."

Mrs. Johnson felt her body tense, since she, herself, did not have a Masters.

"Then she told me her plans, which includes all kinds of new teaching philosophies, writing workshops, Japanese Math, F and Ps…"

"What?"

"Project based learning. I had no idea what she was talking about."

"Sounds like a lot of work to me," Mrs. Johnson grumbled as she took a gulp of wine.

"And that's not the worst of it. I am now teaching fifth grade."

"Really?" Mrs. Johnson could not contain delight. "That means you'll be right across the hall from seventh grade. We won't have to send notes down with the students or send each other texts."

"Forget about notes and texts. We are not allowed to use our cell phones at all. Or drink water or enjoy coffee in our classrooms, which must be decorated to Mrs. Logan's specifications. I looked over the fifth grade curriculum. I don't know anything about geometry!" she wailed.

"I'll help you," Mrs. Johnson said without too much conviction because she was still feeling very uncomfortable about all the changes. Still Mrs. Hopwood was known to be dramatic.

And as if Mrs. Hopwood could read her mind—and maybe she could, since they had been friends for so long—she said, "I know you think I'm exaggerating. But just wait. When are you meeting with her?"

"Tomorrow."

"Good luck to you." And then Mrs. Hopwood hung up, leaving Mrs. Johnson with a dial tone.

Mrs. Johnson poured herself another glass of wine and began to plot a way to get rid of Mrs. Logan.

SEVEN

MISS TURNIPSEED WAS feeling very uneasy. Mrs. Logan had left an hour ago to attend a principal's meeting, and she didn't tell Miss Turnipseed that she could go home.

Some other secretary might take advantage when their boss left early and duck out themselves. But Miss Turnipseed was not that sort of person. For one thing someone might call and, if the call went to voice mail, and Mrs. Logan should pick it up at a later time, she might wonder why Miss Turnipseed hadn't answered. For another thing, Miss Turnipseed was sixty-three years old, and it was important for her to keep this job, at least until her Social Security and Medicare came through. Working for Mrs. Logan wasn't easy, but Miss Turnipseed had done it for six years, and she only had three years to go.

There was something else that was bothering her, like a pin prick in her brain. She had overheard Mrs. Logan tell Mrs. Hopwood that she would be conducting Corey Checks on all of the staff. Surely, though, Mrs. Logan had not meant Miss Turnipseed. First of all, she was not a new employee. She had worked for years with Mrs. Logan, and, if Mrs. Logan hadn't been pleased, she would not have asked Miss Turnipseed to come along with her. Also Miss Turnipseed was not a teacher, so she presented no danger to the students.

As for the rest of the staff, Mrs. Logan had every

right to be suspicious. The truth was Miss Turnipseed was uncomfortable, knowing that she was the only person right now in the school. She had read all about the murders three years ago. An eighth grade teacher had been poisoned in the teachers' room and, shortly after, a janitor had been murdered by the boiler.

If that stroke of bad luck wasn't enough, two teachers had accompanied some students to Sicily, where one of them was kidnapped, as they tried to solve an international murder.

No wonder Father Felix had been given the axe.

But Mrs. Logan was determined to leave that all behind, even if it meant leaving some of the teachers with the past.

Miss Turnipseed was not a snoop, well, not really. But reading through files and sifting through trash cans was one of the few pleasures she had in a rather dull, uneventful job. When Mrs. Hopwood left yesterday, Miss Turnipseed was curious, because according to the Google search she had done, Mrs. Hopwood had been one of those teachers involved in those grisly murders.

What Father Felix had written about her was scanty. Mrs. Hopwood's yearly evaluations showed she was an imaginative, creative teacher, although her classroom management was sketchy. Her space was nicely decorated with students' work, but everything she hung up was crooked. She was often a season behind in her bulletin boards, but she seldom took sick days and she was never late. A few parents had complained that she didn't take their concerns seriously, and she seemed more interested in coming in with a stunning outfit than whether or not their children did their homework. The students, however, adored her because she always made class work fun. But she had a flair for the dramatic and coupled with her best friend, Mrs. Johnson, they loved trouble.

Mrs. Hopwood was everything that Mrs. Logan despised.

Miss Turnipseed knew exactly how Mrs. Logan worked. If she wanted to fire a teacher, she could seldom do that outright for the union would be on her in a New York minute. It involved a long and complicated paper trail, and Mrs. Logan hated long and complicated. So instead Mrs. Logan would simply switch the teacher's grade.

For instance, if a teacher had been teaching seventh grade, she would suddenly send them into kindergarten. A teacher, who was used to instructing teenagers, would suddenly find herself in front of whiny, needy children, who wouldn't sit still, and who couldn't be occupied for any more time than it took to color a picture outside the lines. The same was true for an elementary school teacher who found herself in an upper grade. Teenagers could be hard to manage, difficult to frighten and the curriculum demanded a firm knowledge of higher mathematics and science.

Miss Turnipseed crept into Mrs. Logan's office and saw on the corner of her desk she had carefully laid out Mrs. Johnson's file. Mrs. Johnson was to come in first thing in the morning, and Mrs. Logan was obviously prepared.

Miss Turnipseed could have sat in Mrs. Logan's desk to read the file but she thought that was rather audacious. Instead she took the file to her own little office space, slumped down at the corner and began to read.

Except for the fact that Mrs. Johnson was known

to "stir the pot" and incite Mrs. Hopwood—who according to Father Felix didn't need much urging—Mrs. Johnson's evaluation was glowing. She was an excellent math teacher and always went the extra mile to make sure her students understood the material. Nothing got by Mrs. Johnson, and her students were never allowed to take the easy way out. If her children weren't performing, parents were informed and together they came up with a concrete plan. Her classroom management was excellent. She never had to raise her voice. Her students just knew that she meant business. Parents never argued with her. It was apparent that Mrs. Johnson knew exactly what she was doing, and they trusted her implicitly

Although now and then, Father Felix had scrawled at the very bottom, Mrs. Johnson would overstep the boundaries and argue school policies with him, which was annoying and rather exhausting.

Miss Turnipseed rose and went into Mrs. Logan's office to replace the file exactly where she found it.

She did this with a certain satisfaction, because she had the distinct feeling that Mrs. Logan was going to be doing some snooping of her own.

EIGHT

BERTHA BUTTERWORTH SIPPED her coffee and looked at the calendar. Ten days until school opened and fifteen days until she was due in the dining room, since the first week was only half days.

Bertha was anxious to go back to the cafeteria at St. Polycarp. She missed her lady friends, who chatted vigorously as they doled out the shepherd's pie, the chicken wings, the pasta, and the ham sandwiches. And she missed her weekly paycheck. In the summer it was difficult to make ends meet, since she didn't get paid.

Unlike some of the teachers, she was not unhappy, when she heard that Father Felix wasn't returning. She hadn't thought he was a particularly good principal. For one thing he was very moody and not at all consistent. When he was angry, every little thing bothered him, from the portions the dining room ladies doled out to the students, to whether or not the milk was ice cold.

And when he was feeling chirper, he didn't do a thing to control the noise and the bedlam in the dining room, nor did he take any interest in the disrespectful way that the students spoke to the lunch ladies.

Mrs. Butterworth's mother always used to say, "Be careful what you wish for." And that was certainly turning out to be true. Because Father Felix's replacement was to be none other than Mrs. Logan, who used to be principal of St. Jude's School.

According to the word on the street, Mrs. Logan was supposed to run the school with an iron fist. She was known to be unreasonable and unyielding. She seldom supported the teachers, and she ignored the lunch ladies completely.

If her methods had been so superior, then why had St. Jude's closed?

And there was something else—something that nagged at a part of Bertha's mind, like an uncomfortable pebble that had been stuck somewhere in her brain.

Well, she thought it would come to her, probably in the middle of the night, when she had one of those dreams.

NINE

"I DON'T KNOW why you're freaking out." Mrs. Johnson was sitting in Mrs. Hopwood's classroom, watching Mrs. Hopwood set up. "Just remember that those fifth graders are just your second graders three years later."

"That's why I'm freaking out. I remember that class. Devon Donahue used to stand at the bottom of the stairs and look up the girls' dresses. He was seven. Melanie Santana threw a chair at Amelia Simpson and gave her a black eye. Angela Teger's mother actually complained to the Bishop about me, saying that I forced her daughter to eat all of her peas. Like I really care whether a kid eats her peas."

"What you hang up is supposed to be student driven." Mrs. Johnson took a large bite of her buttered bagel.

"How can it be student driven when the students haven't even started school yet?"

"And it's crooked."

Deborah Harris, who taught first grade, burst into Mrs. Hopwood's classroom, kissed both women on the cheeks, and then asked how their summer was.

Mrs. Hopwood muttered uneventful. She had spent most of her days watching endless reruns of *Murder She Wrote* and *Monk*, occasionally hitting the mall, shopping for new clothes. Mrs. Johnson, on the other hand, had plenty to say, most of it centered around her twins. They had started swimming lessons, and they were doing splendidly. They were in the advanced tennis group. They had learned how to write their names and do simple subtraction. They were well prepared for kindergarten and, although she would have loved for them to go to St. Polycarp, she and her husband felt they should attend the school for the gifted.

"That sounds wonderful!" Mrs. Harris said and, then in a quieter tone, asked Mrs. Hopwood and Mrs. Johnson if they had met Mrs. Logan.

"We met." Mrs. Hopwood was having a hard time stapling on a Welcome Sign. She couldn't hold the stapler straight therefore, instead of going into the wall, the staples flew all over the room, missing Deborah by mere inches.

"I think," Mrs. Johnson said, as she finished the last of her coffee, "that she looks like a woman who knows exactly what she is doing."

It took quite a bit of self-control for Mrs. Hopwood not to hiss. After her meeting with Mrs. Logan, Mrs. Johnson had gone on and on about how Mrs. Logan didn't possess a sense of humor and it was going to be a long year.

"She is not supposed to be a nice person," Deborah whispered. "Her husband ran away with another woman. He couldn't stand her anymore."

"Excuse me." A young, skinny woman stood at the threshold of Mrs. Hopwood's door. She wore her beautifully highlighted blonde hair in a French twist. Her gray pencil skirt and a black cashmere sweater looked expensive. So did her silver accessories, including an oversized watch, which read Cartier. She was carrying a folder.

"I thought I should introduce myself." She strode briskly into Mrs. Hopwood's classroom. "I'm Addison Fiore, the new second grade teacher."

Right then and there Mrs. Hopwood decided that she didn't like Addison. Well, if the truth be told, she was prepared not to like her at any rate, because she had stolen Mrs. Hopwood's second grade class.

"Which one of you ladies is Mrs. Hopwood?"

Before Mrs. Hopwood could answer, Mrs. Johnson pointed a finger at her.

"I have some questions for you." And Mrs. Hopwood did not like her tone either. It was accusatory. "You left a lot of books in your classroom, mostly workbooks. I wonder what you wanted to do with them."

"Do with them?" Mrs. Hopwood repeated blankly.

"I think," Mrs. Harris said quickly, "she was planning to use them. I mean she just received notice last week that she'd be teaching fifth grade—"

"You're welcome to them," Mrs. Hopwood interrupted.

"That's very kind of you but I don't want them. There's a bunch of novels, entire sets, but my children won't all be reading the same book at the same time. Rather, they'll be doing book clubs. As far as the Math workbooks are concerned, I will be creating my own material, depending on my student's needs. I didn't see an easel in the classroom. I like to write a Morning Message, you know, for Responsive Classroom. Do you have any notebooks left over from last year for writing responses? And, oh, I looked in your closet. I'd like to empty it out to make room for my own supplies. Why don't you come up and get what you want before I trash everything?"

Mrs. Hopwood was rendered mute, so Mrs. Johnson took over. "We have a faculty meeting in fifteen minutes. She'll go up after that."

"Perfect." Addison smiled with very white teeth. "Oh by the way," she said as she exited the classroom, "that welcome sign you put up is crooked."

MRS. HOPWOOD WAS SEETHING. On the way to the faculty meeting, she stopped at her mailbox. Nothing but junk, and she was purposely ignoring Addison, who was colliding with her, while she tried to get to her own mailbox.

Mrs. Hopwood took all of the catalogs and proceeded to the wastepaper basket in the hall. She couldn't miss the glare Miss Turnipseed gave her as she threw out her trash. Well, where was she supposed to put her garbage?

"Did you have a nice summer?" It was Bertha, the cafeteria lady who was asking her the question everyone asked, even though no one was particularly interested.

"Just fine," Mrs. Hopwood put on a false smile.

"The faculty meeting is about to begin," Mrs. Logan barked as she strutted out of her office.

Suddenly Bertha stopped in the hall and stared. At first Mrs. Hopwood thought she was staring at Miss Turnipseed. But maybe it was Addison. "You look familiar," she said.

"You don't," Addison said, as she dodged out of sight and hurried into the library for the upcoming meeting.

MRS. HOPWOOD COULD barely concentrate on what Mrs. Logan was saying. Several times she tried to catch Mrs. Johnson's eye but Mrs. Johnson seemed very engaged, even nodding now and then in agreement at a comment from Mrs. Logan.

Didn't her friend understand how difficult things were about to become at St. Polycarp? There were times when both teachers had their differences with Father Felix, but when all was said and done, he liked them, he respected them and he listened to them. Two years ago he had taken them to Sicily with him. All right the trip turned out to be a disaster, but still he had thought enough of both teachers to pay their expenses. And now…?

Well now, it was very apparent that Mrs. Logan wanted her own teachers around. She had hired two others beside Addison Fiore and they, too, were young and pretty and talked about morning meetings, and student driven curriculums, and learning lessons based on differences—things that Mrs. Hopwood didn't know anything about.

"I cannot stress," Mrs. Logan was talking in a slow, maddening tone, as though she was addressing first grade students, "that you are never to leave the classroom unattended for any reason. But I guess you know that. If there is an emergency, you may send a student to Miss Turnipseed and she will arrange coverage." She pointed her French manicure nails down to a file card. "Each one of you will have lunch duty three times a week and recess duty as well. Unless it's below twenty degrees or above ninety degrees, the children will go out. They need the fresh air and quite frankly, so do you. While you're on lunch duty, you are to actually sit with the children and make sure that they are eating a colorful plate. Each child is to eat two vegetables, one piece of protein, a serving of fruit, or they cannot have dessert. This is monitored carefully, because the parents are strict about the diets of their children. After lunch, there is an hour and a half of literacy. We will be using the Wilson Method to teach reading and to teach spelling. If you are not acquainted with that method, I know you, Addison, Dylan and Taylor are, come see me after this meeting and I will give the necessary books. Take the weekend to read through them. If there is something you don't understand, one of the three ladies can help you. You are entitled to ten days off, which includes sick days as well as personal days. I don't expect anyone to use them all. The school year is only one hundred and eighty days. That's a half a year, when you are getting paid for doing absolutely nothing. If you must call in sick, do it that morning. Not the night before, because there is no way that you will know how you're going to feel in twelve hours. Don't be late. It's imperative that you be here at least fifteen minutes before the children. We can't allow your students in the classroom without you. I don't have to tell you what chaos will ensue. Children, who are late, will get weekly detention. If you are late, as well, you will be monitoring that detention.

"One last thing, if you haven't signed a paper giving me permission to conduct a Corey Search on you, please come by my office now, and Miss Turnipseed will give you the forms. Does anyone have any questions?"

As her sense of foreboding increased, Mrs. Hopwood had a question, which she didn't dare ask. How soon could she get a gun?

Because, at this point, she wanted to shoot herself.

TEN

THE FIRST DAY of school was always slightly nerve racking to Mrs. Johnson. It didn't matter that she had been teaching seventh grade for eight years. Every year a different class tumbled in, rambunctious and eager to learn, and it was up to her to teach them, and to discipline them.

This class was no better or worse than any of the other classes she had in the past. There were smarty pants girls, who on the verge of puberty, flirted with the smarty pants boys, while the boys were busy ignoring them. There were brownnosers and studious children, quiet girls, who always did everything right and who, unfortunately, Mrs. Johnson ignored, because she was too busy disciplining the misbehaved.

She passed out the text books. There was no way was she going to let Miss Fiore's teaching style influence her own. She explained about the temperamental pencil sharpener, told them to stay away from the radiator, which could scald them in the winter, and cautioned them to keep their desks neat and clean.

The day went by just as it had for the last eight years, with nothing unusual about it, except for what had happened at three-thirty, after Mrs. Johnson had dismissed her students.

Mrs. Johnson was writing some math problems on the board—in preparation for morning work—and no, she wasn't about to write a morning message, and she had never owned an easel nor had she ever intended to get one. As soon as she finished she was planning to stop across the hall to Mrs. Hopwood's room. She had heard a great deal of racket after lunch. Mrs. Logan clearly was not a woman who was going to tolerate a great deal of racket in the classroom.

When Mrs. Johnson turned around to face her desk, she was slightly startled to see a disheveled older woman, with two pink rollers in her hair, standing in front of her. "Are you the seventh grade teacher?" she demanded.

"Yes, I'm Mrs. Johnson."

"I am here to pick up my son, George."

"George," Mrs. Johnson repeated thoughtfully. She didn't remember having a student named George, and that would be a name she would take note of, since it was the name of her favorite uncle. "I don't think I have a George. Are you sure he's in seventh grade?"

The question seemed to anger the woman, and she waved an orange handbag at Mrs. Johnson. "I guess I know what grade my son is in!"

It took Mrs. Johnson several minutes to find her class list, which was buried under the latest issue of *Star* magazine. "I'm sorry. Maybe he goes by another first name…"

"His name is George Geoffrey Arlington."

Mrs. Johnson shook her head and managed to smile feebly. "I'm afraid he's not in my class. Maybe another school?"

The woman twisted her mouth into a sour expression and began opening and closing her handbag. "I don't understand. I brought him here myself. I saw him walk in the front door."

"Perhaps we should talk to Mrs. Logan." Mrs. Johnson would only be too happy to lay the entire thing on her lap. If nothing else to learn how Mrs. Logan dealt with a crisis.

"I know Mrs. Logan very well. She taught my son in fifth grade."

Mrs. Johnson led the way, not missing the look Mrs. Hopwood gave her, as she entered the hall. She was obviously waiting for Mrs. Johnson to stop by in order to listen to her litany of complaints.

Nevertheless, Mrs. Johnson marched down the stairs in the direction of the principal's office, but Mrs. Logan was not at her desk.

"Where is my little boy?" the woman suddenly bellowed, as she rubbed her bottom lip. "What have you done with my little boy?"

Her cries raised an alarm, and Addison Fiore came racing out of her classroom.

"Mrs. Arlington, how are you feeling?" she asked.

"How am I feeling?" Mrs. Arlington repeated angrily. "I am feeling confused. This woman," she looked at Mrs. Johnson, as though she might spit, so in defense Mrs. Johnson stepped back, "is trying to tell me that my son doesn't exist."

"That is not what I said. I only claimed that he wasn't in my class." Then doubt washed over Mrs. Johnson. "At least I don't think he's in my class. How do you know Mrs. Arlington?" she asked Addison, who ignored her question.

"Why don't you have a seat in Mrs. Logan's office?"

Addison said kindly. "I'll ask Miss Turnipseed to call George and ask him to pick you up."

"What are you talking about?" Mrs. Arlington shouted. "How can George pick me up? He's only thirteen. I am here to pick him up! And his awful teacher, Mrs. Logan. She never calls on him in class! And she always marks his spelling wrong, just because she doesn't take the time to read his handwriting."

"Wait here, Mrs. Arlington, while we get this sorted out." She guided Mrs. Arlington into Mrs. Logan's office and then closed the door behind her.

"What is going on?" Mrs. Johnson could not contain her curiosity.

And maybe she was a little too curious, because Addison gave her a rather nasty look before replying.

"Mrs. Arlington's son, George, did go to a Catholic school, twenty years ago. He's married now, and he has three daughters. Her mind is slipping, and she thinks he is still a little boy. Her husband died a few years ago, and she remembers the time when George was young as the happiest time of her life, so she relives it over and over. She goes from school to school looking for him. Last year it was St. Jude's and this year—"

"The poor woman," was the only thing Mrs. Johnson could say.

"Oh, here is Mrs. Logan. She'll know what to do."

Mrs. Johnson didn't want any part of it. She turned around and started towards the staircase. But not before she heard Mrs. Logan reprimand Addison for letting someone into her office, when she was not there.

Mrs. Johnson couldn't help but be somewhat gleeful that Addison was being reprimanded.

When Mrs. Johnson returned to her classroom, she

noticed that Mrs. Arlington had left her bright orange purse behind, which meant another trip down to the reception area.

But by the time she got down there—having chatted with Mrs. Hopwood—Mrs. Arlington had already left.

ELEVEN

MISS TURNIPSEED KNEW Mrs. Logan rather well. She also knew that for some reason Mrs. Logan was not in a good mood. Her thin lips were pressed together in a slight grimace and her hand was raking through her blonde, floppy curls. It might have to do with Mrs. Arlington turning up suddenly and being left alone in her office. Mrs. Logan did not like it when people were left alone in her office.

Mrs. Logan quickly escorted Mrs. Arlington out the front door, and minutes later Mrs. Johnson came storming into the area, holding Mrs. Arlington's purse, claiming that Mrs. Arlington had left it in her classroom. She practically threw it at Miss Turnipseed, as though Miss Turnipseed didn't have enough on her desk, with class lists, and lesson plans and agendas for future meetings.

Addison was in the hall closet, frantically looking for more bulletin board paper, and she offered to drop the purse off on her way home. "I know she lives with her son and it's only a few blocks from me. It's the least I can do for the poor woman."

But Mrs. Logan declined and, in an icy tone, she responded. "I have to call George anyway. He should know about the incident. I'll have him pick up the bag."

Then Mrs. Logan went into her office and slammed the door.

Miss Turnipseed could hear Mrs. Logan on the phone, and she was definitely irritated. This being a brand new school, she wanted parents to like her. She was a political animal and, through her snooping, Miss Turnipseed knew that Mrs. Logan's ambition was to be the superintendent of schools. That was going to take some doing, since the Catholic diocese had never appointed a lay person to such a high position. But Mrs. Logan was determined to break that hard and fast rule.

And she wasn't about to take any tainted baggage with her.

You would think that the teachers would stay a little later on the first day of school, but no, most of them were out the door, fifteen minutes after the students left. The exception was Mrs. Johnson and Mrs. Hopwood, who both remained in the fifth grade classroom and seemed to be bickering. And Addison Fiore, who was busy redecorating her classroom, stringing what looked like a clothes line from one end to the other and hanging up drawings with clothes pins.

"I'm going to go around to each classroom," Mrs. Logan told Miss Turnipseed when she opened her office door, "to inspect them. I want to make sure that everything is neat and orderly. If there is something important happening, you will know where to find me. You can send all my calls straight to voice mail."

Miss Turnipseed nodded. She was trying to revise the class lists to include students who didn't show up until the last minute, and new students who hadn't registered at all.

And after a half an hour, she finally had the list complete—hopefully because Mrs. Logan did not like mistakes. She could hear Mrs. Logan down the hall, screaming at the janitor about the girls' room trash can being dirty, and he needed to scrub both the inside and the outside, even if there was a bag in there.

Miss Turnipseed rose, went over to Mrs. Logan's office, opened the door and dropped the neatly printed list on Mrs. Logan's desk. At that precise moment Mrs. Logan's private phone rang, and Miss Turnipseed did not dare pick it up.

The right thing to do was to immediately vacate Mrs. Logan's office, but Miss Turnipseed listened instead.

"This message is for Lenora Logan from George Arlington. I can leave work early and I will be by in about fifteen minutes to pick up my mother's handbag."

The caller had hung up, just as Miss Turnipseed heard the clicky clack of Mrs. Logan's kitten heels coming down the corridor. Quickly she exited the office and ran straight into Mrs. Logan.

"Oh by the way," Mrs. Logan said, "do you have those permission slips for the Corey Checks from the teachers?"

Sometimes Miss Turnipseed didn't know where she put things, but today they were right there in a bright yellow file. She handed them to Mrs. Logan.

Mrs. Logan turned and headed into her office. Then she stopped.

And so did Miss Turnipseed's heart, which seemed to tighten.

"If you haven't done it already, would you please fill out one for yourself?" she asked.

TWELVE

Mrs. Hopwood hated teaching fifth grade. And it was only her fourth day. She had come in a little later because her dog Dagny was constipated and she had to bathe her before leaving for work. So she didn't have time to stop at Mrs. Johnson's room and, before she could even run to the bathroom, a group of boys burst into the room.

The boys ignored her, but not the girls, who came tumbling in with their short plaid skirts and their hoodies and their ballet flats.

"How come you haven't turned on the smartboard?"

Mrs. Hopwood looked at the white board in front of her. She had no idea how to use it and no desire to learn.

"Do you need help?"

"You're not supposed to touch the smartboard. You know that, Dior. Besides, what makes you think you know how to use a smartboard?"

"Because I went to tech camp."

"Please have a seat," Mrs. Hopwood said in a feeble voice.

Too feeble because the students were clearly ignoring her.

There was only one thing to do and that was to assume her Catholic school teaching voice. "Everyone sit down!" she said loudly and firmly.

The twenty students—thirteen of them boys—looked

at her, stunned, then annoyed, and finally resigned, as they slumped into their seats.

"Today at the beginning of school year, we're going to talk about ourselves," she said. And she could tell by the grins on their faces that this was a subject they enjoyed.

The girls hoped to be dancers, or fashion designers, or singers. They would audition for *American Idol*, or *America's Got Talent* or *You Think You Can Dance* and they were all going to win. The boys planned to own computer companies, some of them had already started to make apps, or they were going to be basketball stars. A few of them were headed to Hollywood to become actors.

But when she started teaching math, their interest diminished. Mrs. Hopwood had to raise her voice several times, because the students would simply not listen. When she told them to do something, they ignored her. When she threatened to call their parents on her prep, they laughed in her face.

And the last thing she wanted to do was to involve Mrs. Logan, who immediately would come to the conclusion that Mrs. Hopwood could not manage her class—which was turning out to be true.

While the class finally left for art, Mrs. Hopwood didn't bother to write up lesson plans—although they were due in two days. Instead she wrote up rules for a short story contest in writing and then ran across the street and bought a roll of stickers to give as a prize.

Motivated by the stickers—which at first the students moaned and groaned and said they were too babyish— writing was the best period. At least it was quiet and, when it came time to vote, they all participated. A boy won and then he passed out stickers to his friends. Mrs.

Hopwood figured out what must have happened. He had bribed his classmates to vote for him to share his prize.

Mrs. Hopwood didn't care. Last period she gave them a word search and said the first one who finished would have no homework for the night.

It wasn't a horrid afternoon, but she didn't know if she could do this for 185 more days.

She walked to the window and looked out at the park across the way.

And that's when she saw him. A man dressed in black, black hat, black pants, black blazer, staring up at her, his eyes glittering with malice.

She quickly turned away and went over to her desk. The students were still busy with their word search, whispering amongst themselves, even though she told them that they could not exchange any information.

She opened her first drawer, reached for her cell phone, tapped her finger on messages and wrote a text to Mrs. Johnson.

There is a creepy man outside my window. I don't like the looks of him at all.

Within minutes Mrs. Johnson responded.

What is he doing?

Looking at me with a hateful expression, as though he is sneering.

Is he still there?

Slowly Mrs. Hopwood went to the window. He was

still there, his arms crossed, his posture stiff. If he had mouthed something, if he waved, if he moved, she would not be so spooked—but just standing.

Quickly she moved away.

She grabbed her phone and wrote:

Yes, he is.

Maybe you should tell Miss Turnipseed.

What can she do?

Call the police.

He's not doing anything wrong.

He's loitering on school property. He might be a danger to the kids.

"Mrs. Hopwood, I'm done."

"You have to wait."

"I'm done too and I was done first."

"You have to wait. Both of you."

"I'm done and he copied."

"I did not. You copied from me!"

"Bull!" One of the bigger boys, Jerry Savani rose and went over to Terrace Lipman, his fist closed.

Mrs. Hopwood was trying to finish her text.

I don't think he's after me but now he is lowering his chin, looking downward, like into the classroom below. Maybe I should warn…

"Excuse me."

Suddenly the classroom, which had erupted into chaos, was quiet.

Mrs. Hopwood whipped around to see Mrs. Logan standing behind her.

THIRTEEN

BERTHA BUTTERWORTH WAS cleaning up in the kitchen, when her cell phone rang. It was the supplier, telling her that they would not be delivering anymore orange juice, unless the school paid the bill in full. Evidently, Father Felix had owed the company for three months and never settled the debt.

Bertha had to break this news to Mrs. Logan, which she wasn't eager to do. She had a feeling that Mrs. Logan was the type to shoot the messenger.

Nevertheless, Bertha had always thought of herself as formable, so after taking a long, deep breath, she went up the stairs to the principal's office.

She could hear Mrs. Logan's voice, before she turned the corner in the hall. At first Bertha thought she was reprimanding a student.

"I just don't understand what the problem is. I tried to be very explicit about my expectations, and it's as though you haven't heard me at all."

"I'm sorry."

Bertha recognized Mrs. Hopwood's voice.

"It's only the first few days of school, and already I have had some complaints. One of the teachers went up to the second floor to use the teacher's rest room, and she heard you screaming at the children. I don't approve of screaming." Although Bertha noticed that Mrs. Logan herself was using a harsh, grating voice.

"Screaming doesn't accomplish anything and, after a while, the students just tune you out. And I understand that you held a contest."

"Well, it was a short story contest and I didn't give out food. I gave out stickers. The prize encouraged them to write…"

"You should be doing Writer's Workshop. Did you read those books at all?"

"I…"

"And what about the word search?"

Again Mrs. Hopwood was quiet. Bertha was wondering who the spy was and guessing it was probably one of the new young teachers, Addison, Taylor or Dylan.

"Contest and competition are not things I encourage. Competition stresses the children and pits one against another. That is not part of my strategic plan."

"Strategic plan?"

"I will be explaining it on parents' night next week. Please pay particular attention. I will also be giving you a hard copy, which you will read and date, attesting that you understand my expectations. And then there is the matter of the cell phone you were using. I don't know who you were texting, but I made myself clear. Mrs. Hopwood, I don't want to put unkind remarks in your file. I know that file can follow you wherever you go. However, as much as I want to be supportive of my teachers, my first obligation is to the students and their parents. So I am letting it go this time, but please understand, I will be watching you."

Bertha heard the sound of a chair scratching against the floor. She didn't know how Mrs. Hopwood could do so many things wrong in such a short period of time. Not that she had any affinity for Mrs. Hopwood. It wasn't that Bertha disliked her. It was only that Mrs. Hopwood tended to ignore the kitchen staff completely. She brought her own food, so there was no need for her to try to be nice to the dining room ladies.

"Oh, one more thing," Mrs. Logan said. "I am in the process of completing a school handbook. Everyone will be given a copy, parents, teachers, staff, even the dining room ladies." She had said *even* the dining room ladies. As though they were right down there on the list with the school mascot, which last year was a hamster. "Let me read to you what it says. Shoes should in no way interfere with the daily schedule or make it difficult to accomplish simple tasks. This, again, applies to the faculty as well as to the student body."

"Are you talking about my high heels?" Mrs. Hopwood asked, her tone uncertain.

"Exactly. Tomorrow please wear sensible shoes. If you don't have any, maybe your *friend*," Mrs. Logan put a particular emphasis on the word friend, "Mrs. Johnson can lend you some. You look to be about the same size. You may go."

Quickly Bertha ducked under the stairs. There was no question about it. Mrs. Logan was going to run a tight ship.

But then again, Bertha had nothing to fear from her.

So she marched up to the office, delivered the news about the orange juice and left quickly, when Mrs. Logan began to curse under her breath.

FOURTEEN

MRS. JOHNSON WAS not fond of parent/teacher night. For one thing, it meant they all had to stay late. Having to be in their classrooms by eight o'clock sharp—Mrs. Johnson was usually there by seven thirty so she could have coffee with Mrs. Hopwood, although lately Mrs. Hopwood was coming in later and later—and then leaving at eight at night meant that Mrs. Johnson would be working a twelve hour day.

Mrs. Johnson did not like working a twelve hour day.

When the teachers had a late night, Father Felix always ordered in food for dinner. Sometimes it would be pizza from that expensive Italian restaurant down the block, sometimes it would be Chinese or big, overstuffed deli sandwiches. There was always a delicious dessert and an assortment of soft drinks.

Mrs. Logan wasn't doing any of that, so Mrs. Johnson and Mrs. Hopwood had to be content with salads from the local deli, salads which were more greens than chicken and cupcakes, which were a tad bit stale and tasted musty.

Mrs. Hopwood was not in good spirits, since she could not wear the shoes that she preferred. "I have two hundred and fifty pairs," she lamented. "And I'm forced to wear these." She looked down at her glittery white kitten heels. "I suppose the next thing she'll be complaining about is the color. The parents won't understand. They expect me to wear high heels."

"They'll be expecting a lot of things," Mrs. Johnson said. "And all their hopes will be dashed, when they meet Mrs. Logan."

MRS. LOGAN SPOKE at length about her plans for the school in a flat drone, like a dying refrigerator. Listening to her, one would think that St. Polycarp was on its way to being the best Catholic school in the diocese, and the students were lucky to attend. She even promised that getting admittance was going to become very competitive. She had definite goals, a strategic plan, which she would put in action as soon as she met with the PTA.

Mrs. Johnson spotted Mrs. Arlington sitting in the audience, listening intently as Mrs. Logan rambled on, as though George was still a student. And it occurred to her, just briefly, that maybe Mrs. Arlington's delusions might be a tad dangerous.

The parents were sitting almost comatose, yawning and squirming in their seats, which made Mrs. Johnson feel quite sleepy. Yet she kept smiling. And smiling.

She smiled when they clapped, barely moving their hands, and she smiled when the speech was over and the parents sauntered over to the table to eat bakery cookies, mini cupcakes, brownies and hot coffee and tea.

She grinned at Miss Turnipseed, who was busy, arranging the napkins into a circle, as though anyone cared.

She managed to flash a quick smile at Addison, who was trying to talk to Mrs. Arlington, but Mrs. Arlington was too busy watching the food disappear.

Mrs. Johnson would have loved to grab a brownie,

but she did not want to look greedy. She hovered at the end of the line, edging into the chattering crowd, only when she reached the table, the brownies were all gone. Only a few stale biscotti remained.

She was careful with her teeth, so instead she went up to her classroom and prepared to smile some more.

MRS. JOHNSON KNEW most of the parents and they knew her. She had taught their older children, and she would probably teach the younger ones. When they asked her what she thought of Mrs. Logan, she told them that she had the utmost respect for the new principal, and she was certain that this was going to be a banner year.

While standing at the door, she overheard what was going on in Mrs. Hopwood's classroom. And it wasn't good. The parents wondered why she was now teaching fifth grade, and some of them balked at the fact that she would be teaching their children for a second year.

They were concerned that Mrs. Hopwood didn't understand the higher math—Mrs. Johnson knew the concern was not without merit—that the children would not respect someone who had taught them when they were so young and who might remember them as they were and not the wonderful pre-teens they had become. They feared that the girls would pay more attention to her wardrobe and her accessories than to what she was teaching.

Mrs. Hopwood tried to reassure the parents, but she tended to end each statement in an upward tone, as though everything was questionable. This did nothing to set their fears to rest.

Mrs. Johnson would definitely have to speak to Mrs. Hopwood.

But not now. The evening was already over. And thankfully, Mrs. Logan made an announcement on the loud speaker, thanking the parents for coming and inviting them to pick up their pamphlets in front of her office.

But that didn't mean that the parents left. Some of them still lingered, a small knot of people, talking to each other, whispering, asking Mrs. Johnson questions, like what they would be learning in Social Studies this year. And since Mrs. Logan was changing the entire curriculum, it was not a question which Mrs. Johnson felt confident about answering.

After the parents left, Mrs. Johnson went into her room to clean up the paper plates and the coffee cups the rude and inconsiderate parents left behind. She moved the chairs back, in order to prevent chaos in the morning, and then she went into Mrs. Hopwood's room.

And she found Mrs. Hopwood, slumped against her desk, crying. She had never seen Mrs. Hopwood crying before. Not when she discovered dead bodies, not when she was in danger herself from killers, not when her son was in trouble. She was steadfast and confident. But not anymore.

"I just don't think I can do it." Mrs. Hopwood took out a crumbly used tissue from her neon lime green purse and blew her nose. "Those parents were so mean to me. They don't trust me at all. And here's the truth," her bottom lip was trembling, "they're right. They shouldn't trust me to teach fifth grade. I have no idea what I'm doing!"

"Listen to me," Mrs. Johnson assumed her teaching voice. "I got a news flash for you. Most people, whether it's teachers, or lawyers, or politicians, hopefully not doctors, they don't know what they're doing either. Everyone is faking it. That's why the world is in such a terrible state."

"But I don't even know how to fake it!"

"I will teach you. We'll stay after school for half an hour a day. I'll go over the math with you. I'll tell you how to handle the students and the parents. The main thing is that you mustn't let anyone think you can't do the job. Especially Mrs. Logan. If she even suspects that you don't have the confidence, well, it won't be a good thing. You can do this," Mrs. Johnson said. "You can totally do this."

But as confident as Mrs. Johnson sounded, she had to admit that she had her doubts. For one thing Mrs. Hopwood didn't look like a teacher. With her blinding white sheath and her white pearls and her white hoop earrings, she looked as though her biggest problem was not getting dirty. When Father Felix was in charge, he tolerated Mrs. Hopwood's colorful and fashionable outfits, sometimes even admiring them.

But with Mrs. Logan, Mrs. Hopwood's fashion trend would definitely not be an asset.

Mrs. Johnson would have to speak to Mrs. Hopwood about her choice of clothing. One step at a time.

Mrs. Johnson glanced at the classroom clock and noticed that it was going on nine. In less than eleven hours, they had to be back here, bright eyed and bushy tailed.

"We better go," she said to Mrs. Hopwood. "I'll give you a ride home. Try to get a good night's sleep."

Mrs. Hopwood glared at her, as Mrs. Johnson

grabbed her handbag. She was going to leave her tote there since she was hardly going to have any time to correct papers or make up lesson plans.

THE SCHOOL WAS deserted and it gave Mrs. Johnson a rather eerie feeling. She could hardly forget that just a few years ago, it had been the setting of two murders. But as Mrs. Logan said, it was a new year and everything was going to be different.

And then as she and Mrs. Hopwood were going down the back staircase, she caught a glimpse of Mrs. Arlington exiting the door.

"Excuse me," Mrs. Johnson said loudly. "You are not supposed to be in this school."

But if Mrs. Arlington heard her, she gave no indication as the door closed behind her with a soft hiss.

"She's going to be a problem," Mrs. Johnson mumbled.

"Should we sign out?" Mrs. Hopwood wondered.

Mrs. Johnson figured that they should. Father Felix wasn't too strict about things like that, but it wasn't a good idea to start breaking rules so early in Mrs. Logan's term. Especially for Mrs. Hopwood.

The front hall was empty, except for Bertha Butterworth, who was cleaning up, throwing away coffee cups and half eaten cookies and muttering under her breath as she glanced at the clock.

Addison was signing out and they waited patiently for her to finish. Mrs. Johnson nodded when she mumbled, "Have a good night."

Mrs. Johnson looked up just as Bertha Butterworth grabbed a brownie off of Mrs. Logan's desk. She was mourning the fact that she hadn't seen it first, although if Mrs. Logan was looking forward to eating it, Bertha would be in big trouble.

Instantly Mrs. Johnson heard the clicky clack of shoes coming down the hall. She knew that they belonged to Mrs. Logan, and she was thankful that she could easily tell when Mrs. Logan was approaching.

Next time she would know enough to stop texting.

Mrs. Logan seemed surprised to see them. "What are you ladies doing here?"

"We were talking to parents," Mrs. Johnson said quickly.

Bertha didn't answer at all, probably because her mouth was full of chocolate. So instead she just pointed to the large trash can, which she was carting along.

"Well, good night," Mrs. Johnson said, noticing how Mrs. Hopwood had been struck dumb.

"I hate this place," Mrs. Hopwood grumbled as she descended down the stairs.

Mrs. Johnson was not feeling good about Mrs. Hopwood's glum mood. If something should happen, and Mrs. Hopwood should quit, or get fired, Mrs. Johnson would hardly know what to do. Mrs. Hopwood had been her best friend for years. She spent more time with Mrs. Hopwood than she spent with her husband or her children. Going to work without her, well, that would be unthinkable.

They had just walked to the car, when Mrs. Johnson looked up and saw Mrs. Logan waving from her office window.

"What does she want?" Mrs. Hopwood said in a bitter tone.

"Maybe we forgot something?" Mrs. Johnson guessed.

The window flew open, and Mrs. Logan stuck her head out. "Oh my God!" she said. "Can you ladies please come in here?"

"She seems frantic," Mrs. Johnson said. "We better go back in. Something must have happened to her."

Mrs. Hopwood only said one word. "Karma."

FIFTEEN

Miss Turnipseed was getting ready for bed. She had already put on her flannel pajamas, secured a brown hairnet to the top of her head, set the air conditioner on low and the television to the Lifetime channel, when the sirens blared past her house.

Miss Turnipseed knew exactly what to do.

She picked up her phone, quickly accessed the speed dial and waited for her second cousin, once removed, to answer. Patrick was a policeman and every other Thursday night, Miss Turnipseed took him to dinner. If the truth be told, that was where she spent most of her money. But she enjoyed his company and thought of him as a nephew, more than a distant cousin. As an only child, with no children of her own, she enjoyed playing aunt to the young man.

Besides it was not without perks. Patrick frequently confided in her about police matters, so Miss Turnipseed knew exactly what went on and when, whose husband was abusive, whose teenager was picked up for shoplifting, who got drunk at the local bar and had to be driven home, who had restraining orders against them.

Patrick answered right away.

"I hear sirens," Miss Turnipseed said, breathlessly. "Right in the neighborhood. Is it my building?"

"No, but it's your school."

"St. Jude's!"

"I thought you were at St. Polycarp."

"You're right. I'm still not used to that. What happened? Did someone get sick? A parent? A teacher?"

"I'm not sure. We're on our way."

"Can you call me back when you have more information?"

Patrick hesitated.

"I'll call you back in exactly one hour." Miss Turnipseed placed the receiver in its cradle and waited.

SHE TRIED READING but she couldn't concentrate. She watched a little television but it was difficult to hear all those commercials. It seemed to her that these movies were two thirds long and the ads were another third. It wasn't fair. Especially when television was hardly free these days, with the price of cable going up.

In exactly an hour she tried Patrick again. This time it went straight to voice mail, which was a little irritating. Of course, she left a message, but she doubted he would be returning her call anytime soon.

This Thursday she would be taking him to a fast food restaurant.

Luckily, it was time for the late evening news and she switched the channel, just in time to learn what had happened at St. Polycarp.

Bertha Butterworth, one of the dining room staff, had died in the lobby of the school.

The cause of death was unknown.

SIXTEEN

AFTER MRS. LOGAN rapped on the window, Mrs. Hopwood and Mrs. Johnson rushed back into the school to find poor Bertha Butterworth dangling over on one of the new chairs Mrs. Logan had ordered. The half-eaten brownie had fallen to the floor, and Mrs. Hopwood had inevitably stepped on it, not only dirtying the brand new beige carpet but her own white glittery shoes as well.

"What happened?" Mrs. Johnson asked, in a calm, controlled voice.

"I don't know." Mrs. Logan was speaking rapidly and shaking her hands—Mrs. Hopwood knew that Mrs. Johnson was earning points for taking charge of the situation. "One moment she was eating the brownie and the next moment she had collapsed on the chair."

Mrs. Hopwood gazed at Mrs. Johnson. She knew exactly what Mrs. Johnson was thinking. Several years ago the eighth grade teacher, Miss Pinkerton, had been poisoned right upstairs in what was then the teachers' room which had since been turned into a space for the public school learning specialist.

Mrs. Johnson mumbled that it was probably a sugar attack or the beginnings of a stroke—Mrs. Hopwood knew why she did not mention heart attack. Mrs. Hopwood's father had died suddenly and she herself feared the deadly disease, although Mrs. Hopwood had to admit she wasn't frightened enough to give up cheese or eggs or milk chocolate.

The ambulance came and whisked poor Bertha Butterworth away, but they didn't put the siren on as they left, which Mrs. Hopwood could only surmise was not a good sign.

And then Mrs. Johnson insisted that they go to the hospital, which seemed insane to Mrs. Hopwood. Yes, she was curious but she could be curious at ten in the morning as well as ten at night.

Besides, the hospital would not give out any information except that she had passed on, and everything that could have been done for her had been done.

Mrs. Johnson offered to call Bertha's husband, since Mrs. Logan barely knew the dead woman. This action necessitated going back to the school to look up the number.

After the phone call had been made—Mr. Butterworth shrieked so loudly that Mrs. Johnson dropped the phone—when Mrs. Johnson was driving Mrs. Hopwood home, Mrs. Johnson blurted out, "I can't believe that this is happening again! It's like this school is cursed!"

"I can't believe that they don't know how poor Bertha died and yet they're still going to reopen tomorrow morning."

"Well, they're suspending lunch. Mrs. Logan agreed to order pizza from down the block."

"Do you think," Mrs. Hopwood hesitated, "do you think that something was put in the brownie?"

Mrs. Johnson stopped the car dead, which irritated Mrs. Hopwood because she really wanted to get home. "Well, if that's the case, then it was Mrs. Logan who the killer was after, because I saw Bertha take that brownie off of her desk."

"Are you sure?"

"Of course, I'm sure. And I will tell the police so."

Mrs. Johnson revved up the engine and Mrs. Hopwood fell forward into the dashboard. "Now, I really have a reason for quitting," she mumbled.

Mrs. Hopwood did not sleep well that night. No matter how hard she tried, she simply wasn't sleepy. Finally she gave up and turned on the television. She finally fell asleep around four thirty, only to have the alarm clock ring an hour and a half later.

She rose, feeling dizzy and slightly nauseous. At this rate, she wasn't sure how she would make it through the entire year. Could she get another job teaching? *Probably not this late in the year.* Could she get another job that was not teaching? *Probably not.* What else could she do?

Maybe she would get lucky and get fired. Then she could collect unemployment. But that probably was a paltry sum and, with her son, Alexander, in college, they needed every cent.

She turned on the television, while she sipped her hazelnut coffee and chewed on her whole wheat English muffin. The coffee was only lukewarm and the muffin tasted like cardboard.

She couldn't do this for another 180 days.

She almost dropped her coffee cup when she saw a newscaster standing outside of St. Polycarp. He was gleefully announcing the murder of Bertha Butterworth, who was a long time employee of the school, a dining room associate, who was much loved by the students and the staff alike. Evidently, she had eaten a poisoned brownie.

The newscaster, who was speaking rapidly, did not mention the fact that the brownie was originally meant for the principal, Mrs. Logan. Well, maybe that was something that the police wanted to keep secret.

Or maybe Mrs. Johnson hadn't told them yet.

Mrs. Logan must be freaking out, Mrs. Hopwood thought, and in spite of the dire circumstances and the death of poor Bertha, Mrs. Hopwood couldn't help but feel somewhat buoyant. If Mrs. Logan was upset, then she would be distracted, and she wouldn't be as concerned about crooked bulletin boards or whether or not the fifth graders were learning their math.

BUT THE BUOYANT mood deflated in a matter of minutes, once she thought the facts through. Maybe the poisoning of the brownie was just random. Why, anyone could have eaten it. Like herself, like Mrs. Johnson. Maybe the poison was in more than one brownie. Maybe Bertha wasn't the only one to get sick or to die.

And what kind of poison were they talking about anyway? Food poisoning? Like a bad egg that found its way into the batter?

Mrs. Hopwood quickly finished her breakfast and threw on her clothes. The sudden turn of events had made her heart beat just a little faster. She couldn't do 180 days of straight teaching.

But if those days were laced with trouble, well, that she could do with her eyes closed.

SEVENTEEN

GEORGE ARLINGTON WAS very quiet, as he tiptoed into the kitchen and started to prepare his morning cup of coffee. No way did he want to risk waking up his three young daughters, or his wife, Marsha, who was desperately in need of sleep. Especially since she had gone out last night, her book club running over the usual time.

He especially did not want to wake his mother.

He loved his little girls, and God knows they were good. But they were at that age, six, eight and ten, when they were constantly arguing with each other, and sometimes it seemed as though all Marsha did was intervene. When she wasn't trying to cook and clean and look after the first Mrs. Arlington.

And George loved his mother too. Marsha knew when she married him, that he was a mama's boy. And she didn't seem to mind at first. In fact, she liked that George was so devoted to his mother. She would always say, "The way you treat your mother is the way you treat your wife."

But the truth was that Marsha had never signed up for this. Mrs. Arlington was getting old and dementia had set in. George could not imagine putting his mother in a nursing home, so he insisted that she come and live with them.

He could see the resentment in Marsha's eyes and it had created a rift between them.

A rift that he had deepened.

There was no doubt in George's mind that Marsha could not be expected to watch his mother constantly. Not when she was busy with her own family, and right now George could not afford a full time caretaker.

Or even a part time one.

Last night, when he came home from working ten hours on some stock trades—George was an investment advisor—he learned that his mother had gone out. She didn't come home until after nine, and, when he questioned her, she had no idea of where she had been. And with Marsha not being home, it was easy for her to sneak out. They could hardly expect the babysitter to watch his mother as well as the three girls.

But George had a good idea where his mother had been, because he saw the pamphlet in her handbag.

She had been at St. Polycarp, attending parent night, as though she was still a parent responsible for a student. George could only hope that she didn't continue to bother Mrs. Logan, the way she had when Mrs. Logan was the principal at St. Jude's, the way his mother had just dropped in on the first day of school and then left her purse behind. Up to now, Mrs. Logan had been patient, but sooner or later, she was bound to get a restraining order on his mother, and who could blame her?

He also had to hope that his mother didn't get hurt, while she wandered the city unattended.

Or that she didn't hurt someone else in the process.

EIGHTEEN

Mrs. Johnson didn't waste a moment, talking to Mrs. Hopwood. She wanted to tell her friend that she had called the police after midnight and what she said blew the case wide open.

Mrs. Johnson had seen Bertha take that brownie right off of Mrs. Logan's desk, and, if Mrs. Hopwood had been paying more attention, why she would have seen it too. There wasn't a doubt in Mrs. Johnson's mind that the poisoned brownie was meant for Mrs. Logan and, thanks to Mrs. Johnson, the police came to the same conclusion.

The truth was that Mrs. Johnson wanted to call Mrs. Hopwood last night, but she knew better. You also couldn't talk to her in the morning at home, because she had planned her getting ready down to the minute, and she became very crabby, if she was suddenly off schedule.

Mrs. Johnson loved her best friend dearly, but no one could ever call Mrs. Hopwood flexible.

Mrs. Johnson did not want to talk in the school. For one thing she didn't trust Mrs. Logan. There was an intercom system, which Father Felix had installed, but it broke soon after and he was too cheap to get it fixed—which was more than fine with his teachers. But when Mrs. Johnson had come to set up her classroom, she saw a mechanic unscrewing something in

the ceiling. Mrs. Johnson was guessing that the intercom had been fixed and, before Mrs. Logan made that
public knowledge, she would probably use it to spy on
teachers, to turn it on when the teachers were unaware
that anyone was listening.

Therefore Mrs. Johnson waited for Mrs. Hopwood
in her car.

Mrs. Hopwood didn't drive which was probably a
good thing, since just walking for her was difficult, due
to her love of spiked heels. When she saw her friend
lumbering down the street, Mrs. Johnson leaped out
of her car and ran in front of Mrs. Hopwood who released a slight gasp.

"You scared me half to death!"

"I've been thinking…"

Mrs. Hopwood released an exaggerated sigh.

"In my car," Mrs. Johnson insisted, "where we can
talk safely."

Mrs. Hopwood made some weak protests but she
settled in the car—dragging a bright yellow shopping
bag with her. The moment the door closed, Mrs. Johnson said that she had a theory about who might want
to kill Mrs. Logan.

Mrs. Hopwood just stared at her friend.

"Let's think about this reasonably," Mrs. Johnson
continued with as much gusto as she could manage at
seven forty on a rainy, chilly Thursday morning. "I
have thought about it. I'm sure everyone has thought
about it including Mrs. Logan and, of course, the police. It had to be someone who was in the school."

"Not necessarily."

Mrs. Johnson hated it when Mrs. Hopwood argued.
But she was forced to ask, "What do you mean?"

"Yes, it had to be someone in the school."

"That's exactly what I said."

"But it doesn't necessarily have to be someone we saw," Mrs. Hopwood commented. "There were a lot of people roaming around—maybe someone with a grudge against Mrs. Logan who might not be noticed."

"But surely Mrs. Logan would have noticed someone who hated her enough to want to kill her."

"I don't know," Mrs. Hopwood arguing again. "I have a feeling that there might be a lot of people who might want to kill Mrs. Logan."

The children were clamoring down the walk and Mrs. Johnson figured they might as well go in. Just as she was getting out of the car, she saw a police cruiser pull up. This sight made her somewhat gleeful.

Maybe they would all be questioned, and then Mrs. Johnson would have a better idea of what was going on.

And best of all, she would get to tell her story one more time.

NINETEEN

Miss Turnipseed was not feeling good about the turn of events, although she was more than eager to share her opinions with the detectives, who had come to the school to question the staff.

"How long have you worked for Mrs. Logan?" Detective Hargrove asked Miss Turnipseed, when they were behind closed doors in the teachers' room.

Miss Turnipseed hesitated a bit before answering. She didn't like this detective. For one thing, she was a young woman—heavily made-up—wearing a skirt that was too short, a sweater that was too tight, and it was red too. She wore too much jewelry and she was chewing and snapping her gum. She wasn't at all professional and, after all, this was a murder investigation.

"Did you not understand the question?" This policeman, whose name was Detective Pancretto, was easier to talk to. He had a kind face and a little pad and pen and he was dressed nicely too. His khakis were freshly pressed—crease and all—his blue tie looked crisp against his white shirt, and his hair was cut short.

Miss Turnipseed would direct her comments to him.

"I worked for her for six years at St. Jude's and she brought me to St. Polycarp."

"Had she ever had any trouble before?" the female detective asked.

"Trouble?"

"What we want to know, Miss Turnipseed," the male detective again, "is did anyone, at any point, ever threaten Mrs. Logan?"

"Not that I can remember but, of course, Mrs. Logan is a very private person."

A cell phone rang and the female detective took it out of her handbag. "I have to take this," she said

When she left the room, Miss Turnipseed breathed a sigh of relief. "My cousin is a policeman, Patrick Stoller. Maybe you know him?"

"I'm afraid not."

"He's with the second precinct."

Detective Paneretto actually sat down as he shook his head. "Did you notice anything unusual on parent/teacher night?"

"No, I didn't. Except," again Miss Turnipseed paused, "that woman—"

"Mrs. Arlington?"

Miss Turnipseed nodded.

"Mrs. Logan told us about her," the detective urged.

"Well," Miss Turnipseed was going to say exactly what she thought, "I cannot imagine her poisoning anyone. The poor thing just follows Mrs. Logan around because she thinks her son is still in the fifth grade. I doubt very much that she's capable of making brownies and putting poison in them. Besides, why would she do such a thing, if she really believes that Mrs. Logan is her son's teacher? But she was there that night, hanging around those brownies."

"How are the new teachers getting along with Mrs. Logan?"

Miss Turnipseed would not have said anything in a million years had he not asked her.

"Well, of course, it's been difficult for them," Miss Turnipseed lowered her voice to a whisper. "The word is that Father Felix, well, let's just say, he didn't run a tight ship. That worked for some teachers and others..."

"Like?"

"Well, I don't want to be talking out of school, but I know that Mrs. Hopwood is having some problems with Mrs. Logan. I overheard Mrs. Logan reprimand her for the way she dressed and there might have been some teaching concerns as well. I think you know yourself, Detective, that it's not unusual for a new boss to come aboard and want to change things."

"Are you trying to say that Mrs. Logan was going to fire Mrs. Hopwood?"

"No, she couldn't even if she wanted to. I believe that Mrs. Hopwood has tenure, and you know the union, which makes it impossible to get rid of bad teachers. Not that Mrs. Hopwood is a bad teacher. I really couldn't say. But she did transfer Mrs. Hopwood from the second grade to the fifth grade, and sometimes when teachers are given a new assignment, well, they leave of their own accord."

"Interesting."

"And maybe you don't know this," Miss Turnipseed looked around and then began to whisper again, "but several years ago, this exact school was the scene of another poisoning, and Mrs. Hopwood was one of the people who solved the case." Miss Turnipseed would not say what she was thinking—that sometimes the people who solved the case were somehow involved in the crime itself.

"Yes, we know all about that," Detective Paneretto said dryly.

Miss Turnipseed saw Detective Hargrove standing by the threshold. "Is that all? I have to return to the front desk. All this excitement, well, there has been a lot of phone calls from the parents, as you can imagine."

"Sure, you can go now." Detective Paneretto dug into his pocket and took out a business card. "If you think of anything else, will you please give me a call?"

"Of course." Miss Turnipseed stood suddenly, feeling edgy. This entire sordid affair had taken a definite toll on her. "And if I see anything unusual, or overhear anything unusual, should I also give you a call?"

"Absolutely. Keep your eyes and ears open."

As Miss Turnipseed made her way to the front office, she felt a tiny stab of guilt. Mrs. Hopwood was taking her fifth grade class down to lunch, and she herself looked rather piqued.

But there was no denying the fact that Mrs. Hopwood had been present when Bertha Butterworth actually ate the brownie, that she and Mrs. Logan did not get along, and that her clothes, which may be fashionable, were inappropriate for an elementary school.

So the police could draw their own conclusions.

TWENTY

Mrs. Hopwood was very much looking forward to being questioned by the police. For one thing, it meant that she would get out of teaching for a few blessed minutes. Mrs. Logan had the librarian, Mrs. Sugarman, cover for her.

She sat down with the full intention of being cooperative and learning as much as she could about the murder of poor Bertha. But it only took her a few moments to be put on the defensive by Detective Paneretto.

"So you were there when Bertha Butterworth ate the brownie?" It sounded like an accusation.

"Well, yes, I saw her take a bite. But then Mrs. Johnson and I left. We came back when Mrs. Logan was rapping on the window."

"Did you see the brownie on Mrs. Logan's desk before you left?"

Mrs. Hopwood hesitated, and the way that Detective Paneretto stared at her with wide eyes, she was afraid that he took her pause as an admission of guilt. "I don't remember."

"How do you and Mrs. Logan get along?"

Mrs. Hopwood looked at the brightly clothed woman in the corner. She seemed to be taking notes on her phone, but up until now, she hadn't said a word.

"I barely know Mrs. Logan. I've only been working for her less than a month. She seems fine."

"Fine? I understand you had some issues with her."

If Mrs. Johnson had said such a thing, than there was going to be another murder at St. Polycarp.

"I had no issues with her."

"You didn't mind when she switched your grade?"

For a moment Mrs. Hopwood considered lying. She could claim that she had requested the switch last year from Father Felix. After all, Father Felix was in Rome. By the time they contacted him—she decided against it. Lying might be dangerous. "Well, of course, at first I was quite taken aback. I have taught second grade for a number of years and I really like that age group. However, in retrospect, it will probably turn out to be a good thing. Sometimes we get used to doing things a certain way, in a certain routine, and we don't push ourselves, expand our abilities, so to speak."

It was a nice speech but she could tell by Detective Paneretto's hard smile that he wasn't buying it.

"What do you think of Miss Turnipseed?" The woman detective suddenly sat down very close to Mrs. Hopwood, who could now smell her musky scent.

"This is my partner, Detective Hargrove."

Mrs. Hopwood managed to nod and then she said quickly, "I really don't know her. She seems very competent."

"What about Bertha Butterworth?" Detective Hargrove was eying her with suspicion.

"I didn't know her very well either. I mean, I know she was a dining room lady, and she was very good to the children, but I never really—"

"Talked to her," Detective Hargrove finished the sentence in a manner that suggested that Mrs. Hopwood was somewhat of a snob. "Mrs. Johnson?"

"What about Mrs. Johnson?"

"How do you feel about her?"

Mrs. Hopwood thought this was a very peculiar question, but she wasn't about to make trouble. "Mrs. Johnson and I are very close friends."

"Would you do anything for her?"

"Well," Mrs. Hopwood figured it would be best not to hesitate too long, "within reason."

"And do you believe she would do anything for you?"

"I guess."

"That's all for now," Detective Paneretto stood up. Mrs. Hopwood almost expected him to say "don't leave town." Instead he stood at the doorway, indicating that she should go.

Go and return to that horrible class, when all Mrs. Hopwood wanted to do was talk to Mrs. Johnson.

SHE HAD DISMISSED the students and was on the way across the hall, when she saw Mrs. Johnson conferring with an anxious mother. "I don't like the fact that my child can't do algebra," she said shaking her head.

"She'll be fine," Mrs. Johnson answered in a soothing voice.

But the woman was not easily consoled. "Her brother had no problem with math. He could do multiplication problems in first grade."

"We don't like to compare. Everyone gets what she needs and everyone learns at her own speed."

"That sounds like a lot of rhetoric." She crossed her arms. "I know at other schools, they give more math homework, so the children have a good math sense by the time they enter eighth grade."

"It's only the second week of school."

"I know that. It's only the second week of school and already there's been a murder."

Mrs. Johnson spotted Mrs. Hopwood and gave her a weak smile.

"Please don't worry, Mrs. Brown, I'll work with your daughter."

Mrs. Brown seemed temporarily appeased, although she glared at Mrs. Hopwood, as she stomped down the stairs.

THEY SAT IN Mrs. Johnson's classroom, and Mrs. Hopwood gave her a friend a recap of what had occurred during her interrogation. She wasn't surprised that Mrs. Johnson had a similar experience.

"It's as though they suspected us of something," Mrs. Hopwood lamented. "Like if we were going to kill Mrs. Logan, we would do it with a poisoned brownie. Everyone knows the best way to kill someone is to make it look like an accident."

Mrs. Johnson made a disgusting sound with the bottom of her throat. "Don't say that to anyone else! They might think you're serious."

"Well, who do you think did it?"

"Probably someone who she had past dealings with. Someone who didn't like her. Because let's face it, Mrs. Logan is not a likable person. Did the detectives ask you about Mrs. Arlington?"

"Whom."

"Whom what?"

"It's whom she had past dealings with. And you shouldn't end a sentence with a preposition."

"Oh, give me a break! Did the detective ask you about Mrs. Arlington?"

"Who?"

"You know," Mrs. Johnson got up to gather her belongings, "that crazy woman who thinks her son still goes to school here."

"No, he didn't." And Mrs. Hopwood was wondering why.

As though Mrs. Johnson could read her mind, and she probably could, she said quickly, "Well, after all, she came to me initially. And remember, she was here last night."

"Last night?" Mrs. Hopwood said thoughtfully. "Somehow it seems as though it happened a long time ago."

"Well, my money's on her," Mrs. Johnson said firmly.

"That would make it easy," Mrs. Hopwood agreed.

"But as Father Felix used to say, nothing is ever easy and everything is a battle."

TWENTY-ONE

"YOUR WIFE IS on line six, Mr. Arlington."

Yes, he had heard his cell phone vibrate, and he had chosen to ignore it. He was too busy, trying to make sense of the figures in front of him. No matter which way he added or subtracted it just didn't come out even.

More than not even.

Like over one thousand dollars—just gone.

"Your wife?"

"Yeah, I got it." *But I wish I didn't*, George thought as he picked up the phone. He was sure he was going to hear a list of complaints about his mother or the girls.

"Yes, Marsha," he tried to get the impatience out of his voice.

"Something terrible has happened." His wife sounded hysterical—more than her usual hysterical. "The police are here."

George felt his stomach plummet. "Is my mother missing?"

"No, she's home. But they think she might be responsible for the murder of Bertha Butterworth."

"Who the hell is Bertha Butterworth?"

"She was a cafeteria lady at St. Polycarp."

"Why would my mother murder a cafeteria lady?"

"It's complicated. They came here to question her. And you know how your mother keeps opening and closing her damn handbag? Well, they found something in it. Just please come home, right away." She slammed down the phone.

George grabbed his suit jacket, closed down his computer and left his office. "Tell Mr. Foskett I have a family emergency."

His secretary frowned and George knew what she was thinking. Mr. Foskett would not be happy that there was another family emergency.

Well, no one would be happy.

Except for the account he was auditing.

WHEN GEORGE SAW the three police cruisers in front of his house, his stomach turned over. This was evidently very serious, although he couldn't imagine how his mother could be involved in killing someone—unless...

Unless this Bertha aggravated her to such an extent that she hit Bertha over the head with some sort of deadly weapon. But surely no one could hold her accountable.

When he entered the front door, he found a bewildered Marsha in the kitchen with his three terrified daughters and his mother, who was enjoying a cup of coffee and a Scooter Pie.

And there were police all over the house.

"What are they doing?" He was trying to keep the anger out of his voice. "Hey guys," he called to the cops in the hall, "what are you doing? You can't search without a warrant."

The cop stopped and stared at him. "Your wife gave us permission."

George turned towards Marsha. "What were you thinking?"

"We have nothing to hide."

A woman came into the kitchen. George surmised that she might be a detective, because she wasn't wearing a police uniform and had on a short black leather skirt and a tight white sweater. She introduced herself as Detective Hargrove, as she held his mother's orange handbag.

"What are you doing with that?" His mother jumped off the couch with the intention of grabbing the purse, but the detective handed it over to a police officer. "They have stolen my pocketbook! I need a policeman. Another policeman."

"What's going on here?"

"This is your mother's purse. When she opened it, we found fluoroacetate in it."

"What?"

"It's an industrial poison."

"That's impossible!"

His six-year-old, Catherine, started to wail.

"There is no way my mother could have such a substance."

"When am I going to get my pocketbook back?"

"Someone must have put it there."

Except for Catherine's crying, the room had become quiet. They were all staring at George. "It's impossible," he muttered into the silence.

"Nevertheless," Detective Hargrove said, "we're going to have to take her in for questioning."

"She's not well," was all George could murmur.

"We'll have a physician examine her, of course, and you're free to call a lawyer."

"Please," George pleaded, "why would my mother kill a cafeteria lady?"

"We think she poisoned a brownie meant for Mrs.

Logan, whom she did know, and whom she did blame for keeping her son from her."

"I'm her son—"

"We know all that," Detective Hargrove said. "But *she* doesn't, and that's the point."

"She's not capable of murder!" George bellowed.

"That's for a doctor to decide. You can follow us in your car."

He looked at his wife, Marsha, who merely shook her head. And then George saw something else in her eyes. Just a flash of relief. His mother was going someplace, maybe for a long period of time.

Which meant that Marsha was free.

And then he began to wonder.

TWENTY-TWO

MRS. JOHNSON WAS ready to retire when the doorbell rang, which irritated her greatly. She had just put her twins to bed, and she was enjoying her nightly glass of red wine. Her husband was working late again and she was relishing the peace and quiet.

Her first thought was the pesky neighbor from above who frequently reported on the twins' nanny when she saw the nanny in the park with the children. The neighbor said that the nanny spent a lot of time on her phone, often spoke sharply to the boys, and dragged them home against their will.

Mrs Johnson knew that the nanny was not exactly Mary Poppins, but she showed up every day, never asked to leave early, never tried to negotiate a raise and often did the breakfast dishes. Without the nanny, Mrs. Johnson could not work, and if Mrs. Johnson could not work, she would miss the income and her social life, which revolved around the school.

It wasn't the upstairs neighbor.

It was the two detectives, who had questioned her earlier that day.

Mrs. Johnson invited them in and offered them a glass of wine, which they declined. They didn't even sit down. She didn't feel good about this at all.

"Has there been any developments in the case?" she asked, trying to make her voice confident.

The two detectives eyed each other before Detective Paneretto asked, "We just want to clear up a little matter."

"Of course."

"Did you take Mrs. Arlington's purse at any time?"

The question caught Mrs. Johnson by surprise. "I never saw her purse on the night Bertha was poisoned. I did see Mrs. Arlington in the audience and running down the stairs. Well, she wasn't really running, but she was going rather fast, I mean, for a woman her age." Mrs. Johnson hated that she was babbling and stopped immediately.

"We're not talking about the night she was murdered. We're talking about last week, when she left her purse in your classroom."

It took Mrs. Johnson a moment to remember. "Yes, I did. And I returned it immediately to Mrs. Logan. She called Mrs. Arlington's son, and I'm assuming that he took the purse. Why?"

"Just wondering," Detective Hargrove said.

"I never opened it or looked into it. I had no reason to."

"Okay," Detective Hargrove seemed more satisfied than Detective Paneretto, who was casting a curious glance around her apartment, as though he suspected that she was hiding another poisoned victim. "If you can think of anything else, give us a call."

"Yes, of course. I want to help any way I can. Why it could have been any one of us who ate that brownie! I wanted a brownie myself but there was none left. It's a good thing—" *Stop,* she told herself, *stop trying to be their friend.* She walked them to the door and held it open for them.

And the moment they left, she called Mrs. Hopwood.

SHE KNEW THAT she was going to wake Mrs. Hopwood since Mrs. Hopwood frequently retired around nine o'clock, but Mrs. Johnson considered this an emergency, and she told that to Mrs. Hopwood when she answered the phone— sleepy and disoriented.

Mrs. Johnson got right to the point. "The police were here."

"What?" Mrs. Hopwood seemed to have perked up.

"They asked me about Mrs. Arlington's purse."

"What do you know about Mrs. Arlington's purse?" Mrs. Hopwood seemed wide awake now.

"Remember last week when she came into my classroom looking for George? Well, she left her handbag behind. I found it as I was getting ready to leave, and I gave it to Mrs. Logan, who I'm sure called her son to pick it up. But for some reason, the police think I tampered with it."

"Why would you do such a thing?"

"Of course, I wouldn't. I have the feeling that they think I took something from her purse or maybe put something into it. The police weren't at all forthcoming. Why would they be if they thought I was a suspect?"

"Why would you kill Bertha Butterworth?"

"Please!" Maybe Mrs. Hopwood wasn't as awake as Mrs. Johnson had thought. "It wasn't Bertha who was supposed to be killed but Mrs. Logan. Remember?"

"But Mrs. Logan likes you. Of course, she doesn't like me."

"Then you should be the suspect, not me."

"And," Mrs. Hopwood hesitated.

"And what?"

"The police did ask me if you would do anything for me. I did say within reason."

"Thanks a lot!" Mrs. Johnson said.

"Well, I doubt if they think that you would actually murder for me. Would you?"

"Of course not!"

"Besides, they're probably going to arrest Mrs. Arlington and that will be the end of it."

"I doubt it," Mrs. Johnson said dryly. "You know there is no end to trouble and we are about to have plenty of it."

TWENTY-THREE

Miss Turnipseed knew without a doubt that Mrs. Arlington hadn't poisoned Mrs. Logan's brownie. The whole idea was absurd. The poor woman, who spent her days searching for her little boy, would have no reason to kill the one link she had to the past. Besides, where would she even get the poison? The police had arrested the wrong person.

Why weren't they questioning Mrs. Johnson and Mrs. Hopwood?

After all they had been mixed up in another poisoning right at this very school. Father Felix probably had something to do with it as well, and perhaps that was why he had been sent clear across the Atlantic to Rome. The Church knew how to cover things up. But they hadn't gotten rid of those two teachers, and that was a mistake. Instead the police had arrested someone else, who was still claiming to be innocent.

They were probably serial killers who fed on one another.

She tried to steer the police in their direction, but the detectives just didn't seem too clever. Too young, she supposed, and inexperienced, especially the woman detective.

Didn't they ever watch TV? Didn't they know what seemingly normal people were capable of?

Today was the church service, and she and Mrs.

Logan were going together. So were most of the teachers. She was certain that Mrs. Johnson and Mrs. Hopwood would be there as well. Murderers often attended wakes and funerals of their victims to admire their handiwork.

And Miss Turnipseed would be watching them closely.

MUCH TO MISS Turnipseed's surprise, there was no coffin. She heard several of Bertha's relatives say that the police wouldn't release the body. Bertha's relatives all looked very much like her. Solid and strong with round faces and big, poppy eyes.

Miss Turnipseed had only seen Bertha briefly, when Bertha was alive, and she had been smiling. But these relatives weren't smiling. Their expressions were hard and their postures stiff.

They were angry.

Mrs. Logan and Miss Turnipseed sat in the back of the church, and the teachers sat behind them. No one spoke to them and Miss Turnipseed saw Mrs. Johnson approach a tall, balding man with a high forehead. She had to smile to herself, when she saw the man scowl at Mrs. Johnson and refuse to shake her hand.

After the long funeral Mass ended, a slew of relatives raced up to the pulpit to talk about poor Bertha.

"My cousin was a saint. She would do anything for anyone. And in the end, she took a bullet meant for someone else, someone she barely knew." Mrs. Logan's face flushed with this comment.

"My sister loved life. She loved to visit with her nieces and her nephews to read to them, to play video games. She loved to bake with them. She loved to eat, and she especially loved desserts."

Miss Turnipseed was thinking that if she hadn't been so greedy, she would probably still be alive.

"My aunt was a curious person. She always took an interest in other people, what they were doing, what they were feeling."

And then her husband came up. A man, who looked very much like a large handkerchief, with white hair that pointed up and watery blue eyes behind wire framed glasses, took the pulpit. "I loved my Bertha!" he wailed and then aided by Bertha's niece, sank down into the pew.

After the service family and friends were invited to Moe's Pizzeria to continue reminiscing about Bertha, but there was no question that Mrs. Logan would not be welcome, so of course, Miss Turnipseed could not attend either.

She wondered if the two teachers would show up. What she knew about them was that they were nervy, so they would probably be there, asking all sorts of crazy questions.

TWENTY-FOUR

"I DON'T THINK we should go," Mrs. Hopwood said. "They seem like an angry bunch."

"Well, you would be angry too," Mrs. Johnson argued, "if a relative of yours was dead, just because she ate a poisoned brownie meant for someone else."

"I'm not saying that they don't have a right to be angry."

"Well, why would they be mad at us?" Mrs. Johnson argued. "We didn't do anything wrong. I was always nice to Bertha. I asked about her two cats and her dead dog. She even gave me seconds when they were serving grilled cheese sandwiches. She actually liked me."

"But her family doesn't know that." It was Saturday and Mrs. Hopwood wanted to go home. She needed to do her grocery shopping for the week and wash and blow dry her hair, and mop the kitchen floor. Going to a pizzeria with a bunch of strangers, who were mourning a woman she barely knew, was not on her agenda. "I think it was nice of us to come to the funeral but beyond that—"

"We'll only stay fifteen minutes, just to show our faces. And I'll give you a ride home."

"You lie."

THE RESTAURANT WAS CROWDED, and they couldn't find seats. It was also hot and noisy. Mrs. Hopwood followed Mrs. Johnson, who stopped at a table to talk to Bertha's niece.

"We are so very sorry," she said, speaking for the two of them. "We loved Bertha. She was like family to us."

The niece, Camilla, who looked a little like Bertha herself, pinched her lips and then started to talk about how smart her aunt was. "I know that some people thought she was just a dining room lady."

"We never saw her like that," Mrs. Johnson protested as she grabbed a piece of pizza from the tray and was now chewing rather noisily.

"She was very smart, maybe too smart for her own good. Would you excuse me? I need to talk to Uncle Lester."

"Can we go now?" Mrs. Hopwood asked, as Mrs. Johnson grabbed another piece of pizza and a bottle of orange soda.

THOROUGHLY EXHAUSTED, MRS. HOPWOOD didn't rise until nine on the following day. She decided to check her e-mail—which turned out to be a mistake. Mrs. Hopwood longed for the day when computers were not in the classroom and parents and principals were not allowed to contact you 24/7, over trivial matters. And this seemed to be a trivial matter, although Mrs. Logan, who was copied on the e-mail, might not think so.

I understand you gave a multiplication test to the students last week, just to see what everyone knew and what you needed to review. You gave Antonio a hundred, told him it was great and pasted a sticker of what looked like a dead rat on the paper.

Mrs. Hopwood knew it was supposed to be a cute mouse but her water bottle leaked on it.

But either you corrected them in a careless manner, or you yourself do not know the multiplication tables. You failed to mark two of them wrong, when they are clearly incorrect. Attached please find the paper in question and you will see what I mean.

It is hard for me to teach Antonio the importance of studying, when he receives a great and a messy sticker, when his quiz was anything but.

I hope this won't occur again.

Mrs. Hopwood clicked on the attachment and saw a copy of the test with the two incorrect answers circled in a bright red pencil. All right, so she had made a mistake. But really, who had the time to look over every single problem—*apparently not Mrs. Hopwood.* When her own son, Alexander, was in elementary school, and he came home with a sticker and a great on his paper, she got down on her knees and thanked the Lord. And she rewarded her son with an ice cream sundae. She wasn't looking for trouble.

At least not this kind of trouble.

Oh well, Mrs. Hopwood thought, she would have to be more careful from here on in, when correcting papers.

One more thing to be careful about.

"AMELIA?"

"What time is it?" Mrs. Johnson was definitely sleepy.

"It's after nine. I'm sorry I woke you."

"It's all right. I want to go to the ten thirty Mass. You should go too. When was the last time you attended Mass?"

Mrs. Hopwood decided that subject was to be best avoided, and instead told Mrs. Johnson about Antonio.

"I suppose you didn't have him in second grade, since he just came last year," Mrs. Johnson said. "I had his older brother, Luca, last year. I'll tell you one thing, that mother is trouble."

"Like I don't have enough trouble. I'm thinking that if we find out who tried to kill Mrs. Logan, she will be eternally grateful to us and she'll let our little deficiencies slide."

"I don't have any deficiencies. Besides, the police think it was Mrs. Arlington."

"Yes, it might be," Mrs. Hopwood agreed. "I do feel sorry for her. But it might also be someone from Mrs. Logan's past."

"But we don't know anything about Mrs. Logan's past."

"But what we do know is that it was someone there that night. And it's hard to believe that Mrs. Logan wouldn't have recognized a person who didn't belong."

Mrs. Johnson was silent. For a moment. "So what exactly are you saying?" she finally asked.

"I don't know," Mrs. Hopwood confessed.

"Go to church."

TWENTY-FIVE

"SHE DOESN'T BELONG in a mental institution!" George told his wife. "My mother has a form of dementia. That doesn't make her a killer!"

"I agree." George could tell that Marsha was trying hard to be calm, "If it wasn't for the fluoroacetate in her purse."

"Someone must have put it there! It's the only explanation."

"But who?" Marsha fired back at him. "The purse was only away from her for a short while. And it was in the school the entire time. That teacher, whatever her name is—"

"Johnson, I think."

"Well, she gave it right to Mrs. Logan."

"That's what Mrs. Johnson claims," George argued. "But supposing she is not telling the truth?"

"Why would Mrs. Johnson want to kill Mrs. Logan? She barely knew her. Mrs. Logan had only been the principal there for a few days."

"I've given this a great deal of thought." George hesitated as Marsha gave him an intense, fevered stare. "Let's suppose that for some reason that there is something in Mrs. Johnson's past, something we don't know about but something Mrs. Logan is about to find out. So Mrs. Johnson framed my mother for the crime. She put the fluoroacetate in my mother's purse, before she gave it back to Mrs. Logan. Are you with me?"

"I'm with you." Marsha could barely keep the hostility out of her voice. "How would Mrs. Johnson know that your mother was going to be present at the parent/teacher evening? We didn't even know. Your mother sneaked out. And furthermore, how would she know that your mother was going to bring that exact purse? None of this makes sense."

"She sneaked out because you weren't watching her!" George said. "You were at that stupid book club, where you probably do more gossiping than you do reading."

"I'm not even going to respond to that!" Marsha released a quick, disgusted snort. "Except to say that now and then, I deserve a night out!"

George couldn't think of a valid argument for a battle he had already lost. So instead he said, "I'll tell you what doesn't make sense. Let's just say my mother hated Mrs. Logan, because she thought Mrs. Logan was being unfair to me as a young kid. So she goes and buys this poison, although when she did this and how she did this, who knows? So she puts it in her purse. How would *she* know that she would have the opportunity to sprinkle some on a brownie?"

"Well, maybe your mother was hoping she would have a chance sometime."

"You know my mother, Marsha, you know her better than anyone. Do you really think she has the mental capacity to plan something like this?"

Marsha was silent.

"I just don't see it. We have to get her a lawyer and we have to get her out."

"Maybe," Marsha hesitated. "Maybe she's better off where she is."

"What are you saying?"

"Well, she's getting help there. We couldn't help her at home."

"This isn't a hospital, Marsha! It's a prison!"

"What can *I* do?" Marsha asked.

"Nothing. You can do nothing. But I'm going to tell you what I'm going to do. I'm going to find out who tried to kill Mrs. Logan, if it's the last thing I do."

TWENTY-SIX

Mrs. Johnson was busy on the computer, which she had no qualms about being, since Mrs. Logan was at the police station. She was doing a search on Bertha Butterworth, which turned up nothing.

On the other hand, Mrs. Lenora Logan was all over the internet. She had graduated from an Ivy League school and had been a sixth grade teacher for fifteen years at St. Therese, before becoming assistant principal. She taught fifth grade for twelve years at St. Jude's before becoming principal, where she remained until it closed last year.

During her tenure at St. Jude's one of her teachers, Clara Edwards, vanished upon leaving the school. Although the police investigated briefly, they came to the conclusion that no foul play was involved. Edwards' family, however, was not convinced.

When Mrs. Johnson's students began to storm into the classroom, she clicked off the site and began to teach them how to write a business letter.

Mrs. Hopwood had lunch duty, so Mrs. Johnson did not see her. But as soon as school dismissed, she hightailed it to Mrs. Hopwood's classroom. But a quick peek inside told her that Mrs. Hopwood was not alone.

She was talking to a parent.

"Thank you for meeting with me, Mrs. Hopwood."

"What can I do for you, Mrs. O'Hara?"

"Well, let me begin by saying that I am actually representing the parents at a meeting we had this morning."

"So you're not here about Brigid?"

Mrs. Johnson stood in the hall, thinking that this was not going to be good.

"No, I'm not. I'm speaking on behalf of the class. But since you did bring up Brigid, did you tell her that it's not all about her?"

"Well," Mrs. Hopwood hesitated, "she was holding up the line, when it was time to go to the cafeteria."

"Her feelings were very hurt. She's young for her age, you know. She's a February birthday. She should really be in fourth grade but she's so smart that we started her early."

"Do you want me to tell her I'm sorry I embarrassed her?" Mrs. Johnson detected hostility in Mrs. Hopwood's voice.

"I wish you would. Anyway, some of the mothers are complaining because you scream at the children."

"Well, I wouldn't say screamed."

"That's what the children say. But it's not only the kids who are complaining. Some of the teachers have mentioned it to Mrs. Logan."

"I won't do it again."

"I hope that you don't. Tell me, Mrs. Hopwood, do you like teaching?"

Mrs. Johnson thought that poor Mrs. Hopwood had been tortured enough. "Excuse me," she entered the room. "I'm sorry to intrude, but we have a meeting. Remember Mrs. Hopwood?"

A moment of surprise flashed across her friend's

face, but she found her voice soon enough. "Yes, I'm so sorry, Mrs. O'Hara. If you have any other problems, you know where to reach me."

"Well, yes, I guess I do. It's nice to see you again, Mrs. Johnson." She stood, obviously flabbergasted by the turn of events.

Mrs. Hopwood gathered her school bag and her lemon yellow sweater, shut the light in her classroom, as Mrs. O'Hara exited, not too gracefully.

On the way to the car, Mrs. Johnson admitted that she had taught Aiden O'Hara in seventh grade. "Don't you remember how much trouble I had with him? He was always in Father Felix's office. That mother is a pain in the neck for you and I. Good luck."

"For I? You mean for me. Object of a preposition takes the objective case."

Mrs. Johnson ignored the correction in grammar. "Anyway, I found something out about Mrs. Logan. While she was teaching at St. Jude's, one of her teachers disappeared."

"Oh." Mrs. Hopwood flung open the car door. "And that is relative because?"

"It wasn't just a normal disappearance. The teacher's family thought there might have been foul play. And get this, she disappeared after she left the school. She just never went home." Mrs. Johnson settled herself in the car and then gazed up at the window, where Mrs. Logan was staring down at them.

Mrs. Hopwood looked up as well. "It makes me kind of sad," she admitted. "You know how many times you and I looked up there and saw Father Felix waving to us?"

"Now, he's waving to the Pope." Mrs. Johnson

started the car. "So I'm thinking that maybe the attempt on Mrs. Logan's life has something to do with the missing teacher. Like for instance—I hate bike riders. Look at this one. He's going the wrong way on a one way street. They don't obey any rules and they're completely unpredictable. They don't pay attention to lights, they ride on the sidewalks and they make sharp turns. Mark by words. They kill a lot of people."

"Don't you think the police have considered that?" Mrs. Hopwood asked.

"The police don't seem to care about the bikers. Maybe they are bikers themselves."

"I mean about Clara Edwards!" Mrs. Hopwood rolled her eyes.

"I'm sure they've done some research. I mean, if I can learn all of this by searching through the computer, they can also. But I think I'm going to do a little digging on what happened to Clara Edwards."

"Clara Edwards," Mrs. Hopwood repeated thoughtfully. "I wonder why that sounds so familiar."

"We have to help, we do," Mrs. Johnson said. "After all, the next time the killer makes a mistake it could be with one of us."

"Or maybe," Mrs. Hopwood sounded vaguely excited. "The next time the killer won't make a mistake and poor Mrs. Logan will be the one murdered. That would mean we'd get a new principal, wouldn't it?"

Mrs. Johnson stopped the car and stared at her friend. "Don't say that aloud," she warned. "Or better yet, don't even think it."

TWENTY-SEVEN

Miss Turnipseed was sure that she was going to have nothing more to do with the police. But she was wrong.

He came that morning when she was getting ready for school. The knock on her front door frightened her. Miss Turnipseed was not used to having visitors and at seven in the morning. When she looked through the peephole, she saw Detective Paneretto standing outside. Well, at least he was alone, and not with that terrible lady.

Still she left the chain on. "Can I help you?"

"I need to speak to you for a moment, Miss Turnipseed. May I come inside?"

"I'm going to be late, if we talk now. Perhaps if you come by the school later on this morning?"

"I'm sure that Mrs. Logan will understand. After all, we're doing our best to protect her."

Miss Turnipseed had no recourse, but to admit the detective, although she wasn't sure that Mrs. Logan would understand at all. She expected her secretary to be there promptly at seven thirty, to answer the phones, to deal with irate parents, to supervise absent teachers.

If the detective continued to be rude, she would have to remind him of her cousin, Patrick. That would make him jump to.

"I just have a few questions."

"I told you everything I know. I wasn't there when

the…the accident," Miss Turnipseed still could not bring herself to say murder, "occurred."

"You mean when Mrs. Butterworth actually ate the brownie. But you were downstairs when the brownies were being laid out."

Miss Turnipseed did not like the direction this conversation was going. Not in the least.

"Well, actually we're not asking you about the other night," which relieved Miss Turnipseed. "May I sit down?"

Miss Turnipseed nodded, but she wasn't pleased, not at all. She had to put her face powder on, take off her housecoat, finish her tea, and slash on her crimson lipstick. Some other woman might relish in the fact that she was going to be late for school. Some other woman might not care.

But Miss Turnipseed took pride in her work. And besides, she did not want to answer any more questions.

"We are asking about the disappearance of one of your teachers."

Miss Turnipseed was surprised, so she said nothing.

"I think her name was Clara Edwards."

"That occurred at another school," Miss Turnipseed said coldly. "And it has nothing whatsoever to do with St. Polycarp."

"Maybe yes, maybe no. Could you tell me what happened?"

"Nothing happened. She wasn't a very good teacher. She had no class management skills and to tell you the truth, I think she was rather frightened of her eighth graders. Parents complained about her all the time. There was so much noise in her classroom, you could barely hear her speak. Mrs. Logan was getting ready to fire her and then one day, she just didn't come into work. I can't speak for Clara, but I think she was relieved."

"But according to her sister, she simply vanished."

"Well, it's not for me to say, of course, but from what I understand, Clara and her sister hadn't spoken in over a year. So her sister would hardly be the judge of whether or not something was missing from Clara's apartment."

"I guess you got a point there," Detective Paneretto admitted.

"Other than her teaching ability, I have to tell you that Clara was a lovely person. She and I were working friends, so to speak. The day she disappeared she wanted to meet me—to give her advice. Maybe she was dating someone and maybe it wasn't working out. Not having a wealth of advice on that subject myself, I doubt if I could have been much help. I couldn't meet her because one of my cats was sick. The cat passed on. And Clara never came to school the next day."

"I see." Detective Paneretto's voice was flat. Could he be suspecting her?

Miss Turnipseed tried another tactic. "I am trying to be cooperative. It's in my best interest. Why I could have eaten the brownie. And, if someone is bound and determined to kill Mrs. Logan, well, I'm at the front desk. If they come in guns blazing or waving a knife, I'm liable to die right alongside of her. I want this person caught as much as you do, more than you do."

"I'm sure you do." Thankfully, he was heading for the door. "And just so you know, I don't suspect you, Miss Turnipseed." He closed the door behind him.

She didn't believe a word he said.

TWENTY-EIGHT

"I'M TELLING YOU," Mrs. Johnson insisted to Mrs. Hopwood as they ambled to a full faculty meeting. "I really believe that the teacher's disappearance has something to do with the attempted murder of Mrs. Logan."

Mrs. Hopwood didn't buy it. "Why would someone try to poison Mrs. Logan because one of her teachers disappeared?"

"Maybe," Mrs. Johnson stopped for a moment, "maybe Mrs. Logan made the teacher disappear."

"Why would Mrs. Logan make a teacher disappear, just because she wasn't good at her job? She could just fire her. Here goes, another dull faculty meeting."

"If we're lucky," Mrs. Johnson mumbled.

"WELCOME, FACULTY." MRS. LOGAN stood at the head of the library. "We have a few announcements and then Taylor," she turned towards Taylor, who was patting her perfectly blown highlighted chestnut brown hair, "will explain about our new curriculum mapping. We will then break into groups and you will work on planning for the next two months."

Mrs. Hopwood heard Mrs. Johnson sigh behind her.

"Now for the announcements. I want to make this perfectly clear, especially to some of the teachers who have been at St. Polycarp for a while. We have discussed this before, but it bears repeating. Please try not to call in sick. If it's an absolute necessity, then lesson plans should be emailed to me before school day begins. If you have to be out for two days or more, you need a doctor's note before you can come back. Those teachers who insist upon breaking the rules, well, we will just have to dock your pay."

Mrs. Hopwood released a slight gasp and everyone stared at her.

"We don't want to do this. It makes a lot of work for poor Miss Turnipseed, not to speak of the diocese. And it is certainly true that a few rotten apples can spoil the barrel." She paused and looked around. Mrs. Hopwood noticed Mrs. Johnson lowered her eyes.

"I also want to caution you about making friends with the parents of our students. They are not our peers, they are our employers. At my last school, some of the teachers went out to dinner with parents. While this may seem like a good idea, I am here to tell you, it is not. While speaking, you may say something inappropriate, something about another family, for instance, or repeat gossip about another student. You may open a door, which should stay closed. Now Taylor will explain the curriculum mapping and she will pass out the list, so everyone will know what room you're going to meet in. That's all."

AND THAT WAS ALL. Then Mrs. Hopwood sat and listened to Taylor go on in a dull monotone about the need to map out the entire year of social studies, which should include class trips and a lot of writing assignments, a lot of carefully monitored research on Google, a lot of integration with math and literacy and one project based lesson, where the students would actually *do* one related activity.

After Taylor finished, Mrs. Hopwood met with Addison for a half an hour of completely irrelevant discussions. Usually these discussions led nowhere—at least when Father Felix was principal—but Mrs. Hopwood thought that Mrs. Logan might actually follow through with some of the plans.

Mrs. Hopwood was jerked out of her trance, when Addison's cell phone rang. Maybe Addison would become involved in a long, convoluted conversation, and they would all get a respite from the causes of the American Revolution.

Addison, however, did not want a respite. Instead she glanced at the phone, shook her head, put it on mute and tossed it on the empty desk beside her.

Mrs. Hopwood could not resist a peek.

Featherston Investments.

Addison was rich and had investments. So what was she doing, teaching in such a poor school?

"I changed my mind," Mrs. Hopwood said to Mrs. Johnson when the meeting ended. "I know now that any former teacher would happily kill her."

"But obviously not one she brought with her." Mrs. Johnson was getting ready to argue.

"Maybe." A thought just flickered through Mrs. Hopwood's muddled brain. "You know how she is doing a Corey Check on everyone? Well, maybe she is about to find something out about someone that she didn't know before."

"I guess it's a possibility. Come on, I'll give you a lift home. Just let me go back to my classroom and grab my school bag."

Mrs. Hopwood plopped down on the hard chair in front of Mrs. Logan's office. She appreciated the ride home, but the truth was by the time Amelia gathered her belongings, checked her e-mails, sent texts to her nanny and her husband and actually emerged from her classroom, Mrs. Hopwood could already have arrived home, if she had taken the bus.

"My mother did not try to kill you!" Mrs. Hopwood heard a male voice behind the door of Mrs. Logan's office.

"I'm not the person who arrested her, George. You should really be talking to the police."

"But you know my mother, Mrs. Logan. You have known her for over twenty years. You know that she's no killer."

"No, George, I'm afraid that's not quite true. I knew your mother twenty years ago, when she was a homemaker with an eleven-year-old son. The woman who has been harassing me for the last couple of years is a stranger to me and most probably to you as well. I have no idea what she is capable of. And may I remind you that the poison used in the brownie was found in her handbag?"

"Someone planted it there."

"But how is that possible? Only two people touched your mother's purse while she was in the school and left it in Mrs. Johnson's room. I doubt very much if Mrs. Johnson would want to kill me, since we just met. And when she gave the purse to me, I put it aside and handed it straight to you, when you came to get it. So you see—"

"My mother is innocent."

Mrs. Hopwood heard the phone ring.

"I'm sorry, George, I have to take this call. All I can

say is that your mother is getting the help she needs and, for that, you should be grateful."

The door burst open and Mrs. Hopwood saw a man emerge. He was dressed in a suit, wearing a tie that was slightly askew. His black hair was uncombed and he was unshaven. Deep circles under his blue eyes made him look tired and overwhelmed.

She recognized him instantly as the man she had seen outside her classroom.

Mrs. Hopwood would never know what made her do it, but suddenly she sprang up.

"Mr. Arlington?"

He stopped and stared at her, a befuddled look on his face.

"I just want you to know, for the record, I believe you."

TWENTY-NINE

WHEN GEORGE GOT into his car, he was actually shaking.

What had the teacher meant when she said that she believed him? Did she mean that she believed that his mother was actually innocent? There was only one reason why she would say that.

She knew who had tried to kill Mrs. Logan, and who had been responsible for the death of that poor cafeteria lady.

George should have stayed and questioned her further, and would have except that another teacher, a pretty African American woman had come marching in the hall, came to an abrupt halt and demanded that the teacher go with her. She shot George a puzzled look and then frowned at the teacher sitting down.

It occurred to George then that maybe the woman on the chair wasn't a teacher at all. She looked a little old to be a mother, but she could be a grandmother of one of the students.

Or she could be an undercover detective.

He had to get out of there. Hanging around the school was not a good idea.

One thing was certain. George had to question the woman, who believed his mother was innocent and then he had to enlist her help.

She was his only hope.

"I'D LIKE TO see my mother, Mrs. Arlington."

"Oh yes. Well, Mrs. Arlington had a very bad day. The doctor had to sedate her."

George felt that familiar tightening in his stomach and then insisted in a shaky voice, "I still would like to see her."

"You can peek in, but I'm afraid she's sleeping soundly. She won't be awake until probably the morning."

George followed the aide down a long, dim hall, which was lined with bodies in various states of undress, some singing to themselves, some muttering to no one in particular, some screaming at their shadows and some just sitting quietly in the corners, crying.

He had to get his mother out of this place.

Somehow he had pictured a small room with two beds or maybe his mother was lucky enough to have a single. Instead his mother was lying in a large space with a multitude of cots. She was the only one sleeping and, when George looked in on her, he wanted to weep. She looked old, frail, helpless. When he was growing up, she took such pride in her appearance, always had her hair dyed a deep, dark brown, never without her black eye liner and her coral lipstick, and never, ever in pants. She was always dressed in little sheaths and colorful flats and bold jewelry.

Laying there in bed with wisps of white hair, her mouth open, some of her teeth missing, she bore little resemblance to the woman who raised him. Mrs. Logan was right. He didn't know his mother anymore.

But one thing he did know. She wasn't a killer.

"She's at peace."

George turned around and spotted a lady standing

behind him. She, too, was an aide and she looked sympathetic, as she gazed at his mother.

"I wish they hadn't sedated her."

"She was quite out of control, and she kept babbling about a missing teacher."

"A missing teacher?" George said thoughtfully. Hadn't he read about a missing teacher at Mrs. Logan's last school?

"I think she thought the teacher had come back for her. Then she started screaming, *Murderer, murderer!* I have to tell you it was very upsetting to the other patients."

George's heart gave a flutter, as he realized that it was just possible that his mother might have seen something. And if that were the case, then maybe she was in danger.

"I'd like to move my mother," he told the aide. "Maybe to another place. Maybe to another hospital, where there is better security."

The aide glowered at him, as though he were a patient.

"If I can get a doctor's permission—"

"I don't think you quite understand, Mr. Arlington. Your mother is not here by choice. She's here because she's a suspect in a murder case. If she were well, she would be in a prison."

"Not necessarily. She might be out on bail."

"There's no question of that." The voice of the aide was clipped and cold. "At any rate, if you want to move her, you would need permission from the DA. I suggest you talk to him. Does your mother have a lawyer?"

"Not one that's good enough."

The aide shrugged and then looked down at her cell phone. "If you excuse me, I have to take this call."

George was more than willing to excuse her, although he couldn't help but wonder if his mother had said more and what it all meant.

In his mind there was only one way that the teacher who had approached him knew that his mother wasn't guilty.

Because she was.

Even if she wasn't, maybe she knew who was. Maybe the teacher who had found her mother's handbag.

He was going to talk to her soon and find out what the hell was going on.

THIRTY

"YOU WHAT?" MRS. JOHNSON screamed over the phone to Mrs. Hopwood.

"I told him that I believed him. You know, that his mother is innocent."

"First of all, you're admitting that you eavesdropped."

"I could hardly help eavesdropping. They were very loud."

"Second of all, what basis do you have for that statement?"

"You."

"What?" Mrs. Johnson was still yelling and her twins stopped doing their homework and stared at her. "None of your beeswax!" she shouted back at them. And to Mrs. Hopwood, she said, "I honestly don't know what you're talking about, as usual."

"We both agreed that poor Mrs. Arlington was probably not the one who tried to murder Mrs. Logan."

"What we say between us is hardly proof. It's just a gut feeling."

"But our gut feelings are usually right," Mrs. Hopwood argued.

"That man is going to think that you know something. He might even think that you're involved."

"Me? I never met the woman. I mean I saw her briefly on parent/teacher night, but you…"

"Don't even go there!" Mrs. Johnson snapped. "You see what you did? You opened up a door that should have remained closed. What we talk about, that isn't something you should repeat to a stranger. There is no telling where this might lead. And why didn't you tell me this in the car?"

"Because I knew you would scream at me." Mrs. Hopwood muttered an apology and then said that she'd see Mrs. Johnson in the morning.

It didn't prevent Mrs. Johnson from seething and from screaming at Jeffrey James, who didn't know one spelling word. She had a very bad feeling about all of this sordid business, and when she walked in the next morning, she realized that her bad feelings were justified.

Mrs. Hopwood entered with a cup of coffee and a buttered bagel, the kind that Mrs. Johnson liked— poppy seeds with lots of real melted butter. The coffee was just as she preferred, two sugars and heavy on the cream.

And Mrs. Johnson might have thought about forgiving her, except just as Mrs. Johnson was about to bite into the bagel, Mr. Arlington appeared at the door.

She had never actually met him, but she knew who he was by the recognition in Mrs. Hopwood's face.

His first comment was directed at Mrs. Hopwood— except he asked her if she was Mrs. Johnson.

It took a second for Mrs. Hopwood to deny such a thing and point a long red manicured finger at Mrs. Johnson.

"I'm Mr. Arlington. Do you mind if I ask you a few questions?"

Mrs. Johnson hesitated, because she really did mind. But Mr. Arlington didn't wait for an answer.

"You were the woman who found my mother's purse?"

Mrs. Johnson was immediately put on the defensive. "She left it in my classroom. I saw it a few minutes after she left the school. I gave it to Mrs. Logan."

"Did you look inside of it?"

"Of course not. Why would I?"

"Can I ask you a question?" Mrs. Hopwood intervened, making Mrs. Johnson annoyed and grateful at the same time. "Didn't the police wonder where your mother got the fluoroacetate? I mean, it's not the sort of thing that you can go into CVS and just buy. Wouldn't there be some sort of paper trail? Unless she bought it on the computer?"

"My mother doesn't know from computers. She's frightened of them. She thinks that they're the devil's work."

Mrs. Hopwood was quick to agree. And then she added, "Well, isn't that a big hole in the prosecutor's case?"

"It should be. But they still insist that my mother be locked up. You told me that you think she's innocent."

Mrs. Johnson couldn't help but glare at her friend.

"Do you want to tell me what you meant by that?"

Mrs. Hopwood paused before saying, "It just doesn't make sense to me. I mean, I never met the woman…"

"I did," Mrs. Johnson interrupted. "She didn't seem quite…"

"Lucid," Mr. Arlington interrupted.

"I can't see her planning something as complicated as this."

"Let me ask you a question," Mrs. Hopwood said in a bossy tone. "Is it possible that on parent/teacher night someone could have taken your mother's handbag for a little while, without your mother even noticing?"

Mr. Arlington hesitated. "It's possible, yes. But the truth is my mother kept a pretty good grip on her purse. It was the one thing she valued. She was always talking about how she needed taxi money, so we made sure she always had a twenty dollar bill in her wallet."

"But if she kept a tight grip on her purse," Mrs. Johnson couldn't help but argue, "then why did she leave it in my room?"

Mr. Arlington had no answer and Mrs. Johnson could hear the unmistakable stampede on the stairs.

"Listen," Mr. Arlington said quickly, "I believe that my mother put down her handbag, and someone planted the poison in it. That must have happened, although I don't know when. It's the only explanation."

He turned around and stomped out of the room.

Mrs. Johnson and Mrs. Hopwood stared at each other as David Dudley strutted into the room. "We're meeting in here," Mrs. Johnson said. "Wait outside!"

With a sullen look on his face, David disappeared into the hall.

"So what are you thinking?" Mrs. Johnson asked her friend.

"I'm thinking that, if there is another explanation, we should find it."

THIRTY-ONE

MISS TURNIPSEED SAW Mr. Arlington run down the stairs. She heard the front door slam and then she saw Addison Fiore stop in the front hall. She exchanged a few words with Mr. Arlington, who was nodding in an irritated way. Perhaps she was expressing her sympathy about the arrest of his mother and he didn't want her sympathy.

No matter. He was going to get it anyway, because something told Miss Turnipseed that Addison Fiore was a nosy parker.

Of course, that didn't prevent Miss Turnipseed from pushing through the clump of students, walking over and greeting Mr. Arlington warmly. He wasn't so warm.

"Is there anything I can help you with?" she asked, as Addison frowned and headed towards her classroom.

"You can help my mother by pointing the police in another direction."

"Well, I would if I could. But I have no idea..."

"You know Mrs. Logan. You know whom she pissed off."

Miss Turnipseed could not resist recoiling at his crude language.

But if Mr. Arlington was bothered by her frown, it didn't stop him from continuing. "You also know my mother. She didn't do this. She couldn't do this."

"I already told the police what I think. And they have no interest in listening to me. I'm sorry, really I am."

The office door burst open and Mrs. Logan stormed into the reception area. Miss Turnipseed had been working with her long enough to know when Mrs. Logan was angry. "Is there anything I can help you with, George?"

"No, I'm finished here." As he left, he added, "For the time being."

"I'd like to see you in my office, Miss Turnipseed."

Miss Turnipseed didn't think this was a good time to be in anyone's office. She had to be at the front desk for the latecomers and the straggling teachers, but she would never consider arguing.

She knew it was serious when Mrs. Logan closed the door and asked her to sit down. She held her breath and hoped that this wasn't about why she hadn't handed in her Corey Check.

"I saw you talking to Mr. Arlington."

"I just asked if I could help him." Miss Turnipseed breathed a silent sigh of relief.

"Well, I don't want you to help him. For the past years, I've had to endure his mother coming in here and accusing me of being unfair to her little boy. Then his mother tries to poison me and actually kills that poor cafeteria lady."

"Bertha Butterworth."

Mrs. Logan grimaced when she heard the correction, but Miss Turnipseed thought that, after all, the poor cafeteria lady had a name. "At any rate, I don't need her son around now disrupting the school. It has endured enough scandal and the diocese doesn't like to draw attention to its schools. You know that."

Miss Turnipseed knew all about the diocese.

"The next time he comes here, tell me immediately. I may have to get a restraining order against him."

"Don't you think that's rather harsh?"

The tone that Mrs. Logan took with Miss Turnipseed was rather harsh. "I am principal of St. Polycarp. That means, Miss Turnipseed, my job and my priority has always been the students. It's been that way since," she paused, "since Bruce and I parted ways. I feel very bad for George and his mother, and I'm more than willing to forgive her for trying to kill me. But I cannot have him coming here and disrupting the learning of my students. Is that understood?"

Miss Turnipseed nodded.

"Fine, as long as we understand each other."

Miss Turnipseed stood. Something inside of her told her that she shouldn't even say it, but she couldn't resist. "They were asking about Clara."

Mrs. Logan's face paled beneath her bronze makeup.

"Who? Mr. Arlington?"

Miss Turnipseed shook her head.

"Those two nosy teachers?" Mrs. Logan asked, slumping in her chair.

"No."

"I don't have time to play games and you have work to do," Mrs. Logan said.

"The police. They came to my apartment this morning."

"I don't understand." Mrs. Logan's gray eyebrows knitted together. She looked faintly befuddled and, for a moment, vulnerable. "Do they think Clara was the one who tried to kill me? Or do they think Clara had ties with Mrs. Arlington?"

"I don't know what they think. They didn't tell me."

Mrs. Logan shot Miss Turnipseed a nasty look.

Maybe, Miss Turnipseed thought, *she had gone too far.* She should be on her best behavior, just in case Mrs. Logan went through with that Corey Check— just in case she learned the secret that Miss Turnipseed had been hiding all these years. She would fire Miss Turnipseed in a New York minute. But right now Mrs. Logan wouldn't be firing anyone. Not when someone was trying to murder her. Still, if the police were looking for a motive, then they would soon find out that Miss Turnipseed had one.

She returned to the front desk and scowled at the latecomers, especially the music teacher, Mr. Robbins, who had come in fifteen minutes after his appointed time. That meant that Mrs. Hopwood would be missing some of her morning prep and, knowing Mrs. Hopwood even briefly, she wouldn't be happy.

While Mrs. Logan was making her rounds which consisted of bursting into classrooms, sitting down and taking notes and making teachers nervous—which delighted Mrs. Logan who then followed up with stone-faced criticism, Miss Turnipseed thought about doing something rather daring.

She decided she would have a talk with Mrs. Hopwood.

She chose Mrs. Hopwood, because she appeared a bit unsure of herself. The other teacher, Mrs. Hopwood's friend Mrs. Johnson, always looked grumpy and determined, as though she was on a mission.

Mrs. Johnson might ask too many questions.

Now was the perfect time, when Mrs. Hopwood's students were in music, and Mrs. Logan was no doubt torturing the music teacher about a subject she knew nothing about.

Miss Turnipseed found Mrs. Hopwood sitting at her desk, reading one of the scandal magazines. "May I speak to you for a moment?"

Mrs. Hopwood looked extremely suspicious and slightly aghast.

"I don't know who else to confide in. The police came to see me this morning, and they were asking all kinds of questions about Clara."

Mrs. Hopwood stared at her blankly.

"You know, the woman who disappeared. Clara and I, well, I guess you could say that we were friends, at work that is. Although Clara tried several times to extend our relationship outside of school, meeting for tea, or an afternoon at a museum. I always declined. I felt a little uncomfortable. The day that Clara disappeared she sent a student down to the office with a note for me. She wrote that she wanted my advice on something very important. I suspected she was having man trouble. I was supposed to meet her at the coffee shop on the corner, when school got out. I was going to go, but then my neighbor called to tell me that my cat had taken a turn for the worse. I had no way of reaching her, and I should have phoned her that night. But I thought I would see her at school the following morning and explain. But she never showed up."

"Did you tell the police this?"

"I did. But since I had no idea what Clara wanted to discuss, I wasn't very helpful. About a week later, her sister Grace called me. She wanted me to meet her. I went out of respect for Clara and I have to admit I was somewhat curious. Grace was very hostile. She seemed to think that I knew where Clara was, that Clara had confided in me." Miss Turnipseed took a deep breath.

Mrs. Hopwood stared at her and she too, seemed hostile. "Why are you telling me all this?" she asked in a strained voice.

Miss Turnipseed knew that she had made a bad choice. She should have chosen Mrs. Johnson. "Well, it's, it's that," she stuttered, "I know that you and Mrs. Johnson are close friends and the police are questioning her about having had Mrs. Arlington's pocketbook."

"What does that have to do with Clara and Grace?"

Thankfully before Miss Turnipseed had a chance to answer, she heard a stomping on the stairs and a shrill voice, which she recognized as Mrs. Logan.

"Stop right now! I don't know what the rules of the school were prior my being principal. But I will not have you running up the stairs and screaming like a bunch of banshees. Now you turn around and go back up the stairs and walk up quietly. And if you're not quiet enough, you'll repeat it again and again."

Miss Turnipseed nodded and left the room.

Well, she had given Mrs. Hopwood something to think about.

And now she would have to see if Mrs. Hopwood took the bait.

THIRTY-TWO

"I'M TELLING YOU it was bizarre." Mrs. Hopwood settled herself in Mrs. Johnson's car. "The way she was going on about Clara and Grace."

"Did you ask why she was telling you all this?" Mrs. Johnson started the car.

"I told you!" Mrs. Hopwood was exasperated because sometimes Mrs. Johnson just didn't listen. "It's because you had Mrs. Arlington's purse."

"Then why didn't Miss Turnipseed talk to me?"

"Maybe because you didn't have a prep. I don't know. What I do know is that there is something strange about that woman, with her tea, and her dead cat."

"Did her cat die?"

"Well, maybe her sick cat. Did you ever think she might have tried to poison Mrs. Logan?"

"She worked for Mrs. Logan for years. Why would she wait until now to try and kill her?"

"Well maybe," Mrs. Hopwood said, "she was just waiting for the right opportunity. And she could have planted that poison, when you gave the purse back to her, and before she returned it to Mrs. Logan."

Mrs. Johnson stopped abruptly, causing Mrs. Hopwood to lunge forward. Mrs. Johnson cursed under her breath and then asked, "How did she know that Mrs. Arlington was even going to be there that night?"

"She didn't. No one did except, of course, Mrs. Ar-

lington herself and maybe she didn't even know. But
what Miss Turnipseed *did* know was that Mrs. Arlington would be back sooner or later. She always came
back. Miss Turnipseed was just looking for the right
opportunity."

"And why would Miss Turnipseed want to murder
Mrs. Logan?" Mrs. Johnson challenged.

"For the same reason everyone might. Miss Turnipseed works for her."

MRS. HOPWOOD RETURNED to her silent house. Since Alexander had gone away to college, she was often alone.
Her husband had taken to working late.

Or so he said.

She turned on the television to a repeat of *Law and
Order*, but because she had tuned in when it was half
over, she found it difficult to follow. She was channel
surfing when the phone rang.

She ran towards it, noticing that it was from Mrs.
Johnson. She collapsed on her bed, in the mood for a
long chat.

"I've done some investigating." Mrs. Johnson often
got right to the point. "About what Miss Turnipseed
told you."

"Was she lying?"

"I think she was."

"How do you know? No one knows whether or not
Clara had asked Miss Turnipseed to meet her. That
can't be proven one way or the other."

"Not that part. I read about Clara's disappearance."

"And?"

"It said right there in the paper that she was not involved with anyone."

Mrs. Hopwood was rendered mute.

"So you know what that means?"

"Miss Turnipseed was lying?"

"Someone was lying."

"But Miss Turnipseed just said she *could* have been involved with someone. She didn't say it was for sure."

"I know, but in that case..."

"So now what? What should we do? Or maybe we should do nothing."

"Well, you did kind of promise that poor man."

"George Arlington?"

"That you would try to help him. Not only that, but the cloud of suspicion is on me, just because his mother left her handbag in my room. Besides, another murder at St. Polycarp is not good. If it's not solved, then the school is in jeopardy of closing. And who knows where you and me—"

"You and I," Mrs. Hopwood could not resist.

"Will end up, maybe not even together."

"So," Mrs. Hopwood said, "I'm still going back to my original question. What should I do?"

"I think you and *I* should talk to Clara's sister."

"And where do we find her?"

"For that we have to talk to Miss Turnipseed."

As LUCK WOULD have it, Mrs. Logan was out at a principal's convention the following day.

The fact that she wasn't in the building put Mrs. Hopwood in a rather relaxed mood and she could feel the other teachers breathe a sigh of relief as well. Miss Turnipseed, however, was in some sort of frenzy, trying to take messages and solve problems, which would have been referred to Mrs. Logan.

So when Mrs. Hopwood went over to the desk, Miss Turnipseed glared at her.

But Mrs. Hopwood soldiered on, for hadn't Miss Turnipseed asked Mrs. Hopwood for help?

"I'd like to talk to Grace," she said.

Miss Turnipseed appeared to be looking right through her as she shifted in her seat.

"You know Grace, Clara's sister."

That got Miss Turnipseed's attention. She dropped the newsletter she had been typing and looked up. "I don't know what good that will do. As I told you, Grace was very hostile to me."

"But maybe this attempt on Mrs. Logan's life had something to do with Clara's disappearance." Mrs. Hopwood couldn't even remember thinking it, but suddenly she burst out, "Do you think it's possible that Mrs. Logan knows where Clara is?"

"I don't see how she would and, even if she did, why would someone try and kill her?"

Mrs. Hopwood wasn't sure but she never got a chance to argue, because the phone rang and Miss Turnipseed answered immediately in a very professional voice.

That was the end of her being professional, though. She evidently had to take a message for Mrs. Logan, and it must have been a confusing message, because she asked how to spell the name a number of times, and then had to repeat the message again and again.

Something about geometry homework that had gone wrong.

As soon as she hung up, Mrs. Hopwood said quickly—because she could hear bedlam in her classroom—even

from the floor below—and because the phone was ring-
ing again. "Could you give me Grace's address at least?"

"I'll send it in," she said as she answered the phone
with a quivering voice.

Mrs. Hopwood had a feeling that she would be asking again.

THIRTY-THREE

"MAMA, DO YOU know who I am?"

George Arlington was standing in front of his mother. Just looking at her broke his heart.

"Mama, look at me."

"Where is my little boy?"

It did no good to try and convince his mother that he himself was George. No matter how rational he sounded, no matter how much he managed to convince his mother for the moment, minutes later she would ask the same question.

"Do you know where you are?"

"I want to go home. I want to be in my violet bedroom with the purple velvet quilt and the lilac drapes."

George's mother hadn't slept in a bedroom like that for twenty-five years.

"Mama, I want to take you home. Marsha wants to take you home."

"Marsha? Is that the pretty blonde lady I saw you with?"

George ignored the question, knowing that his mother would forget the answer in a minute. "You're here, Mama, because they think that you tried to hurt Mrs. Logan."

"She never should have given you that fifty on the spelling test. You had the words correct. It wasn't your fault if she couldn't read your writing."

"Mama, this isn't about the spelling test. Do you remember when you went to parent/teacher night?"

"Of course, I remember. I go every year. I am one of those involved mothers. I want to be part of your education. Some day you're going to be a very important man, George."

"Do you remember carrying your orange pocket book?"

"I always carry my orange pocketbook. My orange pocketbook." His mother began to stutter, and grow flustered. "Where is my orange pocketbook now?"

"We'll get it to you, Mom," he lied. The police were probably holding it for material evidence. "Did you give it to someone? Did you give it to Marsha?"

"No! Why would I give it to Marsha? Did *you* give it to someone?"

His mother took a deep, pained breath and closed her eyes.

George was feeling very discouraged. There was no way that his mother was going to be able to help him. But couldn't everyone see that? How could this woman plot a murder? How could she buy poison and plant it into a brownie without anyone seeing? She wasn't capable of such an action.

Still he would try another stab at it.

It meant his mother's life.

"Mom, I want to ask you about the brownies."

Her forehead creased in confusion, and for a moment she looked like a wrinkled old turtle. Then suddenly she perked up. "Are we having brownies for dessert tonight? They're not very good here, you know. I think that they make them with cocoa powder instead of with Hershey syrup. And they don't use real sugar either. Someone said that they actually put in apple sauce. Can you imagine?"

"Do you remember the brownies at parent/teacher night?"

"I had two. They were delicious. I would have taken three, but I was afraid I would get a belly ache."

"Did you give one to Mrs. Logan?"

"Why would I do that? Mrs. Logan could take her own. But I think she was too busy, flitting around, trying to talk to all the parents. She didn't come to me, though, which I thought was rude. Still, it's puzzling."

George felt his heart quicken. "What's puzzling, Mama?"

"What Miss Turnipseed said."

"What did Miss Turnipseed say?"

"She didn't think I heard because she whispered it, like it was a secret."

"What did she say, Mama?"

"She said she couldn't find the brownies."

"Mrs. Arlington," a nurse's aide wearing a uniform that was much too big for her sauntered over and said heartily, "it's time for dinner."

"Who said she couldn't find the brownies?"

"Are we having brownies for dessert? My son said we're having brownies for dessert."

"No, not tonight. Tonight is Jell-O night with whipped cream."

"It's not real whipped cream, though, is it? It's that horrid one that comes in a bowl. Where's my pocket-book? Where is my little boy?"

George heard his mother utter those unanswerable questions, as she was whisked away down those long corridors, following the odor of mashed peas and over-cooked broccoli.

His mother had seen something. Of that he was certain. Somewhere in her memory, she had a clue on how that poor cafeteria lady had been killed.

And one thing that George Arlington had learnt. So did Miss Turnipseed.

THIRTY-FOUR

"WELL, I'LL TELL you one thing," Mrs. Johnson looked down on the note paper which had Teresa Turnipseed's name neatly printed on in purple, "this Grace Edwards is rich."

They were sitting in Mrs. Johnson's car.

"And how do you know that?" Mrs. Hopwood asked.

"Look where she's living. In Beaudoin Heights. That's where all those beautiful Tutors are."

"And here her sister was nothing but a lowly Catholic school teacher." Mrs. Hopwood shook her head.

"Like us."

"So are we going to question her?"

"She probably won't talk to us. Look how nasty she was to Miss Turnipseed. But still…"

"Still, you're curious," Mrs. Hopwood finished the sentence.

"I guess it can't hurt," Mrs. Johnson said, "although that's what you told me when I almost died in Sicily."

"But you're alive and well," Mrs. Hopwood said.

"Barely," Mrs. Johnson murmured.

"OH, GOODNESS, JUST look at that house," Mrs. Hopwood exclaimed as Mrs. Johnson drove up the long circular driveway to an English Tutor that resembled a castle.

She parked the car in back of the gold Mercedes, and she and Mrs. Hopwood headed for the front door.

"I bet she has a maid," Mrs. Hopwood whispered.

"Probably an entire staff," Mrs. Johnson agreed. It took her several moments to find the bell and, when she rang it, the sound of Westminster Chimes floated through the air.

"She could be hiding Clara up there," Mrs. Hopwood pointed to a garret.

"You mean like a prisoner?" Mrs. Johnson asked.

Mrs. Hopwood had no time to respond because the door was flung open by a middle-aged woman wearing a maid's uniform, right down to the starched cap on her silver curls.

"Can I help you?" she asked in an annoyed tone of voice, as she looked the women up and down.

"Yes, we'd like to speak to Grace Edwards." Mrs. Johnson always felt that it was better to be polite.

"What is this about?"

"It's a private matter between us and Miss Edwards," Mrs. Hopwood piped up.

The maid glared at them. After several long seconds, Mrs. Johnson repeated her request.

"I'm Grace Edwards."

Mrs. Hopwood released a gasp and Mrs. Johnson felt like slapping her.

"So, what is this about?" Grace challenged them.

"It's about your sister, Clara," Mrs. Hopwood said quickly.

Now it was Grace who gasped. "Have you found her? Do you know where she is? Is she all right?"

"It's nothing like that." Mrs. Johnson hated to dash her hopes. "Can we come in for a moment?" And then she added, "It's complicated."

With a great deal of reluctance, Grace held the door open.

They stepped on a white oriental rug placed in a large hall, paneled in mahogany. But Mrs. Johnson could hardly take in the sights, because strutting down the stairs was a woman impeccably dressed in a royal blue suit, lots of gold jewelry, and red spiked heels.

"Who are these people?" she asked Grace, not once glancing at Mrs. Johnson or Mrs. Hopwood.

"It's about my sister, Clara."

"Oh." Now the woman did look at Mrs. Hopwood's shoes, which were a cheap imitation of Stuart Weitzman's. She frowned slightly.

"Do they know where she is?"

Grace's eyes darted to both teachers before Mrs. Johnson admitted she wasn't sure.

"Well, I guess you can speak to them in the study. But please make it snappy. The mayor will be here for dinner in less than three hours and you haven't started on the popovers."

"Yes, Mrs. Van Kemp."

As Grace led them to a room further down the paneled hall, Mrs. Hopwood whispered, "Wouldn't you like to have some popovers with your dinner?"

"I don't know," Mrs. Johnson said. "I never had a popover."

Grace opened the door to a small cozy room, furnished in leather. A fire crackled in the corner, flanked by floor to ceiling bookshelves.

Grace hadn't invited them to sit down, but Mrs. Johnson had had a hard day in school trying to teach algebra to a group of seventh graders who were too busy pecking at the iPads, so she slumped down on the sofa.

Mrs. Hopwood plopped beside her, while Grace stood.

"I wonder what Mr. Van Kemp does for a living," Mrs. Hopwood said in a hushed voice.

"Mr. Van Kemp works in a toll booth at the Mass Pike. Mrs. Van Kemp is a lawyer, a partner actually, in the most important law firm in the state."

"Oh," Mrs. Hopwood said.

"So what is this about? You can see I'm very busy."

"As we said," Mrs. Johnson said, suddenly feeling at a loss for words and exchanging a nervous look with Mrs. Hopwood, "it's about your sister."

"Has there been another clue?"

"Well, here's the thing," Mrs. Hopwood intervened. "We think," she pointed towards Mrs. Johnson, "that your sister's disappearance might have something to do with the death of Bertha Butterworth."

"Who is Bertha Butterworth?"

"She's the woman who ate the poisoned brownie," Mrs. Johnson said.

"The one meant for Mrs. Logan," Mrs. Hopwood added.

"Yes, I read about that in the paper. I didn't know her name."

"No one knew her name," Mrs. Hopwood said sadly.

"I still don't understand what this has to do with Clara," Grace said stubbornly.

"You see," Mrs. Hopwood glanced over at Mrs. Johnson, who decided to remain mute, "we're friends with Miss Turnipseed."

"Miss Turnipseed is an evil woman."

It was time for Mrs. Johnson to intercede. "Well, we're not really friends. We work with her. It's like this. Whoever tried to kill Mrs. Logan, well, the murderer must have had something to do with her past."

"At the other school," Mrs. Hopwood interrupted.

"Yes, at the other school. Mrs. Logan had only been at our school…"

"St. Polycarp," Mrs. Hopwood said.

"For a few weeks. So even if Mrs. Logan managed to make some enemies…"

"And we're not saying that she did."

"They would hardly be the sort of enemies who would kill her."

"I still don't know what this has to do with Clara." With a jerky motion, Grace turned the knob and opened the door slightly. "Now if you'll excuse me…"

"But your sister's disappearance is the only odd thing that happened at her other school!" Mrs. Hopwood insisted.

"And how would you know that?" Grace asked.

Mrs. Hopwood had no answer.

"And why do you care anyway? Are you friendly with Mrs. Logan?"

The teachers looked at each other again. Mrs. Johnson decided she would let Mrs. Hopwood come up with the convoluted explanation. "They think that poor Mrs. Arlington, who is suffering from dementia, committed the murder, which is really impossible. So if Mrs. Arlington didn't kill Bertha than someone must have planted the evidence in Mrs. Arlington's handbag. And Mrs. Johnson," Mrs. Hopwood pointed, "was one of the few people who had the means and the opportunity."

"Just the opportunity, not the means," Mrs. Johnson corrected her.

"This is far too complicated. Really you have to go."
She opened the door wider.

"Can you tell us something?" Mrs. Hopwood was
now pleading, "Anything about your sister that might
be useful."

"What do you mean useful?"

"Anything," Mrs. Johnson said. "We've come a long
way." Which was a lie. It was less than three miles
from the school.

To her surprise, Grace closed the door and shrugged
wearily.

"My sister and I lived happily with my father. Then
my father died and we learned that he hadn't paid taxes
on the house in Nebraska for many years. It was a lot
of money and neither Clara nor I could make the payments. The house went into foreclosure. We decided to
move east. I got this job here and Clara found a small
apartment on the other side of town. She never felt safe."

"Well, with gangs and…" Mrs. Hopwood muttered.

"No, it was more than that. She had a feeling that
someone came and went in her apartment. She would
come home and things would be misplaced. Once she
found her canary on top of her headboard, and the
cage was bolted."

"Why didn't she change the locks?" Mrs. Johnson
wondered aloud.

"She did. Three times. It didn't matter. Before she
disappeared, she gave me something to hold for her. It
was a note of some sort. I suspected it had to do with
a man she might have been seeing."

"Where is it?" Mrs. Hopwood almost leaped out
of her seat.

"I don't have it. Someone stole it out of my handbag. I had gone grocery shopping for Mrs. Van Kemp. I had the envelope in my handbag, and when I came home and went to get it, it was missing. My purse was in the front of the cart and, at one point, I remember looking at some cucumbers. I turned around and my cart had been moved. Of course, I panicked. I wasn't thinking of the letter. I was thinking of my money, my credit cards. It didn't occur to me until I got home and looked for the envelope, that it was gone."

"Did you tell the police this?" Mrs. Johnson asked.

"Of course. I went right to the police, when Clara disappeared. And I told them about the letter. They told me that Clara was an adult and she had every right to disappear, if she wished. According to Mrs. Logan, she had been complaining a lot about teaching and wanting to start over someplace else. But I know my sister. She would never have started over without telling me. Now, really you have to go."

"So what do you think?" Mrs. Hopwood asked Mrs. Johnson as soon as Grace shut the front door.

"I think it's a sad story but, for the life of me, I don't know what any of this has to do with the attempted murder of Mrs. Logan."

"What if, what if, what if…"

"What if what?!" Mrs. Johnson slammed the car door.

"What if Mrs. Logan was as frightened as Clara?"

"Something tells me that Mrs. Logan doesn't frighten easily."

"I wonder why someone would torment poor Clara." Mrs. Hopwood snapped on her seatbelt.

"I'm afraid we might never know," Mrs. Johnson said as she made her way down the long, circular driveway.

THIRTY-FIVE

"Why did you do it?"

"Who is this?"

"You know very well who I am, Miss Turnipseed. Why did you sic those two women on me?"

"I..."

"Don't bother to deny it. There is no way they could possibly have known where to find me, unless you told them."

"Mrs. Johnson and Mrs. Hopwood are very fine teachers."

"I'm sure they are, but this isn't an educational matter."

"What I wanted to say, Grace, is that they are very smart. They're trying to find your sister."

"And why would they want to do that? They gave me some long complicated story about poison in a purse and someone name Butterspread."

"Butterworth."

"But they never even met my sister."

"I did. And I can't rest until I know what happened to her. And I would think you would be grateful if anyone looked into what the police are considering a cold case—if they ever even considered it to be a case." Miss Turnipseed promptly hung up the phone.

Something told her that she was in trouble in her attempt to tie the missing Clara to the bungled murder. Miss Turnipseed didn't like to think about it.

BUT SHE DID think about it. All night in fact. She vacillated between being happy that she had approached Mrs. Hopwood and managed to whet her curiosity and being angry that she had involved the two teachers. Because there was no saying where this was all going to end.

When the alarm rang at six the following morning, she could barely get herself out of her nice feather bed. Even her cat, Kit Kat, didn't budge, when Miss Turnipseed nudged him.

The first clue that this was going to be a bad day was when Miss Turnipseed put on the kettle for her candy cane tea and couldn't find the tea bags. That rather puzzled her, because her tea bags were always kept in the same exact place. The second cabinet above the stove on the right hand side.

Could she have put them someplace else without thinking?

Hastily, she checked the other cabinets, the refrigerator, the wastepaper basket, which thankfully she hadn't emptied—although it didn't matter since the tea bags weren't there—and she even peeked into the oven.

Could she have used them all?

No, she was positive that it was a fresh box and, even if she had used the last one, where then was the empty container?

She couldn't spend any more time searching. She was already seven minutes behind schedule. She gave Kit Kat some milk, when she meowed loudly, and she threw two pieces of bread into the toaster.

But the pumpernickel bread with strawberry jam was dry and unappetizing without the sweet tea.

And Miss Turnipseed knew that when her morning did not go well, it was a bad omen for the rest of the day.

SHE WAS SLIGHTLY late getting to work, which meant that Mrs. Logan had to answer the early morning calls, usually about absences, not only from students but from teachers as well. Missing teachers meant that other teachers would have to use their preps to fill in and that meant anger and resentment.

Mrs. Logan had never been a friendly, warm woman but since the attempt on her life, Miss Turnipseed thought Mrs. Logan had become even more distant. She had taken to bringing her own lunches from home. She wouldn't even order from the neighborhood deli and started locking the cooler in her file cabinet. Miss Turnipseed had once taken a message for her from a man who sold guard dogs. And several times Miss Turnipseed had overheard Mrs. Logan phone the police and demand to know what was being done to find the person who had tried to kill her.

On this particularly gray September day Mrs. Logan approached the front desk, holding some papers in her hand.

"This has to go out to the diocese today," she said. "I need for you to make three copies, one for our files, the other two should be enclosed in this envelope with the original. Can you drop it off at the post office on your way home?"

Miss Turnipseed nodded, but she was not pleased. The post office was not on her way home, in fact it was quite out of the way, and at four o'clock, there was usually a long line.

Miss Turnipseed guessed that Mrs. Logan had left the application for additional funds for the learning specialist to the last minute. Her focus and energy on keeping the school functioning had now been switched to keeping herself alive.

"Here," she stuck another paper in Miss Turnipseed's startled face. "Sign here."

Miss Turnipseed did not have to ask what it was for. It was that horrid Corey Check and there was no getting out of it now. Well, maybe she could intercept the mail when the results came in.

What if they came in on the computer?

Well, she could hardly worry about that now. There were too many other fires to put out.

Miss Turnipseed was on her way to the copy machine when a fifth grader came running up to her and said that Devina Diamond had fallen off her chair and chipped her tooth. She was bleeding profusely, and Mrs. Hopwood wasn't sure what to do.

Neither was Miss Turnipseed, and it was not one of the days when the visiting nurse visited.

Miss Turnipseed turned around, papers in hand, knocked on Mrs. Logan's door, and let the excited and somewhat gleeful student repeat the message.

Mrs. Logan rose to her feet, gave an exasperated sigh and marched out of her office. Miss Turnipseed heard her heavy footsteps, as she stomped up the stairs.

Miss Turnipseed had an awful headache. She was sure it was because she had missed her morning tea. The teachers' room was right down the hall and although the tea bags there were old and stale, it was better than nothing at all.

By the time she came back with the weak and luke-warm tea, Mrs. Logan was already descending the stairs with the weeping child.

"My mother is going to be very unhappy. I'm a model you know. I have a booking to do, a print job for GAP. How can I do it with a chipped tooth!" Devina wailed. "Someone is going to have to pay for this!"

"How could you fall off a chair?" Mrs. Logan demanded. "I can expect that sort of accident from a first grader, but you're too old to be rocking on a chair."

"It wasn't my fault."

Miss Turnipseed thought if she had a dollar for every time she heard a child utter those words, she would be a millionaire.

"Arthur Riley kept pinching my ass, and I gave him a slap and the chair tilted. He had been bothering me all morning."

"Why didn't you tell Mrs. Hopwood?"

"I did. She didn't care. She was too busy doing a crossword puzzle."

Miss Turnipseed didn't think that things looked good for Mrs. Hopwood, but that wasn't her problem. Right now Miss Turnipseed's problem was trying to hide her cool tea from the glare of Mrs. Logan, who did not like her staff to drink or eat anything at their desks.

Mrs. Logan took Devina inside and closed the door. Minutes later she announced that she was meeting Devina's mother and they were going to take Devina to the emergency room, because Devina's gum would not stop bleeding. Mrs. Logan hoped to be back before dismissal.

Miss Turnipseed was not happy with this outcome. She had hoped to leave a little early, because of her trip to the post office. Because Mrs. Logan was absent, it fell to Miss Turnipseed to deal with a first grader who had dropped red paint on his friend's sneakers, a third grader who had a fever and threw up in the hall, a parent who complained about serving hot dogs. *Didn't the school realize they were high on the list of food that kids choked on?* And the superintendent who was disturbed when she learnt that Mrs. Logan was not in the building.

Mrs. Logan did not return by dismissal time and it was four o'clock before Miss Turnipseed was able to draw a breath.

It was precisely four o'clock before Miss Turnipseed realized that the application Mrs. Logan had given her was gone.

THIRTY-SIX

Mrs. Hopwood was in trouble and she knew it.

The feeling in the pit of her stomach made her nauseous and dizzy. The only person she wanted to talk to was Mrs. Johnson. But today was a day that Mrs. Johnson had arranged to leave right after dismissal to attend a kindergarten welcome play. She had told Mrs. Hopwood all about it, how proud she was of her rambunctious twins, and how she intended to take them out for pizza afterwards.

Mrs. Hopwood didn't dare share the news with her husband, Montgomery. He would not be sympathetic and would no doubt ask her the same questions that Mrs. Logan was sure to ask while grilling her.

"Why weren't you paying attention?"

"How could you let this happen?"

"Can't you control the class?"

No, she couldn't. And now everyone was about to find that out.

Mrs. Logan didn't waste a moment. She called Mrs. Hopwood out first period the following day and arranged for Addison to cover the religion class. The moment that the fifth graders saw Addison with her sour expression, they became strangely quiet and subservient.

Addison was all of twenty-six years old and the fact

that she was more intimidating than the middle-aged Mrs. Hopwood was sad.

Mrs. Hopwood perched on the edge of the chair, her heart thumping rapidly. She couldn't help but remember the numerous times she had been in this office, in this exact chair, chatting with Father Felix.

This conversation could not be described as a chat.

"I think you know what this is about, Mrs. Hopwood."

"It's about the Devina incident."

"While the Devina incident occurred," Mrs. Logan put an undue emphasis on Devina incident, "I understand that you were doing a crossword puzzle instead of supervising the class."

Mrs. Hopwood felt a flash of anger run through her. "Yes, that's true. I was doing a crossword puzzle with the class. It was something that I had created myself, to use in conjunction with social studies." That was a lie. Mrs. Hopwood had found it on the internet. Either way, Mrs. Logan didn't seem impressed, so Mrs. Hopwood forged on. "Devina and Arthur have this thing going. They love each other and they hate each other, and they are wreaking havoc."

"Then they should not be sitting together!"

"I only let them sit near each other because they told me that they wanted to work on the puzzle and, since they do such little work, I was hoping they would stay on task. They promised that they would."

"And you took the word of a couple of eleven-year-old kids?"

"I like to trust my students."

"Because of your trust, Devina has a damaged tooth and her parents are threatening to sue the school, to sue the diocese, to sue me, and, just so you're aware of it, to sue you as well."

"Me?" Mrs. Hopwood's hand flew to her chest.

"I understand that you are on tenure, Mrs. Hopwood."

"Yes, I have been teaching in the Catholic school system for almost thirteen years."

"So you know that tenure can be challenged."

Mrs. Hopwood paused before replying. Mrs. Logan's mouth was set in a scowl, and Mrs. Hopwood had to admit that her own mouth might also be set in a permanent frown, if someone was trying to murder her.

Except Mrs. Logan had the same expression the first time they met.

"I know tenure can be challenged," Mrs. Hopwood kept her voice calm and even, "but with all due respect, I am a good teacher. You don't know what I'm capable of."

"That's where you're wrong, Mrs. Hopwood. I know exactly what you're capable of. Father Felix left very specific and detailed notes on all the teachers."

Mrs. Hopwood was not sure how to respond to this earth shattering news. She considered Father Felix to be a friend. Had he written something negative about her?

"I also read the papers. I know you were involved in a murder, which took place at St. Polycarp a few years ago, and there was an unfortunate incident, when you accompanied some of the students on a trip to Sicily."

"I solved those murders, Mrs. Logan, with the help of my friend, Mrs. Johnson."

"Yes," Mrs. Logan said dryly. "Mrs. Johnson, your

cohort. It's debatable, whether you actually solved them or merely added fuel to the fire."

Mrs. Hopwood could not think of a snappy reply.

"I just want you to understand one thing, Mrs. Hopwood. I will be watching you."

"You said that before, and I have to tell you that sounds like a threat."

"It's my job."

Mrs. Hopwood rose, her knees shaking. She was furious and she was scared.

Too scared to go back to that horrid fifth grade classroom and talk about inference.

As soon as she got home, Mrs. Hopwood left a message for Mrs. Johnson to phone her as soon as possible. And when Mrs. Johnson hadn't called back and it was close to seven o'clock, Mrs. Hopwood, whose stomach had plummeted to her toes, called again.

"Didn't you get my message?" Mrs. Hopwood asked angrily.

"I did. I was waiting until the twins went to bed. I'm helping them with their homework."

"They're in kindergarten."

"They're in the advanced class and they have homework."

"Mrs. Logan called me into her office."

"Well, that wasn't unexpected. Jeffrey James, what are you doing? How could you possibly think two and one is thirteen? Count on your fingers!"

"She's threatening my tenure."

"Justin Joseph, why is there a hole in your paper!? Well, don't erase so hard. Or better still don't erase at all. Think before you write something down!"

"And she mentioned you."

"Me?"

"She called you my cohort."

"Cohort? That can't be good."

"It wasn't good. Her tone of voice when she said it was mean."

"What did *I* do? The paper is over there. No, Justin Joseph, over there."

"Well, maybe she thinks you put the poison in Mrs. Arlington's purse."

"Why would I do such a thing?"

"Because you wanted to kill her."

"That doesn't even make sense. Jeffrey James, make a straight line. If you can't make a straight line, use a ruler. First of all, I had no way of knowing that Mrs. Arlington would even be at the parent/teacher conference."

"Maybe she told you." Mrs. Hopwood was grasping at straws and she knew it.

"Yeah, like she really knew what she was talking about. And furthermore, why would I want to kill Mrs. Logan? You know darn well that I'm not a viable suspect. You're just trying to make yourself feel better. Justin Joseph, don't wrinkle your homework!"

Mrs. Hopwood merely muttered, "You're right."

"As far as I'm concerned, there is only one way you can get back into Mrs. Logan's good graces."

"I can't be the kind of teacher she wants me to be. That's just not in me."

"Believe me, I know that better than anyone. That's not what I'm talking about."

"What then?"

"You have to find the person who is trying to murder her."

"You're absolutely right," Mrs. Hopwood agreed. "I will find that person. And then I'll do everything in my power to give him a second chance."

THIRTY-SEVEN

"YOU'RE LATE," MARSHA SAID as soon as George walked into the house.

"I was visiting my mother."

"How is she doing?"

"She's in a nuthouse with the criminally insane. How do you think she's doing?"

Marsha was silent—for a moment. "I made your favorite, breaded pork chops, whipped garlic potatoes, string beans with almonds and mushrooms. I have a little bit more time now..."

"Now that my mother isn't living with us anymore."

"I'll warm up your dinner."

"I'm not hungry."

"George, you're being childish."

"Childish?! My mother is accused of murder. I'm upset and you think I'm being childish?"

"Look," Marsha was playing with the dish towel she had in her hand. "Your mother is getting help."

"Oh really?" George headed for the stairs. "You think she's getting help in that place?" He paused and then whipped around. "You're trying to make me believe that she did it, as though that would cross my mind, even for one moment. Knowing my mother, do you really think she could have done something like that?"

"I knew your mother, George. I knew the woman

she used to be. But she's not that woman anymore. No one knows what she's capable of."

"Somewhere buried deep inside that woman is my mother. And my mother never harmed a living soul. She wouldn't even kill the water bug we found in the bathtub. But you're happy now, aren't you, Marsha?"

"That's not fair!" she bellowed. "But since you asked, yes, having her out of the house is a whole lot easier for me and for the girls. They couldn't bring their friends over. They were embarrassed by her, what she would say, the way she looked. Why she wouldn't bathe, or comb her hair, or dress decently. She wouldn't accept my help or even yours. I was afraid of her, George, afraid she would leave the gas on in the kitchen, or light a candle in the living room, and we would all burn in our beds."

"Were you afraid that she would poison us?" And then George said, although he barely remembered thinking it, "How badly did you want her out of the house, Marsha?"

"What is that supposed to mean?"

George took the stairs two at a time, because, the truth was, he wasn't sure what it meant. But somewhere in the back of his mind, a horrible idea was flashing through his brain.

Because he suddenly remembered.

HE REMEMBERED THE night of the parent/teacher evening, when his mother had slipped out of the house. It was a Thursday evening and he was working late. They had hired a sitter to watch the girls, because Marsha had gone to her book club meeting. But what if she hadn't gone? What if she had gone to the school instead?

And then he recalled the day after Bertha Butterworth's funeral, the day that the police had come barging in.

That day at nine o'clock the bank called to say that their mortgage was ten days overdue. Marsha paid all the bills, and George knew that sometimes she had to juggle finances. But one thing they couldn't fall behind in was their mortgage. So he phoned her.

She wasn't home. Marsha never went out before eleven. She had her coffee and read the newspaper, as soon as the girls boarded the school bus. Then she did an hour of yoga with some DVD she bought. After that she phoned his sister in Oklahoma for a leisurely chat.

Then she waited for George's mother to take a nap.

George kept trying and finally reached his wife at eleven thirty. She said she had gone out to buy a quart of milk. But George had used milk in his cereal and he hadn't noticed that they needed more. Besides, she often asked George to pick up an item or two on his way home from work.

Of course, it was ludicrous to think that Marsha could have killed Mrs. Logan. Why would she do that? Just to put the blame on his mother in an effort to get her out of the house? That was rather extreme.

But she could have somehow bought the poison, after the newspaper identified it. She could have placed it in his mother's purse. That would have been easy enough to do.

Marsha knew how his mother felt about Mrs. Logan. She had heard his mother rave on and on. She also knew that his mother had been there the night an attempt had been made on Mrs. Logan's life.

No, he was being silly.

Wasn't he?

Marsha had never understood the deep ties George had with his mother. When her husband left, she had raised George single handedly, cleaning houses during the day and working as a matron in a fancy hotel bathroom uptown, where rich women threw dollar bills in a bowl, while she handed them paper towels.

She was always there for George, attending every school function. She even managed to send him to college. And now when the tables were turned, how could he desert her?

George knew one thing with absolute certainty.

If it was between his mother of thirty-three years and his wife of twelve, the choice was easy.

THIRTY-EIGHT

Mrs. Johnson was dreading her meeting with Mrs. Logan. It was about the standardized test that was coming up, and there was no reason to think that Mrs. Logan would talk about anything personal. Still Mrs. Johnson knew that the principal was not the easiest person to communicate with.

When Mrs. Hopwood heard about the meeting, she was insistent.

"Can't you pick her brain?"

"Pick Mrs. Logan's brain? What are you, kidding? I'd have more success trying to pick Bertha Butterworth's brain."

"Only Mrs. Logan knows who hates her enough to try to kill her. Maybe," Mrs. Hopwood said as she gulped her coffee and looked at the clock, "it was her husband."

"I don't think she's still married. Remember what Deborah said? He left her."

"No surprise there."

"The problem is," Mrs. Johnson also glanced at the clock and realized that she better skedaddle to her own classroom, "that Mrs. Logan would have recognized anyone that night who had no business being here."

"Maybe."

"Listen, I'll see what I can do."

It was a vague promise, a promise which Mrs. Johnson always made when she wanted to pacify someone and Mrs. Hopwood knew it.

"My life is on the line," she said, and then she added, as she always did, "You owe me."

MRS. JOHNSON WAS never quite sure of what Mrs. Hopwood held over her head. Was it the time she babysat for the twins? Or when she agreed to accompany Mrs. Johnson to that trip to Sicily—when all was said and done it should have been Mrs. Johnson, who came collecting. Or maybe because now and then Mrs. Hopwood helped Mrs. Johnson to correct papers, or when she talked Mrs. Johnson out of buying those gold earrings, which turned out to be stolen.

Nevertheless, Mrs. Hopwood was one hundred percent Sicilian and, because of that she would always expect to be paid back—and she frequently reminded Mrs. Johnson about her distant relatives.

So Mrs. Johnson was going to gently probe the subject of Mrs. Logan's attempted murder with her and hope that Mrs. Logan didn't start to talk about Mrs. Johnson's tenure.

THE FIRST PART of the meeting was over in ten minutes. Mrs. Logan wanted to know how Mrs. Johnson had administered the tests in prior years. She gave Mrs. Johnson a number of teacher guides on how to prepare the students, and she reminded Mrs. Johnson that this year she expected the grades to be higher than they were in the past.

Mrs. Johnson, who obviously was supposed to agree, lied and said they would be, and then she said, "I don't think I ever told you how bad I feel about the attempt made on your life."

"Badly."

"Yes, very bad."

"No," Mrs. Logan was vehement, "you used the word bad incorrectly. Feel is a verb and it takes an adverb, not an adjective."

Mrs. Johnson couldn't begin to think of a response to that comment, except from hanging out with Mrs. Hopwood, she knew that Mrs. Logan was dead wrong. Feel was one of those linking verbs, which took an adjective. But no way was she going there. Instead she merely uttered, "I can't imagine anyone who might try to murder you."

"Neither can I, but I can assure you that the police are looking into it."

Mrs. Johnson took a deep breath before she plunged ahead. "Do you think that it has anything to do with Clara's disappearance?"

Mrs. Logan pressed her lips and raised her eyebrows. Her expression remained stony.

"I know Grace," Mrs. Johnson said.

"Grace?"

"Clara's sister. She thinks that Clara came to harm."

Mrs. Logan shook her head. "I told the police at the time, what I told them recently. Clara was a mediocre teacher. She was not on tenure and I had made up my mind not to renew her contract. She always had her nose in a romance book. Even though she was close to fifty, I think she was still waiting for a knight on a white horse to come rescue her. She packed her bags, and her books, boarded a Peter Pan bus and started a new life. There is absolutely no evidence that she was a victim of foul play. And even less evidence that her disappearance has anything to do with the attempt on my life."

Mrs. Johnson stood.

"Please tell that to your friend."

"My friend?"

"Mrs. Hopwood. She should spend more time reading teachers' manuals and less time concocting half-baked theories."

Again Mrs. Johnson was at a loss for words, so she just got up and quietly left.

Mrs. Hopwood was right. She was in trouble as long as Mrs. Logan continued to be principal.

"So YOU GOT no information from her at all?" Mrs. Hopwood asked as soon as she settled into Mrs. Johnson's car.

"No, nothing. She seems to think that Clara ran away, chasing a knight on a white horse." And then Mrs. Johnson added, "Mrs. Logan was going to fire her."

Mrs. Hopwood paled slightly. "It seems that she enjoys firing people. You know, I've been thinking."

"Always a dangerous thing."

"What if Mrs. Logan wasn't the target after all?"

Mrs. Johnson decided not to run the yellow light. She stopped abruptly, causing Mrs. Hopwood to lunge forward. "What are you doing?" she asked, irritated.

Mrs. Johnson decided to answer the question with a question of her own. "What do you mean, what if Mrs. Logan wasn't the original target?"

"What if it was purely random? The murderer wanted to kill someone from St. Polycarp School and he or she didn't care who ate the brownie."

"Well, if that's the case, we're really in trouble because how on earth can we possibly come up with a motive?"

"It could be," Mrs. Hopwood said, "someone who hates the school or is dissatisfied with the teaching and—" She stopped suddenly.

"If that's the case," Mrs. Johnson said, "then you're in real trouble. So if I were you, I wouldn't go eating any brownies."

THIRTY-NINE

WHILE SHE LAY in bed that night, Miss Turnipseed went over everything that had happened the afternoon before.

She could not believe that she had misplaced the application that Mrs. Logan had asked her to mail. Of course, she always had a lot of papers on her desk, so the logical thing was that it just got mixed up with the absent report, or the lesson plans, or the catalogs which promised solutions for a tidy classroom.

If she had to lose something, why couldn't it have been those darn Corey Checks?

Miss Turnipseed retraced all of her steps. She did it calmly and thanked the Lord that Mrs. Logan was in the ER with the devastated Devina. She looked in the file cabinets, on Mrs. Logan's desk—it might have gotten mixed up with the mail—and if Mrs. Logan found it before she did, Miss Turnipseed would be in terrible trouble. She emptied out the trash bin and even went to the teachers' room, thinking she might have carried it, being absentminded, when she got her tea.

She couldn't find it.

It just didn't make sense.

Miss Turnipseed had once seen this movie about little white people, who live in the walls. They come out, unseen, take your belongings, play with them for a while and then return them in the exact spot in which they were taken. Which explained why sometimes when you are looking for an item in one place, and it's not there, and you return a few minutes later, it magically appears. Of course, Miss Turnipseed did not believe in little white people, but she was desperate. She said a few prayers to St. Anthony and then she checked the same places that she had previously checked a second time and then a third time.

These searches were interrupted by phone calls, mostly for Mrs. Logan, but also from anxious parents, who wanted to speak to teachers. And then wayward students had been sent down to the office to be reprimanded by Mrs. Logan, and they were promptly sent back to class by Miss Turnipseed. One third grader had a nosebleed, a first grader had thrown up in the hall and Miss Turnipseed was unable to find the janitor.

It turned out that he had a fainting spell and had collapsed into a bucket of water.

"When will Mrs. Logan be back?" Dylan Moen, the new fourth grade teacher demanded, as though Miss Turnipseed was ill equipped to handle a crisis.

"Soon," Miss Turnipseed said, although she was hoping it was not too soon because she had to find the application.

Except she didn't find the application, and Mrs. Logan did not return.

At least she hadn't by four o'clock, when the school had emptied out.

Miss Turnipseed knew that in spite of what her mother had always said, "Everything has to be somewhere," that simply was not true. Sometimes things disappeared forever, never to be seen again, as though there really were white people in the walls. Miss Turnipseed knew exactly what she was going to have to do.

She was going to lie.

She knew it was a sin, but after all, she had begged St. Anthony for help, and he didn't come to her aid, so she almost felt justified. She was going to pretend to have mailed the application and claim that somehow it got lost in the mail.

Although she wasn't quite sure how she was going to explain the lack of copies.

The thing she was most worried about was that Mrs. Logan would find the application first, but that wasn't too probable because Miss Turnipseed had done a thorough search.

She left quickly because, in case Mrs. Logan returned, she did not want to be at her desk. Mrs. Logan might ask about the application.

While Miss Turnipseed waited for the bus, a very unsettling thought crossed her mind. Was it possible that dementia was setting in, the way it had for Mrs. Arlington? After all, she couldn't find her tea bags this morning and she could have sworn she had bought a new box.

And it wasn't the first thing she had misplaced.

Was she doing other things, things that she could barely remember?

But that wouldn't explain what actually happened to the missing items.

Nevertheless, she was going to have to force herself to pay more attention in the future.

At least that was the plan.

FORTY

"CAN I ASK you a question?" Mrs. Hopwood approached the front desk rather cautiously.

"I am very busy," Miss Turnipseed said in a rather haughty voice,

"It won't take long. I was wondering if there is a list of people who attended on parent/teacher night."

"The police already asked me that and I told them that Mrs. Logan never puts out a sign-up sheet."

"Was there anyone there whom you didn't recognize?"

"That's an odd question. How would I know who should be here? I don't know the parents in this particular school."

"That's true. Well, was there anyone you recognized from your former school?"

Miss Turnipseed released an exasperated sigh. "The police asked me all those questions and the answer is no, there was no one there I recognized. For most of the evening, I was downstairs helping the caterers with the food."

"Did you see anyone...?"

"No, I did not see anyone sprinkle anything on a brownie. Mrs. Logan has been using these bakers for years, they're very professional." She shot Mrs. Hopwood a condescending smile. "I think it's time for you to get back to your classroom."

Mrs. Hopwood was not happy with this remark. Who was Miss Turnipseed to tell her to get back to her classroom? She was the school secretary and was supposed to be serving the teachers, not giving them orders.

Nevertheless, she had a point. It was time to return to the classroom. She was in the process of doing that, when she saw Addison, walking down the hall.

"Excuse me, Mrs. Hopwood. Can I speak to you for a moment?"

"I have to return to class." Mrs. Hopwood began to walk up the stairs with Addison trailing close behind.

"It will only take a minute. As you know my classroom is right below yours."

"I know where your classroom is located." Mrs. Hopwood could not keep the bitterness out of her voice. She wanted to add it had been her classroom for seven years.

"Well, what I want to ask is could you possibly keep the noise down? We have quiet time every afternoon after lunch, and sometimes I feel as though the students are going to come through the ceiling, with the scraping of the chairs and the stomping."

Mrs. Hopwood wanted to stomp on Addison. "I'll see what I can do, but as you can plainly hear my class is usually quiet."

Mrs. Hopwood marched down the hall, thinking that her class was unusually quiet. And that was because Mrs. Logan was crammed into one of the back seats.

She was sitting at Jeremy Sitomer's desk, because Jeremy was, as usual, absent. The problem was that Jeremy's desk was overflowing with papers and torn books and stale gum and maybe even half eaten candy.

"Today we're going to talk about writing," Mrs. Hopwood said in a falsely cheerful tone.

"Why?"

"I thought we were doing social studies."

"Can we work on our horror stories?"

Mrs. Logan was writing something frantically in her notebook, as the students continued to call out.

"Yes," Mrs. Hopwood's voice became louder in an attempt to drown out their comments, which she knew was a mistake. When a classroom became noisy, a teacher was supposed to be quiet and wait until everyone was calm, before speaking. But Mrs. Hopwood feared if she did that, she would have to wait until Thanksgiving. "We are going to work on our Halloween stories, but before we do that…"

"Can I read mine out?"

"I want to hear Dory's."

"Is that the one where Mrs. Hopwood gets beheaded?"

"Before we start writing, we're going to talk about setting. Everyone take out their writing books."

It was a mistake because it wasn't only Jeremy's desk that was a mess. It was everyone's.

"I can't find it. I think someone stole it."

"I left mine at home."

"That's my book."

"No, it's not."

"It's mine. Look, it has my sticker on it."

"Then where is mine?"

Now Mrs. Hopwood did stop. She stood in the front of the class in a confrontational stance, with her arms folded and she waited. Some of the girls stared at her, but the boys paid little attention. One of them even rose, went over to the wastepaper basket and began shooting crumpled papers into it.

"Let me know when you're ready," Mrs. Hopwood said.

"Maybe at three-fifteen," Bruce Holland bellowed.

"Bruce, you may leave the room."

"And go where? Mrs. Logan is here."

"In the hall."

Bruce shrugged and then said he would be happy to. And then with a smirk, he strutted out without a care in the world.

Mrs. Logan was still sitting in the backseat. She had gotten a hold of someone's notebook, probably Jeremy's and she was reading through it.

She looked horrified.

"All right," Mrs. Hopwood said because there was a very brief lull in the class, as the students started to stuff debris into their desks feverishly. "We're going to talk about our favorite horror movies and where they are set."

The class liked this and, although they were still shouting out, they were at least on task as Mrs. Hopwood recorded their answers on the board.

When Mrs. Hopwood gave them the opportunity to continue with their stories, the class was finally quiet and mute.

But it was too late. Mrs. Logan had already left.

No doubt taking Mrs. Hopwood's teaching career with her.

WHEN SHE ARRIVED HOME, there was a message on her answering machine to call Alex. A message from her son was never good news. Alex hadn't given his mother good news since he told her that he was finally potty trained.

"What now?" she asked with bated breath.

"I moved out of the dorm."

"You what?"

"I had to get out of there, Mom. My roommate is a psycho."

"Well, you were getting along so well with him at the beginning of the year."

"That's true. But he's selling pot and, if he gets caught with all that stuff in our room, I'm going down with him."

Mrs. Hopwood did not like the sound of that—at all. "You have to report him to the Dean."

"Mom, you are so out of touch."

"No, listen to me, Alex. I know all about loyalty and not ratting on your friends, but this guy is committing a felony."

"Actually, it's only a misdemeanor."

"Whatever."

"I can't report him."

"Why not?"

"Because I'm one of his customers."

Mrs. Hopwood sank down on the floor.

"Just now and then. And not anymore."

"Where are you now?" She could hardly get the words out.

"I took an apartment off campus with Otto."

"Otto?"

"He's this cool guy from Djibouti."

"Where?"

"It's an island off of Africa."

"You mean he's not even an American?"

"Mom, you are like, so prejudiced. Anyway, I need three thousand dollars."

"What?"

"You know, first month rent, security deposit, application fee."

"Alex, we have already paid for your dorm room."

"I know, but I just explained why I can't stay there."

"I don't have three thousand dollars."

"Ask Dad."

"No, you ask Dad."

"He doesn't like me."

"He likes you fine."

"No, he doesn't. He likes you. He married you. Anyway, I got to go. Otto and I are meeting up with some guys at a pool room."

The connection was broken.

Slowly Mrs. Hopwood put back the phone in its cradle. She doubted very much if Montgomery was going to give Alex three thousand dollars, after they already paid for his room and board on campus. It wasn't as though Alex was a stellar student. So far he was maintaining a low C average.

She heard the front door slam and she glanced at the clock. It was barely five, too early for Montgomery to be home. Was he sick?

Maybe he had something contagious, and she would catch it, and she would have to be out for months.

She thought he might be, when she saw his slack expression, and the way he was slumped over.

"What's wrong?" she asked.

His answer was simple and to the point. "I just lost my job."

FORTY-ONE

GEORGE ARLINGTON HAD never felt more confused in his life.

In the last couple of weeks, everything he believed in had changed. His mother was no longer living with him and he no longer trusted his wife.

Yet George knew that he hadn't lost his mother the moment that the police came and arrested her. He had lost her little by little, day by dragging day, while her mind was growing weaker and weaker.

Still she did not deserve to end her days in a mental institution. At the very least she should be with her son, her grandchildren, with people who loved her and would care for her. Now and then she did have waves of consciousness. What would she think when she woke up and found herself in a psyche ward? Would she hate George for allowing that to happen to her?

Was his wife guilty of putting the poison in his mother's purse? There was a very good possibility. He had seen his mother with that purse. She never let it out of her sight. She held on to it as though it was the only connection to her old life, and it probably was.

The only time she lost it was in Mrs. Johnson's classroom.

Could Marsha possibly be guilty of more than just planting evidence? Could she have gone that far?

Maybe. If she found out what George had been up

to for the last two years. Well, that was over. Still Marsha might not know that, and she was a woman, who clearly took revenge.

No, he was being crazy. Marsha would never kill an innocent person. Someone else had done it. Someone else had planted that poison.

If George could find the real killer, than his mother would be cleared. And the murderer would be able to say whether or not he had tried to frame George's mother.

He. Well, maybe it wasn't a *he*. Maybe it was a she. And for some reason Miss Turnipseed came to mind. George didn't know her very well. She certainly hadn't been school secretary when he was in elementary school. But she had served Mrs. Logan a number of years at St. Jude's.

But why would Miss Turnipseed try to kill her boss? How would that benefit her? She might lose her job, and considering her age, she probably would find it difficult to be hired in a similar position, or any position at all.

Unless—unless Mrs. Logan had made out a will and Miss Turnipseed was a beneficiary.

He knew nothing about Mrs. Logan and her life. Mrs. would indicate that she had married, but somehow he doubted if Mr. Logan was still around. Did she have children? Relatives? Did she have money that could be distributed after her death?

George knew that all of this was just crazy theories. He also knew that the police were conducting their own investigations. But sometimes investigations could take years and years, and, by the time they found the murderer, if ever, his poor mother would be dead and buried.

And what about Mrs. Logan? Was she putting pressure on the police? Wasn't she afraid that another attempt might be made? And this time he or she might be successful?

What George had learned upon becoming an adult—something that was reinforced every single day of his life—is that things took forever to happen. No one had a sense of urgency and, whether you were waiting on the other end of the line for help with your computer, or waiting for someone to get back to you about a recent payment, or waiting for the doctor to call on the results of a biopsy, people took their sweet time.

But his mother was running out of time.

It was absurd to think that Marsha would murder Mrs. Logan just to frame his mother.

And then he found that text.

FORTY-TWO

"DON'T YOU UNDERSTAND what trouble I'm in?" Mrs. Hopwood said softly.

"Why are you whispering?"

"Because I don't want Montgomery to hear me. He's devastated enough."

"I don't understand," Mrs. Johnson said. "How can they fire him, just like that?"

"They said that they could just lay him off, but then they said he wouldn't be able to collect unemployment. They told him that if things pick up in January, they might be able to hire him on a part time basis to do some taxes."

"That's horrible. And he's been there so long."

"It doesn't matter. He says that they are hiring a bunch of kids right out of graduate school. They're all computer geeks, and you know Montgomery. He's never been tech savvy. I didn't even tell him about the three thousand dollars that Alex wants. We don't have that kind of money to just throw away, especially now."

Mrs. Johnson hoped that Mrs. Hopwood wasn't hinting for a loan. "I'd like to help you out, but we can barely make the rent ourselves. And with the twins' tuition…"

"I know. We are going to have to apply for a second mortgage on our house, but who knows if we'll get it."

"I think Alex should take a semester off." It was

Mrs. Johnson's firm opinion that Alex took advantage of his parents, and that firm limits should have been implanted long ago. "He obviously doesn't seem to be doing too much studying."

"I agree. Oh, Montgomery is coming. By the way, you didn't take any of my magazines, did you?"

"What magazines?"

"You know, in my classroom. I had a pile of them for the kids to read when they finish their assignments and my Teen Vogues are missing."

"What would I do with Teen Vogue? One of your delightful girls probably snitched them."

"I guess that's the least of my problems," Mrs. Hopwood said glumly.

IT WAS THE least of her problems, and Mrs. Johnson didn't want to tell her friend what she had just learned from her neighbor Linda Lee, who worked for the superintendent.

The diocese was very unhappy about the death of Bertha Butterworth. It was the third poisoning at St. Polycarp in four years, and rumors were rampant. Parents were complaining and demanding that the cafeteria be closed, and students be allowed to bring their own lunches. Although there never had been an attempt made on a pupil, the death of a cafeteria lady was close enough.

There was even talk of St. Polycarp closing midyear, and then they would all be out of a job.

It didn't matter that the first murderer had been caught, or that the police thought they had the second killer in custody—poor Mrs. Arlington. Scandal was scandal and murder was murder.

The truth was that Mrs. Johnson loved St. Polycarp and was totally devoted to it. She almost felt as though it were one of her children. She couldn't let anything happen to the school.

Although she wasn't clear about what she could do.

ON THE FOLLOWING day it was pouring, torrential rain beating down. Mrs. Johnson was running late because it was difficult to get her twins out of bed, dressed, breakfasted and ready for school. When she arrived, she didn't have time to visit Mrs. Hopwood. She barely made it into her own classroom.

She was taking attendance when a flustered Mrs. Logan came in.

"I wonder if you could do me a favor," she asked Mrs. Johnson.

And Mrs. Johnson said, "Of course" because she didn't want to get on the bad side of Mrs. Logan.

"Miss Turnipseed is not here today."

"Oh, is she sick?"

"I really don't know. She left a message on the answering machine. It's very unfortunate. I think this is the first time she's been absent in years. Anyway, I have a meeting with a parent—someone from Mrs. Hopwood's room." Mrs. Logan's jaw tightened at the mention of Mrs. Hopwood's name. "I know you have a prep at nine-twenty and I wondered if you could watch the front desk for me, answer the phone, take care of late comers, etc. I hope the meeting won't be long."

"Of course." Mrs. Johnson smiled but she felt it was a strain. She had been looking forward to her prep. She wanted to grab a cup of coffee from a nearby deli and pick up an almond croissant for Mrs. Hopwood, in an effort to cheer her.

Well, maybe she wouldn't be there for long.

But the moment she arrived at the front desk and overheard what was going on in Mrs. Logan's office, she knew that wasn't happening.

IT WAS ROSALIND'S parents whom Mrs. Logan was talking to and Mrs. Johnson had taught the older brother last year. Mr. and Mrs. Brokowski thought their children were brilliant and their main complaint was that the school did not challenge them, therefore they could not reach their full potential.

"I don't know what is going on in that classroom," Mr. Brokowski said. "But I do know that there is not a lot of learning taking place. She never returns their Math homework. I don't think she corrects it, because she probably doesn't know how."

"Whose idea was it to take her out of second grade?" Mrs. Brokowski had a high, shrill voice, which made Mrs. Johnson cringe. "She was fine in second grade, which is really just a year of review. But to put her with these pre-teens, that is an entirely different matter. It's just a matter of time, before someone gets hurt."

"Someone did get hurt," Mr. Brokowski said, "remember Devina Diamond? She chipped her front tooth and now her modeling career is on hold."

"We are working with Mrs. Hopwood," Mrs. Logan said calmly and then she said something else but Mrs. Johnson couldn't hear it, because the phone rang.

It turned out to be a third grade parent, who relayed a long message about not having her ex pick up her son, because there was a nasty custody battle going on, and the child might never be returned.

After that Taylor came to the front desk to complain that the copy machine was broken again and demand that Mrs. Johnson call the company. Mrs. Johnson retorted that she was not the school secretary, she was just doing Mrs. Logan a favor, and if Taylor wanted the copy machine fixed, she should call the company herself. And then Mrs. Johnson handed her the Rolodex.

Taylor stormed off.

The phone rang again. The diocese was on the other end of the line and they wanted to know what happened to the application for additional funds. Mrs. Johnson was taking the message when the mailman came with a certified letter for Mrs. Logan from a lawyer.

Mrs. Johnson signed for it and took the rest of the mail, which consisted of two bills, five catalogs from teacher supply companies and a letter addressed to Mrs. Logan with no return address.

The seventh grade class was on the stairway, which meant that Mrs. Johnson's prep was up. She wasn't sure what to do. She couldn't leave the desk unattended, nor could she let her class run wild.

She asked them to wait in the hall.

While they were waiting and, while she was threatening them, Mrs. Logan's door opened and two parents emerged. From the disgruntled look on their faces, Mrs. Johnson surmised that Mrs. Logan had not placated them.

Quickly she delivered the messages to Mrs. Logan and handed her the mail.

She was halfway to her own classroom, when she heard Mrs. Logan scream.

FORTY-THREE

KIT KAT ALWAYS waited patiently for Miss Turnipseed by the front door. So Miss Turnipseed was a little surprised when she entered her apartment, and the cat was not in sight. A dreaded feeling came over her. In her haste and her confusion had she left the toilet lid up, and had Kit Kat jumped in face first and then drowned?

With a heavy heart and dropping shoulders, Miss Turnipseed tiptoed towards the bathroom. To her relief the toilet lid was down.

What about the refrigerator? Miss Turnipseed could not remember opening it, but she might have, and the cat might have jumped in unnoticed, and Miss Turnipseed might have slammed the door and, when she opened it now, the cat would be dead, frozen, as stiff as her two week old cheese.

She drew a deep breath and opened the refrigerator door. No cat in sight.

Miss Turnipseed continued to call for Kit Kat as she looked under the bed, in the closet, even in the hamper, and with a fluttering stomach, in the oven—although she knew that wasn't a possibility because she never cooked in the morning. She examined every inch of the sofa, behind the bookcase, in the bathtub, took apart her bedding, and even looked in her bureau drawers.

But Kit Kat was nowhere to be found.

So Miss Turnipseed called her cousin, Patrick.

OF COURSE, SHE did not tell him about the missing cat. She didn't want him to think she was turning into a dotty old lady. Instead she just said that her apartment had been broken into. And that was the truth.

When Patrick came, he arrived with another young officer, Officer Shea. They looked around, and asked if the robber took anything.

"He did. He took my tea bags," she did not miss the smirk on Officer Shea's face, "and he took my cat."

"Your cat?" Officer Shea repeated. "He is probably hiding in the apartment somewhere. Cats do that. My mom has a cat."

"I looked everywhere. He is not in the apartment."

"Maybe he went outside," Patrick suggested kindly. "When you opened the door, he just escaped."

"You know Kat Kat." Which wasn't quite true. Patrick had never met the cat. "He wouldn't do that. Kit Kat is frightened to be outside his home."

Officer Shea asked her if she was sure she had a cat.

"Of course, I'm sure." She turned towards Patrick and rolled her eyes but Patrick's expression was blank. She took both officers into the kitchen and showed them the bowl of milk, which she had left out this morning, the milk which had probably soured, waiting for the cat who never came.

"We'll look around," Patrick said "and if the cat is in this apartment, don't worry, we'll find him for you."

So they looked. They searched in the same places that Miss Turnipseed had searched. And just like the way she had wished, when she was searching for the application for additional funds, she prayed that the little white people had taken Kit Kat for the adventure of a lifetime, and they would now return him by placing him under the night table.

But the officers were no more successful than she was.

And their only replies for her frantic questions were shrugs.

"It's a mystery, all right," Officer Shea said. But from his tone Miss Turnipseed was thinking it was a mystery he wasn't interested in solving.

"There is only one explanation," Patrick said. "Teresa, the cat slipped out of your apartment, when you opened the door and you just didn't notice."

"I would have noticed," Miss Turnipseed said firmly.

Officer Shea was vehement. "Ma'am, there is no sign of a break-in."

"What about my tea bags?"

The two policemen stared at each other. Miss Turnipseed saw a hint of a grin on her cousin's face, which infuriated her. She wondered if she should continue the Thursday dinners.

She turned towards Patrick and then pointed to Officer Shea. "Does he know that I am the secretary at St. Polycarp School?"

"St. Polycarp," Officer Shea repeated thoughtfully, "why does that sound familiar?"

"Because there was a murder there," Miss Turnipseed responded coldly. "A woman was poisoned."

"And you think that has something to do with your missing cat?" Patrick asked.

"I don't know, but it's possible that someone is trying to drive me crazy." She hadn't remembered even thinking that, but when she said it, Miss Turnipseed realized that it was a distinct possibility. Suddenly she remembered Clara saying something similar before she disappeared.

"Well," Patrick headed for the door, "I really don't think you have anything to worry about, Teresa. But call us if anything else mysterious happens."

"And what if it's too late?" she retorted back. It was on the tip of her tongue to ask her cousin if there was any way one could erase a prior criminal record from a long time ago. But with his attitude and the attitude of the other policeman, it just wasn't a good time.

And it might never be.

MISS TURNIPSEED COULD not sleep. She was so frightened that she was ice cold and shaking. She kept the light on and put a hot water bottle in bed to alleviate the chill. If someone had broken into her apartment and stolen Kit Kat, then they could easily sneak in again, in the middle of the night, to return the cat.

Miss Turnipseed was in danger, although she couldn't imagine why.

And for that precise reason she decided to call in sick on the following day.

FORTY-FOUR

Mrs. Hopwood did not know what was going on, but whatever it was, she knew that it was important.

While dictating a spelling test—something she liked to do, because at least the class was quiet when she said the words—she happened to glance out the window. She saw a police car parked in back of the school.

Had someone else been killed?

Maybe even Mrs. Logan.

God forgive me, she thought, but with Mrs. Logan dead, her own life would be so much easier.

What she wanted to do was to send Mrs. Johnson a text message, but she could hardly stop the test to do so. So she soldiered on, but decided instead of twenty-five words, she'd only dictate twenty, which brought a sigh of relief from the class.

Then instead of going right to science—which was a lesson on botany, something she had no interest in—she gave out a word search and said that the first person who finished it would be relieved of homework.

Most of the students scrambled to start, and the few who didn't asked if they could read. That was fine with Mrs. Hopwood, as long as they weren't noisy.

She opened her desk drawer and, without removing the phone, texted Mrs. Johnson.

Do you know that there is a police car in back of the school? Do you know what's going on?

I do. I was watching the desk.

Well, what?!

Mrs. Logan received a threatening letter.

No!

Yes!

What did it say?

It said Sorry I missed. Next time I won't.

Oh my God!

She freaked. I had to call the police.

Oh my! I guess that lets Mrs. Arlington off the hook.

Not necessarily. She could have sent it from the hospital.

I can't see her doing that.

Me neither. But who knows what the police will think.

"Mrs. Hopwood?"
Mrs. Hopwood looked up to see two policemen

standing in front of her. Quickly she slammed her desk drawer as Mario Mauers shouted out, "Busted."

"I don't know if you remember us. I'm Detective Paneretto and this is Detective Hargrove."

"I remember you," Mrs. Hopwood muttered. She could hardly forget them.

"I need to talk to you. Detective Hargrove is going to watch your class."

A cheer erupted from her students.

"Good luck," Mrs. Hopwood said as she left the room.

Happy to be out of the classroom, nevertheless, Mrs. Hopwood's heart was racing. She felt sweat making a pathway down her breasts. She wondered why the detective wanted to talk to her. She could hardly shed any light on the letter.

"Mrs. Logan thought we could talk in the art room."

Mrs. Hopwood followed Detective Paneretto into the classroom, decorated with Halloween pictures, done in bright neon colors—skeletons, vampires, clowns, mummies—the surroundings only adding to her tense feelings.

"Have a seat," Detective Paneretto invited.

With weak knees, Mrs. Hopwood sank down and sat up, her spine straight, her hands folded neatly in her lap. She was not going to appear nervous. She had nothing to hide.

"All right, let me ask you a few questions."

"Are you questioning all the teachers?" Mrs. Hopwood did not know why she blurted out such a thing.

The answer made her wish she hadn't. "No, just you."

"How can I help you?"

"I understand you keep magazines in your classroom."

"Well, yes. When the children are finished with their class assignments, they are free to read them. I know some educators feel that children should only read good books, the classics, but I'm of the mindset who believes that anything that makes a kid excited to read should be encouraged."

Detective Paneretto did not seem impressed.

"Why do you ask?" she wondered.

"Mrs. Logan received a threatening letter." Mrs. Hopwood tried her best to look surprised. "The message was written in words, letters which had been cut out from a magazine."

"So that makes me a suspect?"

"Not necessarily so. Could you tell me the magazines you had in your classroom?"

"It's funny you should ask." Mrs. Hopwood smiled. Detective Paneretto did not. "All my *Teen Vogue* went missing from my classroom."

"Interesting." Detective Paneretto's bushy brows rose. "When did you notice that?"

"A few days ago." And then so Detective Paneretto would not think that she was lying, she quickly added, "I told that to Mrs. Johnson."

"Do you remember the issues?"

"They must have been the three recent ones, which would be August, September and the October one just came out."

"That's very helpful." Detective Paneretto stood. "We will let you know what we find."

Mrs. Hopwood remained seated. "Do you think that someone cut letters out of my magazines?"

"It's possible."

"Then that means it's someone in this school."

"Bingo."

Mrs. Hopwood was too astonished to move.

"You better get back to your classroom," Detective Paneretto advised. "Detective Hargrove has limited patience for children."

So do I, Mrs. Hopwood wanted to respond, but, of course, she didn't say that.

A moment later, she wasn't even thinking that.

What she was thinking was that she was now clearly a suspect.

FORTY-FIVE

GEORGE HADN'T MEANT to be snooping, but Marsha had left her phone on the kitchen counter, while she ran upstairs to find Catherine's blue shoe. When it vibrated, he glanced down and saw that someone was sending Marsha a text.

And just like that the text appeared.

Been missing you at book club for the last three weeks. Are you coming this Thursday? I made lemon lush.

Marsha wasn't there, George thought. *She hadn't gone to book club. Not for three weeks.*

So it was possible, no more than possible, that she had gone to the parent/teaching evening. And maybe someone could identify her. If Marsha had been present, there was only one reason why that would be so, to kill Mrs. Logan.

But why had she missed three entire weeks?

It wasn't only that night she had missed, but two before then. There was a pattern there. Maybe Marsha was having an affair. That would make more sense.

Especially if she had found out about his affair.

George knew what he should do. He should confront Marsha, demand an explanation.

And when he heard her footsteps on the stairs, he was going to do exactly that.

And then he saw the morning paper.

SOMEONE HAD ACTUALLY sent Mrs. Logan a threatening note. The newspaper didn't divulge the contents of the letter, but the journalist claimed that this action cast doubt on Mrs. Arlington's guilt.

George could hardly bring himself to believe that his prayers had been answered. His mother was going to be released. And right now that was all he cared about.

He was going to be late for work again. He called in and said that it was matter of extreme urgency. He knew his excuses were running thin, but these were extreme circumstances.

How many times in your life was your mother indicted for murder?

He went straight to the police station. But of course, Detective Paneretto was not in, nor was Detective Hargrove. That was all right. George would wait. And he did wait. For over a half an hour before Detective Paneretto came in, carrying a container of coffee. When he saw George, a spasm of surprise flitted across his face.

"Can I talk to you?"

He didn't answer, just beckoned for George to follow him, which George did gladly, until they came to a small room, with only a table. George slumped down as the detective closed the door.

George wasted no time. "When are you going to let my mother go?"

"Pardon?"

"I read about the note that Mrs. Logan received. It's obvious that my mother never wrote that note. She couldn't have. Even if she was able to think clearly, she would not have had a chance to mail it."

Detective Paneretto took a gulp of his coffee and then wrinkled his nose. "Cold," he said.

George was not interested in the temperature of the coffee. "So my mother is innocent."

Detective Paneretto paused a moment before responding. "Not necessarily."

Now it was George who said, "Pardon?"

"Of course it's possible that the person who tried to poison Mrs. Logan, and who succeeded in killing Bertha Butterworth, is the same person who wrote the note. But it is equally possible that someone who doesn't like Mrs. Logan is just trying to screw with her head, trying to torment her. This person doesn't want Mrs. Logan to rest easy, just because we have your mother in custody."

George felt as though a nest of bumble bees were whirling in his head. "So you're not going to let my mother go?" He could barely get the words out.

"I'm afraid not, at least not at this time."

"What does that mean? At least not at this time? What time? Ten years from now? My mother is elderly. She doesn't have long to live. She shouldn't have to die in that hell hole, paying for a crime, she didn't commit."

"I understand what you're saying, Mr. Arlington." Detective Paneretto was struggling to put the lid back on his coffee. "But she's getting help there."

"Getting help there?" George was aware that his voice was getting louder and shriller. "You're joking, right? Have you been there, Detective Paneretto? Do you have any idea what kind of people she's been thrown in with? Do you have a mother, Detective Paneretto?"

With a slight shake of his head, Detective Paneretto snapped the lid on, and flung his coffee into a nearby trash bin, where it made a soft thud.

"Would you want your mother in a place like that?"

For one moment George could read a flicker of sympathy in the detective's bland, pale face. "I understand," he finally said and George breathed a sigh of relief. "So I'm going to tell you what I'm going to do. I'm going to speak to the DA. If you want to move your mother to a private facility, as long as it's secure, we might be able to do that. I don't know what sort of insurance she has…"

"That's not what I want!" George bellowed. "I want my mother to come home!"

Detective Paneretto jerked back, as though he was startled. "You have quite a temper, Mr. Arlington. Does that run in your family?"

George hung his head low. He felt dizzy, nauseous.

"Here's the problem, Mr. Arlington. The poison which Bertha Butterworth ingested is an industrial poison, and we can't tie that poison to anyone but your mother."

"But how could my mother, who is mentally incapacitated, execute such an act? Besides someone else could have put that poison in there to implicate my mother."

"Someone like who, Mr. Arlington?"

This was it. The moment when he could say something. He could tell the detective about his suspicions concerning Marsha.

But before he could utter a word, Detective Paneretto said, "There is something else, something you should be aware of. Yesterday, after I returned from St. Polycarp, I had a visitor."

George felt his chest tighten.

"It was your wife. She pleaded with me, not to let

your mother come home. She's afraid of your mother, afraid for your children. You might want to keep that in mind."

George couldn't speak. There was nothing he wanted to say. He rose, and, without even uttering thank you, he left the building.

You're afraid of my mother, Marsha? he thought. *You should be afraid of me.*

FORTY-SIX

MRS. JOHNSON HAD just dismissed her class and, after trying to soothe a concerned mother about a flunked Math test, she intended to drop by Mrs. Hopwood's classroom. When she passed Mrs. Logan's office, she saw the principal sitting at her desk, staring into space with watery eyes.

Mrs. Johnson decided that a little comforting wouldn't hurt. "Are you feeling all right?" she asked rather gingerly, as she stepped over the threshold.

"How would you feel if someone was threatening your life?" she snapped.

Mrs. Johnson thought it best not to answer the question. Instead she said, in a soothing tone, "I am so sorry that this is happening to you."

Mrs. Logan shook her head. "I think you should know that I heard from the police."

Mrs. Johnson wondered if she dare sit down.

"They seem to have identified the magazine where the cut out letters came from. Those magazines were in Mrs. Hopwood's room."

Mrs. Johnson decided not to sit down.

"Well," she fumbled for words, "Mrs. Hopwood told me that someone had stolen some magazines from her classroom."

Mrs. Logan's only response was a grunt.

"Look, I've known Mrs. Hopwood for years."

"Is this the part where you tell me what a wonderful person she is?"

"No, I mean yes. I mean, of course, she's a wonderful person but she is also a smart person. If she was going to threaten you and, that is a big if, why would she use a magazine, which could have easily been traced back to her own classroom? She could easily have torn up a golf magazine or a race car one."

"This isn't my opinion." Mrs. Logan's tone was clipped and cold. "This is what the police told me." Mrs. Logan paused, and then put her head in her hands. Her voice softened, as her shoulder curled over her chest. "Contrary to what you might think, I am not a mean person, Mrs. Johnson. But please understand where I'm coming from. Mrs. Hopwood's teaching skills are shaky, and there is a possibility that she might be involved with the attempt on my life. If you were me, would you want someone like that around?"

Mrs. Johnson could only shake her head as she headed towards Mrs. Hopwood's classroom.

But Mrs. Hopwood had already left.

WHEN MRS. JOHNSON got home and settled the twins with cookies and chocolate milk, she phoned her friend.

Mr. Hopwood answered and said that his wife had gone out for a walk to clear her head.

Mrs. Hopwood hated to walk, so Mrs. Johnson surmised that she was on the brink of a breakdown.

"Did Julia tell you that they laid me off?" Mr. Hopwood asked.

"Yes, she mentioned it. You'll find another job."

"Yeah, right. You know what I think? I think we should move down south. The cost of living there is much cheaper, and it might be easier to find work when I'm not competing with these Ivy Leaguers. Or maybe Oklahoma. I have a brother there."

Mrs. Johnson felt a tingle of panic at the thought. "What about Alexander," she argued. "You're just going to leave him behind?"

"Alexander is tucked away safely at school. He can travel to us on the holidays."

"Did you discuss this with Julia?"

"Yeah, I did. She's opposed to the idea, of course. But really, she could find a teaching job anywhere. Can I ask you a favor?"

"You can ask."

"Could you try to persuade her?"

"Have her call me."

And then Mrs. Johnson hung up.

THE THOUGHT THAT her best friend might be moving thousands of miles away made Mrs. Johnson feel as though a heavy weight had been dropped on her shoulders. She couldn't imagine teaching without Mrs. Hopwood by her side. Why, she was like family. No, she was more than family. You didn't see your family every day, talk to them every night on the phone, spend eight hours a day, one hundred and eighty-seven days with them.

Things were so muddled. She wished with her heart and soul that Father Felix had never left. She wondered if she could FaceTime him in Rome.

When Mrs. Hopwood finally phoned back, the twins were begging for more cookies. She threw the bag at them.

"You should have been there," Mrs. Hopwood said. "The police actually questioned me about those magazines. Like I really would steal my own magazines and start cutting out letters."

"I know."

"I don't understand any of this. How could I have killed Bertha? How could I have planted that poison in Mrs. Arlington's purse? I never had her purse."

"But I did. Is that what you're saying?"

"Of course not. Maybe the police don't think the letter and the murder are related. Or maybe they think we did it together."

Mrs. Johnson decided then and there that she better come clean with Mrs. Hopwood. Better that Mrs. Hopwood find out through her than a newspaper article. "I talked to Mrs. Logan."

"And what did the witch say?"

"I wouldn't call her a witch," Mrs. Johnson warned. "At least not in public."

"This isn't public. It's on the phone. Unless," Mrs. Hopwood paused, "they've tapped our phones."

"Mrs. Logan told me that the police think that the letters came from one of your magazines."

"How could they know that!?"

"I guess they talked to the students about the missing magazines and they got copies, maybe."

"I didn't send that letter!"

"Of course not. But here's the thing. Someone in the school must have."

"Well, we have to find out who that is," Mrs. Hopwood said firmly.

"Absolutely," Mrs. Johnson agreed. "In order to save your job."

"And maybe," Mrs. Hopwood whispered, "…maybe my life."

FORTY-SEVEN

MISS TURNIPSEED WAS living in mortal fear.

She was afraid to fall asleep, because she was afraid that Kit Kat would just magically appear, jump on her bed, and attempt to suffocate her.

She was afraid to eat, because she was convinced that someone had been in her apartment and stolen her cat and maybe even put poison in her food—although how this was possible was something she couldn't imagine. She was the only one with a set of keys and, even Patrick said, there was no sign of a break-in.

But her biggest fear was that the danger was not from a hidden intruder, but from someplace deep inside herself.

Maybe she never had a cat. Maybe her cat had died a long time ago and she was living in the past, like poor Mrs. Arlington.

And the things that were disappearing—like the application Mrs. Logan had given her. Perhaps Mrs. Logan had never given her an application at all. Maybe Miss Turnipseed had merely imagined it.

Maybe Mrs. Logan didn't even exist.

Well, there was a silver lining in all of this. She wouldn't have to worry about the Corey Check. If she was going insane, no one would care an iota about what she had done in the past.

But right now it was the present she was most concerned about.

Miss Turnipseed did not know what to do. She was tempted to stay hidden under the covers, praying that someone or something wouldn't come out from the shadows and harm her.

But if she was suffering from some sort of memory disease, she would have to go to the doctor. And she would have to use her insurance, which meant that if she really did have a job, she had better show up for work.

But first she had to deal with the police.

She was shocked, when Detective Paneretto rang her bell just after four o'clock. His grim face only added to her terror.

She let him in and he asked politely how she was feeling.

"Fine," she lied.

"I understand you took the day off."

"Yes," she sank down on the sofa. "My cat is missing. I actually called the police, well, really I called my cousin, Patrick, to come look for him. I think someone broke in and took him." Suddenly the thought occurred to her. "You didn't find him, did you?"

The look that the detective gave her reinforced the thought that maybe she was losing her mind.

"No, I'm not here about the cat. Mrs. Logan received a threatening letter."

"Oh my!"

"But I'm not even here about the letter, although it does cast some doubt on Mrs. Arlington's guilt."

Miss Turnipseed thought it best not to respond.

"Of course, we have done some background checks on everyone close to Mrs. Logan."

Miss Turnipseed knew what was coming. And she always knew that someday she would have to walk down that long, dark road.

But she never thought it was going to be today.

"So you found out?" She couldn't stop her voice from trembling and her hands from shaking.

Detective Paneretto nodded.

"It was a long time ago and I was so young, barely nineteen. I was a different person then. I thought I was in love with Vito. So when he asked me to keep watch, as he robbed that liquor store, I didn't argue. I was afraid to. One year in a prison and I turned my entire life around. Since then I've led a good life. No one can say differently."

"But Mrs. Logan might not care what happened after you were convicted."

Miss Turnipseed bit her bottom lip and then asked in a scared, little voice, "Does she know?"

"Not yet. But I understand she was doing some Corey Checks, so she will find out."

Miss Turnipseed was terrified to ask, but she did it anyway. "And that gives me a motive?"

"It does."

"It wasn't me," she protested. "I swear it. I would never do anything like that."

Detective Paneretto merely nodded and then he rose. "That's it for now. But don't go anyplace, Miss Turnipseed."

"I won't," she whispered. "I have no place to go."

ON THE FOLLOWING MORNING, feeling like a damp, cold tea bag, she set out for St. Polycarp. The first thing that

Miss Turnipseed noticed was that her desk was in complete disarray. She would never leave her desk like this, so maybe it wasn't her desk at all.

And then she remembered. She hadn't left it so untidy. She hadn't been in yesterday and, more than likely, a parade of teachers had filled in for her. And no one bothered to straighten up.

She hung up her coat, as Mrs. Logan emerged from her office.

"Did you hear the news?" she asked Miss Turnipseed.

Miss Turnipseed could only hope the news wasn't about her. "No, I was in bed for most of the day. I wasn't well."

"You don't look well. You don't have anything contagious, do you?"

Miss Turnipseed shook her head.

"Someone wrote me a threatening note, actually sent it in the mail, the letters cut from a magazine. The police were here for most of yesterday."

Miss Turnipseed tried to look surprised. "Do they know who is guilty?"

Mrs. Logan didn't have a chance to answer because the phone rang and Miss Turnipseed had to pick it up. It turned out to be the kindergarten teacher, Charlotte Young, who said she had a bad sore throat and wouldn't be in. It was the second time Charlotte had called in sick in the few weeks since school began, and Miss Turnipseed could tell by Mrs. Logan's expression that she wasn't happy.

She threw the substitute list at Miss Turnipseed. "Call someone to take over her class," she instructed.

"It's too hard for the other teachers to fill in for such young children."

It took a full thirty minutes for Miss Turnipseed to reach someone available, and another thirty minutes before the harried, older woman arrived. In the meantime the children had been split up and sent to various classrooms and there was a lot of wailing in the background.

Miss Turnipseed was happy about the wailing. She was even happy about the threatening letter. All of this meant that Mrs. Logan was preoccupied and a preoccupied Mrs. Logan would not be asking about the missing application or when the Corey Checks were due to come in.

Miss Turnipseed was in the middle of printing up the teachers' lesson plans when a thin, older woman shuffled into the school. Miss Turnipseed recognized her as Pearl, a woman, who worked in the cafeteria at St. Jude's.

Never one to gush, Miss Turnipseed managed a quick smile. She didn't ask her how Pearl was, because people always asked that question, even though no one really cared. Instead she asked Pearl how she could help her.

"Actually I'm here to help you. I spoke to Mrs. Logan. I'm the new cafeteria worker. I'm here to take the place," Pearl paused just briefly, "of the poor woman who passed to the other side. If you could show me the way to the dining room, I could get started right away. I even brought my own apron." Pearl reached inside her tote bag and dragged out an apron covered with radishes and onions.

Miss Turnipseed peeked in to tell Mrs. Logan— who was on the phone—that Pearl had arrived, and

Miss Turnipseed would show her the way to the dining room—in case Mrs. Logan was looking for her, which was always a distinct possibility.

"My daughter told me that I shouldn't take the job," Pearl said in a hushed tone, as she glanced around uneasily "because of the murder, you know. All I can say is that I will be very careful about what I eat." She laughed in a hearty, almost obscene way.

Miss Turnipseed did not see the humor.

They walked down towards the kitchen where Jane and Norma were peeling anemic looking potatoes. She introduced them to Pearl. They looked Pearl over, then looked at each other, and managed to flash forced smiles.

Miss Turnipseed knew that cafeteria ladies could be a tight group, but one would think that they would be grateful for another pair of hands, after the demise of poor Bertha.

She decided to stop in the teachers' room. She saw one of the parents drop off a box of donuts for a birthday celebration and, sometimes if there were some left over, the teacher would put the remains out for the faculty.

But what if the donuts were poisoned, like the brownie had been?

As she approached the teachers' room, Miss Turnipseed heard two women talking, whose voices she recognized as Addison and Taylor. Of course, she knew them both from the former school and didn't care for either of the young women.

Mostly because they didn't give her the time of day.

"I can't believe it!" Taylor was practically gasping with delight, "but I understand that there is no doubt that the magazine came from Mrs. Hopwood's room. She must really hate Mrs. Logan."

"You think that she tried to murder her!" Addison asked, her mouth thick with something, probably donuts. She obviously wasn't worried about being poisoned.

"Perhaps Mrs. Hopwood just wanted to torment her. Mrs. Logan doesn't like Mrs. Hopwood at all. She practically told me so. She thinks Mrs. Hopwood is an awful teacher, with no classroom management skills whatsoever. How is it going with you know who?"

"He's ignoring me, which I don't understand. I know I could make him happy. But I suppose he has a lot on his plate right now. All I can do is be supportive, if he'll let me."

"It's better if he's ignoring you. You wouldn't want Mrs. Logan to…"

Miss Turnipseed heard two chairs scraping against the floor and as much as she wanted to, she didn't dare listen to any more. But what had Taylor meant when she said—you wouldn't want Mrs. Logan to—to what?

She hurried away from the teachers' room, her head buzzing. Mrs. Hopwood was definitely a villain. And maybe, just maybe, she wanted to put the blame on Miss Turnipseed. Maybe she found the application—perhaps by the copy machine—and instead of returning it to its rightful owner, she simply trashed it in an effort to get Miss Turnipseed in trouble.

Could Mrs. Hopwood have been responsible for the missing cat and the vanishing tea bags? That was harder to explain. But Mrs. Hopwood usually sped out of the building, as soon as her ill-behaved students left, and maybe she was a pro at picking locks. Maybe she did break into Miss Turnipseed's apartment and had taken those items. Maybe she even brought poor Kit Kat to the ASPCA.

Miss Turnipseed would have to drop by the ASPCA, as soon as she could leave school, and she wondered why she hadn't thought of that sooner.

But why would Mrs. Hopwood do such horrible things?

Obviously, she wanted to cast suspicion on Miss Turnipseed and drive a wedge between her and Mrs. Logan. Of course, this was all supposition, but one thing Miss Turnipseed knew. She was not the person who had sent that threatening note. At least she didn't think she was.

FORTY-EIGHT

No sooner had Mrs. Hopwood hung up the phone, when Detective Hargrove appeared at her door. Although Mrs. Hopwood knew that this wasn't a good sign, she invited the detective in and even went as far as offering her a cup of coffee.

She declined.

Luckily, Montgomery wasn't home, because he would be full of questions, and the way Mrs. Hopwood's heart was beating, and her stomach knotting, she was not in the mood for questions.

"We wondered if you would mind coming down to the police station to take a lie detector test?"

"Now?" Mrs. Hopwood asked and she could tell by the somewhat surprised expression on Detective Hargrove's face that wasn't a good reaction.

"You can come anytime tomorrow."

"Of course. I have nothing to hide." And then in a bolder tone of voice, Mrs. Hopwood asked another question. "You think that I wrote that note to Mrs. Logan?" And when the detective didn't answer, she forged ahead. "Just because the words came from a magazine, which happened to be in my classroom, which just happened to go missing."

"We have to explore all possibilities."

"I understand. I'll come tomorrow after school."

The detective slipped out of the door and was gone for

mere minutes before Montgomery came in. Mrs. Hopwood thought the less said the better. She so wanted to call Mrs. Johnson back, but decided to wait until Montgomery retired.

Only at eleven o'clock he was watching some violent crime show on television, so Mrs. Hopwood retired first.

She didn't sleep.

She went over and over everything in her mind. And by the time the clock registered three, she knew exactly who the guilty party was.

SHE GRABBED A coffee on the way to school and waited outside of Mrs. Johnson's classroom. Unfortunately, Mrs. Johnson arrived a little late and a little harried.

"Jeffrey James is not feeling well. He has an awful sore throat. I sent him to school anyway, because the nanny isn't available on Thursdays. Now I feel guilty."

Mrs. Hopwood had no time to talk about maternal guilt, which she knew was ever present and everlasting. "The police came to see me last night."

"No!" Mrs. Johnson struggled with the sticky key to her classroom.

"They want me to take a lie detector test."

"Really! Is it about the magazines?"

Mrs. Hopwood managed to nod as she took a sip of coffee. "What if I flunk?"

"How can you flunk?" Mrs. Johnson flipped on the switch and her classroom was flooded with light.

"Because I'm nervous."

"They probably take that in account."

"You know that as a fact?" Mrs. Hopwood was feeling tired and grumpy and for some reason her eyes stung. "Did you ever take a lie detector test?"

Mrs. Johnson admitted that she hadn't.

"I've been thinking. There are only a few people who could have been involved in the murder of Bertha, which really was the attempted murder of Mrs. Logan, and they were the people who knew her prior to coming to this school."

"Who are we talking about? Those three young teachers, who when you take away lesson plans, probably can't plot out a dinner?"

"No, think about it." Mrs. Hopwood heard a racket on the stairs and guessed that they really didn't have much time for thinking. "Miss Turnipseed."

"Miss Turnipseed?" Mrs. Johnson repeated blankly. "Why would Miss Turnipseed want to kill Mrs. Logan?"

"I don't know. But maybe it has something to do with Clara."

"Clara again," Mrs. Johnson rolled her black eyes.

"This is really important," Mrs. Hopwood spoke with urgency. "When Mrs. Arlington left her purse in your room, and you gave it to Mrs. Logan, was Miss Turnipseed at her desk?"

"I honestly don't remember."

"This is life and death!"

"Well, I didn't know that at the time." Mrs. Johnson marched into the hall. "Can't you see that two teachers are having a meeting? How dare you whoop and holler when we're trying to talk. Do you all want to stay in for recess?"

The hall became quiet.

"You know what I'm thinking," Mrs. Johnson whispered as she returned to her classroom. "I'm thinking that we have that five day break around Thanksgiving and you and I should go to Rome."

"Rome?"

"We should visit Father Felix. I could e-mail him and tell him we're coming. He's very good in cases like this, helping us to solve mysteries."

"I can barely afford to make my house payments and, anyway, by Thanksgiving it might be too late. One of us might be dead." Mrs. Hopwood said that, as she was exiting the classroom, and one or two of the seventh grade girls screamed.

Mrs. Hopwood was very near the screaming stage herself.

Mrs. Hopwood could barely concentrate on her teaching, while thinking about the upcoming lie detector test. She was tempted to use her cell phone to Google information, but decided against it. It might just panic her more and, if Mrs. Logan should catch her, well she was already in enough trouble.

Mrs. Logan, however, was keeping a low profile. She wasn't patrolling the halls, instead her door was shut tight. On the other hand, Miss Turnipseed seemed to be everywhere from the faculty room, to the cafeteria. She even made a pretense of delivering a note to the parents about the upcoming Halloween party, and after dropping the papers off in Mrs. Hopwood's classroom, she stood at the threshold for several minutes, watching Mrs. Hopwood.

Mrs. Hopwood surmised that she was probably trying to figure out something else she might steal to incriminate her.

I wonder if she knows that I know, Mrs. Hopwood

thought. But it didn't matter. Because Mrs. Hopwood was on her way to the police station, where she intended that everyone would know.

THEY KEPT HER WAITING, which made Mrs. Hopwood even more nervous than she already was. When her cell phone rang, she picked it up quickly and discovered that Alex was on the other end of the line.

"Did you send my money?" he demanded.

"I'm afraid not."

"Well, I need it. If I don't have it, they're going to kick me out."

"Your father lost his job."

"You're kidding."

"I'm a suspect in a murder."

"Again?"

"I'm at the police station, waiting to take a lie detector test."

"What am I going to do?"

"I suggest you go back to the dorm."

"I can't do that! My roommate is afraid I'll rat him out. He might try to kill me. He has a lot of mob contacts."

"Mrs. Hopwood?"

She looked up to see a short, ginger haired cop looking down at her. "They're ready for you now." Her tone resembled a nurse in a doctor's office when very bad news was about to be relayed.

"I have to go," she told Alexander. "I'll call you tonight."

Her heart was racing and her muscles tense, as she followed the police officer through a long, dark corridor. Was Alex serious when he said his life was in danger? She had to persuade him to come home immediately. He could finish his college education locally.

"All right, Mrs. Hopwood, please have a seat."

It was very cold in the room, and Mrs. Hopwood was shivering. A red headed man with a freckle on his nose was sitting by a computer. A woman with long black hair and pointy features—she looked like a witch—asked politely if she could place some buttons on Mrs. Hopwood's fingers. Mrs. Hopwood nodded as the woman fiddled with a rather complicated sleeve. Mrs. Hopwood wished Alexander hadn't called. The call had made her jittery, and that was sure to be reflected in the lie detector test.

Detective Hargrove appeared in the corner. "Just answer yes or no," she told Mrs. Hopwood. Her arms were folded, her jaw clenched. She looked hostile.

"Okay, we're ready to start," the witch said. "Just yes, or no."

She asked her name, her age, her address. Mrs. Hopwood knew that they were the easy questions.

And then came the harder ones.

"Do you know who is behind the murder of Bertha Butterworth and the attempted murder of Lenora Logan?"

Mrs. Hopwood wasn't sure what to answer. "I have my suspicions. I think that Miss Turnipseed, who has known Mrs. Logan for some time—"

"Just yes or no," Detective Hargrove was almost yelling.

"I don't know for sure. No."

"Did you ever tear anything out from the magazines in your classroom?"

"Yes. I tore a picture of Jennifer Lopez in a white

gown. I thought if I put it on my refrigerator door it would stop the mindless picking."

"Did you ever cut out any words?"

"No."

"Did you ever mail a letter to Mrs. Logan?"

"No."

"Do you like Mrs. Logan?"

Mrs. Hopwood paused. "No, not really. Well, she doesn't like me."

"Okay, we're done here."

While the witch was disconnecting her, Mrs. Hopwood looked up at Detective Hargrove. "How did I do?"

"We'll be in touch," she said in a threatening tone.

"THEY SAID THAT they would be in touch," Mrs. Hopwood told Mrs. Johnson, whom she had phoned the moment she left the precinct. "That means that they're going to question me again."

"Not necessarily."

"Of course, necessarily. They should have said good-bye."

"Maybe they were impressed by your suspicions."

"I doubt it."

There was something about Mrs. Johnson's voice that was shaky. And Mrs. Hopwood was immediately suspicious. "What's going on?"

"What do you mean?"

"You know something."

Mrs. Johnson hesitated, and Mrs. Hopwood wondered if she would be able to make it home to use the bathroom. "Well?" she managed to ask.

"I think Mrs. Logan is going to fire you."

FORTY-NINE

GEORGE WAS STEAMING MAD, and intended to have it out with Marsha as soon as he went home. But first he had to visit his mother.

It hurt him more than he could say, seeing her propped up in a cot with a thin mattress and a rumpled, ragged blanket. He wondered if he could bring her a comforter and a fluffy pillow, instead of the flat lump she was forced to rest on.

"Mom, I have some of your favorite candy." He took out some licorice pieces and she smiled as she tried to fish out the pink ones with the black centers. He noticed that she was missing several more teeth.

"Mom, I want you to know that I'm going to get you out of here."

"Can you find my little boy? He didn't come home from school."

George ignored the remark. "I know you didn't try to kill Mrs. Logan and the police know it too. You didn't poison that brownie."

"The brownie, at the parent/teacher meeting. I remember that brownie."

George felt the hairs on his neck raise. "Mom, think. Try to remember about the brownie at that meeting."

"They were good brownies. I had one. Everyone took one. I had to wait in line, but I didn't mind. I wanted to talk to Mrs. Logan and to tell her what a smart boy George is and to be sure to challenge him in math."

"Who was in that line?"

"Oh, lots of people, the pretty lady. And people I didn't know. But there was someone I did know."

"Who was that, Mom? Was it one of the teachers?"

"I don't want that African American woman to be George's teacher. She's very rude. I think she stole my pocketbook." Mrs. Arlington abandoned the licorice and started moving her head in a frantic manner. "Where is my purse? Someone stole my purse!"

"Mr. Arlington, it's time for your mother to go to group therapy." A plump woman, wearing broken glasses, sneaked behind him.

George rose from the rickety chair he was sitting in. "You think that will help her?"

"It's required."

"I'm going to get you out of here, Mom, if it's the last thing I do."

"DID YOU SEE the paper?" George asked his wife as soon as he arrived home.

"Yes." Marsha's tone was uncertain.

"My mother is getting out," he lied, "since she couldn't have possibly written that threatening note."

Marsha's skin paled and her eyes grew wide.

So George continued. "So it was all for no use at all."

Now her expression was puzzled.

"What you did," he elaborated

"What did I do?"

George sank on the couch, enjoying the moment.

"You poisoned Mrs. Logan and then framed my mother."

Marsha didn't answer right away. Instead she stood there, looking foolish, her eyes popping, her mouth wide open. Then she began to shake her head.

"Don't deny it, Marsha. I have proof."

Again the shaking of the head, only this time she muttered, "You can't be serious."

"Oh, I'm serious and so are the police." It was another lie, of course. He hadn't told the police. But there was no need for her to know that. Not yet.

"Why would I do such a horrible thing?"

"You wanted my mother out of the house."

"So I murdered someone?" She was whispering now, her voice hoarse and raspy. "I can't believe you think that. I wasn't even there when the murder occurred. I was at my book club."

George leaped up. "That's where I caught you, Marsha. I know as a fact that you were not there on Thursday, nor have you been there for the last three Thursdays."

She didn't bother to deny it. "How did you find out?"

"Does it matter?"

"So you think…" Now it was Marsha who collapsed into the recliner, her voice quaking.

"I think you murdered Mrs. Logan and I think you bought the poison and put it in my mother's purse. You wanted her out of the house and you were willing to do whatever it took to make that happen."

"You don't know me at all," she said softly.

"No, I don't. But what I do know is that someone

framed my mother. It's the only explanation. And no one was in a better position to do that. You lied to me."

"Yes, I did. Would you like to know where I was on that Thursday night?"

"If you're going to give me the name of a man, who might give you an alibi, don't bother."

"I am going to give you a name of a man." Marsha got up, quickly and quietly and went over to her handbag, which was resting on the coffee table. "You can call him." She reached inside and came out with a card. She threw it at George, missing his eye by inches.

He looked down. It was the name of a therapist.

"You can call. I've been going there every Thursday night. I'm not happy George, and I don't know what to do. I thought it was me, but now, now I see what is really going on here. You don't love me. You don't trust me. You don't even know me. And don't think for one moment, that I don't know what you've been up to."

George wasn't sure how to respond, so he just said, "Let us be clear about one thing, Marsha." He was aware that he was speaking through gritted teeth. "If it's between you and my mother, I am always going to choose my mother."

"And what about your children?" she asked. "Because that's the choice you're making, George. You might want to think about that."

She stormed out of the room, leaving the contents of her purse scattered on the floor.

GEORGE SET HIMSELF up on the couch but he couldn't sleep.

What Marsha said kept echoing in his mind. It was true, it wasn't just about his wife. It was about his children as well. If they separated, she'd keep the girls and, knowing Marsha is a vindictive woman, he doubted that he would see them on a steady basis.

Especially because she suspected that he had an affair. The fact that it had been brief and was now over would not matter. She would grab the ammunition.

And maybe he had jumped the gun, accusing Marsha. But who could blame him? He had to find out who was guilty. And if not his wife, then who?

He couldn't leave his mother where she was, in some county psyche hospital with a bunch of crazies, accused of a murder she couldn't possibly have committed.

Once he proved her innocence, maybe he could move her to a nice home.

Somehow deep inside that woman, he knew his mother, who had scarified so much for him, was alive and well.

Was it wrong to abandon her?

Was it wrong to choose his mother over his wife and children?

It turned out he didn't have to make the choice.

Because shortly after midnight, the hospital called to say that his mother had died.

FIFTY

"THEY CANNOT DO that to me!" Mrs. Hopwood lamented to Mrs. Johnson on the phone. "I'm on tenure."

"I know. But Mrs. Logan claims she doesn't feel safe as long as you're teaching in the school. So maybe," Mrs. Johnson's voice rose slightly, as though she was hopeful, "maybe they will just send you to another school."

"I don't want to go to another school!"

"You may not have a choice."

Mrs. Hopwood felt a surge of anger. "And suddenly you and Mrs. Logan are best friends."

"It's not that."

"She confiding in you."

"Yes, I am encouraging that, but it's better to know your enemies. That's all I'm trying to do."

"Then talk her into keeping me."

"Do you honestly want to stay?"

Mrs. Hopwood thought about it. "I want to be at St. Polycarp. It's my home and my home is being invaded. But I want Mrs. Logan to be gone."

"Whatever you do," Mrs. Johnson warned. "Don't say that to anyone else but me."

WHEN MRS. HOPWOOD hung up the phone, feeling sick to her stomach, she glanced down at her cell and she saw that Alexander had been texting her.

I don't understand. Why are u involved in another murder?

It's complicated.

It's always complicated with u, Mom. And 2 b honest, I can live without the drama. Except now it's affecting my life.

You should talk about drama, Alexander. Moving out of the dorm without consulting us, threatening me that you are in dire danger.

I never said dire.

I think you should take a year off and come home. Your father and I need you.

Right.

We can't give you that money right now, Alexander.

Then I don't know what I will do. I'll be in touch. Maybe.

The last statement made Mrs. Hopwood feel rather woozy. She knew her son and she knew that Alexander could be a top rate manipulator. But what if he was in danger? What if the drug selling roommate harmed him?

What if she lost her job and they all became homeless?

What if the real murderer killed her?

She took immediately to her bed and stayed there for the rest of the night.

SHE TOLD MONTGOMERY that she wasn't feeling well, which really wasn't a lie. So he offered to sleep on the couch. Since he had been laid off, he just hung around the house in his pajamas and watched television and searched on the computer, waiting for an e-mail, which never came.

She rose early the next morning and got dressed quietly, careful not to wake him. She didn't want to talk, not until everything was settled, whenever that might be. She decided she'd pick up coffee and a roll on her way to school.

The thought of going to school made her light-headed and dizzy with fear. She had decided that she was going to take the bull by the horns and speak directly to Mrs. Logan. If Mrs. Logan was going to fire her, then Mrs. Hopwood didn't have to worry about tiptoeing around her anymore.

She had just exited the deli and was headed for the school, when she felt a tap on her shoulder. Taken by surprise, she jumped and almost dropped her coffee. She whisked around and saw a disheveled Mr. Arlington, standing behind her.

"I'm sorry. I didn't mean to startle you."

Mrs. Hopwood was not in a good mood, and she was not up for small talk. She got right to the point. "What do you want?"

"Are you the teacher they're accusing now?"

Mrs. Hopwood didn't quite know how to answer that question.

"About the letter."

"I didn't send any letter." And then she added quickly, "I even took a lie detector test and I passed." The moment she mentioned the lie detector test, she was sorry. After all, it was none of his business.

"I understand what it's like to be accused of something you didn't do."

Mrs. Hopwood kept walking.

"I thought you should know my mother died last night."

Mrs. Hopwood stopped walking. "I didn't know. I am so sorry."

"They said it was heart failure—that she died in her sleep."

"Maybe the strain."

"Maybe. Or maybe someone killed her."

"Are you accusing me?" Mrs. Hopwood could not keep the irritation out of her voice.

"Of course not. But Mrs...."

"Hopwood."

"Hopwood, a lot of things which are happening make no sense at all."

Mrs. Hopwood had to admit that was true. "I'd like to think this is all over," she said as she spotted Mrs. Logan getting out of her car, "but I have a very bad feeling that the worse is yet to come."

"Mrs. Logan?"

Mrs. Logan looked up from the desk, where she was examining a group of papers.

"I just spoke to George Arlington."

"I saw you talking to him," Mrs. Logan said in a tart tone. "I didn't know you had a connection to the Arlington family."

"You're my only connection," Mrs. Hopwood repeated in an equally tart tone. "His mother is dead."

Mrs. Logan opened her mouth.

"She died in her sleep," Mrs. Hopwood answered, deciding that she was going to leave out the murder part. No sense in making it more complicated. "So you see, if she was the killer, you can rest easy."

"I wish that were true." Mrs. Logan looked down again at her papers.

"I understand you're thinking of letting me go."

Again Mrs. Logan looked shocked, and it occurred to Mrs. Hopwood that maybe Mrs. Johnson did not want her to mention it. Well, too bad. It wasn't Mrs. Johnson's job that was on the line.

"I just want to feel safe," Mrs. Logan said simply.

"If you're still not safe, after Mrs. Arlington's death and, my passing the lie detector test, then you only have yourself to blame."

Mrs. Logan had no comment but her glare was frightening.

"You should know, Mrs. Logan," Mrs. Hopwood said. "If you do decide to fire me, I won't go gently into the night."

FIFTY-ONE

MISS TURNIPSEED SAW Mrs. Hopwood march out of Mrs. Logan's office. She stopped briefly to nod at Miss Turnipseed. Miss Turnipseed couldn't help but overhear that Mrs. Arlington has passed on. *It was probably for the best,* Miss Turnipseed reasoned, *as the poor woman had lost all sense of reality, and she was probably going to spend the rest of her life in a psyche ward.*

Miss Turnipseed tried not to think of what this might mean for herself since she was having spurts of forgetfulness. She wondered if a disease like that happened gradually, like losing things and misplacing cats, or if you just wake up one morning and think you're thirty years young.

Better not to think about that, Miss Turnipseed decided, as she began to unload her tote bag, taking out her blood pressure pills, her thermos of prune juice, and her mid-morning snack of four graham crackers spread with a light coating of peanut butter and strawberry jelly.

While she put her cleaning wipes down in the corner, she noticed a note from Norma, one of the cafeteria ladies. It was written in very neat handwriting, asking Miss Turnipseed to please come to the cafeteria, as soon as she was able.

Miss Turnipseed peeked in at Mrs. Logan who was busy locking her own lunch in the file cabinet and announced that she was going down to the basement. "I want you to know where I am," she told her boss, "if the phone rings."

She was on her best behavior, just in case Mrs. Logan got it into her head to fire Miss Turnipseed, after she discovered that the application for the additional funds had never arrived. And after she received the Corey Check.

"THERE WILL BE no milk today," Norma announced as she buttered two pieces of bread and slapped them together.

"What do you mean?" Miss Turnipseed was genuinely confused.

"It didn't arrive. I called the milk company and they said, no more milk for us, because we didn't pay in advance, the way we're supposed to."

"Why are you telling me this?" Miss Turnipseed began to wring her hands. "Isn't this a matter for Mrs. Logan?"

"One would think so, but aren't you the one who orders the milk and mails out the checks after Mrs. Logan signs them? At least that's what she told us at the orientation meeting."

Miss Turnipseed couldn't find her voice to respond.

"I didn't want to get you in trouble, Mrs. Logan being so nervous since someone tried to kill her."

Pearl, the new cafeteria lady, edged closer, and Norma began to whisper. "I can tell her myself, if you want me to—if you are afraid of her."

Miss Turnipseed resented the remark. "No, I'll take care of it," she snapped.

She took the stairs slowly. She would not be able

to hide the missing milk, the way she had the application papers. She would have to face Mrs. Logan. The funny thing was that Miss Turnipseed distinctly remembered filling out that milk order and putting it on Mrs. Logan's desk.

Maybe Mrs. Logan was the one who broke the chain. And if she wasn't?

Miss Turnipseed thought of poor Mrs. Arlington again, and she shivered.

"I'M AFRAID, MRS. LOGAN, that there is no milk today."

Mrs. Logan put down her attendance book and looked up, confused and angry.

"The milk company claims we didn't pay." Miss Turnipseed had decided to take the offensive. "I don't know how that's possible, I distinctly remember putting the order on your desk. Do you remember sending out the check?"

Mrs. Logan reached inside a drawer and pulled out a large checkbook. Of course, she would keep records, so it wasn't really good lying. But the scary thing was Miss Turnipseed wasn't sure if she was lying or not.

"No, it's not here. If you had put the order on my desk, Miss Turnipseed, I would have signed it and given it to you to mail. It seems to me, you're getting a little forgetful."

With that remark Miss Turnipseed felt her fingers tingle.

"I suppose I'll have to call them, because every mother will be hollering from here to New York City, if her little darling misses a glass of milk. Get me the number."

That Miss Turnipseed could do.

Or at least she thought she could do.

Where was that number? It should have been in the Rolodex. Why wasn't it in the Rolodex? *Breathe deeply,* Miss Turnipseed thought, as she felt heaviness in her chest, and hoped she wasn't going to have a heart attack.

Maybe she could get it from the file, which should be in the bottom drawer. Yes, there it was, a bright white file, for bright white milk. She grabbed it, opened it and there was the number.

And there was something else—the application for additional funds, buried under that file.

Miss Turnipseed breathed a sigh of relief. She could quickly make copies, file them, mail it tonight, and just say that the post office must have delivered it to the wrong address. She wasn't sure how it managed to find its way to the bottom drawer, but she must have put it there without thinking.

She would worry about what was happening to her mind later.

She grabbed the papers and promptly dropped them.

For underneath the application she found something else that brought terror to her heart.

It was a magazine addressed to Mrs. Hopwood, torn up, with missing pages.

FIFTY-TWO

"DEAD?!? ARE YOU SURE? Dead?" Mrs. Johnson went on feverishly. "Are you sure?"

"I'm only repeating what her son told me outside the school. She died in her sleep, but George thinks she was murdered." Mrs. Hopwood was leaning against the blackboard, as though she might faint at any moment.

"How is that possible?"

"I don't know," Mrs. Hopwood said. "I don't see how someone in the hospital could have killed her."

"Well, did you ask if his mother had any visitors?" Mrs. Johnson demanded as she glowered at the two girls, who were about to burst into the classroom.

"I could hardly do that. I am lucky I could talk to him at all, with Mrs. Logan watching us. By the way, I confronted her and told her, if she was thinking of firing me, she could think again."

"What?" Mrs. Johnson could scarely believe what she was hearing.

"I have to stand up for myself. She can't just fire me. I have…"

"I can't believe you did that. You told her that you knew that she was going to get rid of you. She's going to know that information came from me!"

"Who cares?"

"I care!" Mrs. Johnson lowered her voice as she saw more students looming in the hall. "And you should care too. I'm trying to make her a confidante, so we can both get information. It's important that she's on our side."

"Well," Mrs. Hopwood said as she sidled towards the door, "that worked out real well for me."

WHILE THE STUDENTS were writing about what they thought God wanted from them, Mrs. Johnson was standing by the window, holding up a writing book and texting Mrs. Hopwood.

I think that after school you and I should go and visit George Arlington. I Googled him and I know where he works, Featherston Investments. We can ask him a few questions.

Will you give me a ride home?

Of course. We need to find out what's going on.

Can't text anymore. Mrs. Logan is outside my door.

Meet you in the parking lot at 3:30.

"THIS IS PROBABLY a waste of time," Mrs. Hopwood said in her usual defeatist voice.

"You don't know that," Mrs. Johnson said as they rode the elevator up to the eleventh floor. "At this point, you really don't have anything to lose, do you?"

The elevator stopped with a jerk, propelling Mrs. Johnson into Mrs. Hopwood, who cursed under her breath. Mrs. Johnson let it go. She supposed her best friend had a reason to be in a foul mood. Things weren't going well for her.

"We would like to see Mr. Arlington," Mrs. Johnson said, after she had marched through the glass doors and stopped at the receptionist's desk.

The woman with dyed red hair and sage eye shadow and brown gloss on her teeth asked if they had an appointment.

"No, we don't. But I think he'll see us. I'm Mrs. Johnson and," she turned towards an embarrassed Mrs. Hopwood, who was loitering by the elevator, "this is Mrs. Hopwood. We were friends of his mother."

"Oh, yes. I was very sorry to hear about her death. Personally," the receptionist looked around and then began to whisper, "we're all surprised that Mr. Arlington is here today. You would think he would want to be home with his wife, grieving together. Why don't you have a seat? I'll tell him you're here."

Mrs. Johnson plunked down on a brown leather chair, while Mrs. Hopwood remained standing. She reached for a magazine, but before Mrs. Johnson had a chance to open it, George Arlington walked into the waiting room.

"I can't say I'm not surprised," he said.

Mrs. Johnson noticed that his face was flushed and his eyes bloodshot. A wave of sympathy washed over her. "We would like to talk to you about your mother."

He led the way, Mrs. Johnson following him and Mrs. Hopwood trailing them. He opened the door to a small office and he sat behind a cluttered desk. Mrs. Johnson took a chair across from him, and Mrs. Hopwood reluctantly took the other one.

Mrs. Johnson did not waste time. "You think your mother was murdered?"

George nodded. "I think it's a possibility. Aside from her dementia, there was nothing wrong with her. Her heart was strong and, just a few months ago, the doctor told us she had many good years ahead of her. But, of course, that was before all this sordid business."

"What do you think happened?" Mrs. Hopwood spoke for the first time.

George shrugged and Mrs. Johnson jumped right in. "Did you ask the hospital if your mother had any visitors? Because if your mother didn't die of natural causes, then someone must have come to see her just before she passed on."

"No," George said thoughtfully. "I didn't think of it. I was too shocked."

"Why don't you call now?" Mrs. Johnson suggested and didn't miss the glare Mrs. Hopwood gave her. All right, she knew she was being bossy, but someone had to take the lead. "And put it on speaker."

George fiddled with some papers and then finding the number, he began to dial.

"Morning Glory Hospital."

"Yes, could you connect me to the fifth floor, please?"

"Just one minute."

Of course, it wasn't a minute, not at all. While *The Way You Looked Tonight* played in the background, Mrs. Johnson studied the surroundings. The plaques on the walls said that George had graduated from Middlebury College and got an MBA from Syracuse.

Smart.

"Fifth floor. Can I help you?"

"This is George Arlington."

"Oh yes, Mr. Arlington. We had your mother transferred to the McKinney Funeral Home early this afternoon. That was what you wanted, isn't it?"

"Yes, thank you." He gazed uneasily at Mrs. Johnson. "I was just wondering if yesterday, before she died, my mother had any visitors."

"I don't recall any, besides you, I mean."

Mrs. Hopwood released an annoying cough.

"Let me check the log book. I went out for a late lunch, around three thirty. So it's possible someone did come in and I didn't know. Do you mind if I put you on hold?"

Just once, Mrs. Johnson would like to say, "Yes, I do mind. How long are you going to be? And are you really trying to get information for us while we're waiting?" She diverted her attention to a picture George had on his desk. He was standing by his mother, a stunning woman with dark brown hair and the most amazing hazel eyes. Her smile was wide, displaying perfect white teeth.

Where had she gone?

"Mr. Arlington?"

"Yes."

"As a matter of fact, your mother did have a visitor."

Mrs. Johnson leaned forward, in order to get closer to the telephone.

"Who?" George asked in a raspy voice.

"It was a woman, a woman by the name of Clara Edwards."

FIFTY-THREE

GEORGE ARLINGTON WATCHED as Mrs. Johnson leaped out of the chair and stuck her face into the phone. "Who?" she asked frantically.

"Clara Edwards."

"She's not dead," Mrs. Hopwood whispered

"Is there any way you could be mistaken?" Mrs. Johnson probed.

"That's the name she signed in with," the voice on the other end of the line answered stiffly. "Who is this, anyway?"

"My name is Amelia Johnson." She sneaked a glance at George. "I'm a friend of the family's. No, what I need to know is if it's possible for someone to impersonate Clara Edwards?"

"Who is Clara Edwards?" George wondered aloud.

"Ma'am, whoever you are, please understand this is not a nursing home. It's a prison, albeit, a minimal security prison, but we have rules and regulations. Everyone that comes in has to show a picture ID. If this woman says that she was Clara Edwards, then she was Clara Edwards. Now, if you'll excuse me, I need to return to my job."

As the line went dead, George asked again. "The name does sound familiar. Was she a teacher?"

Mrs. Johnson and Mrs. Hopwood exchanged frowns. "Well?"

"She's not dead," Mrs. Hopwood repeated.

Mrs. Johnson sank back into her seat. "You're right. She was a teacher, who disappeared at the last school that Mrs. Logan was affiliated with. The police think she ran away. Her sister thinks she was murdered. We think," Mrs. Johnson pointed to Mrs Hopwood, who looked rather comatose, "she has something to do with the attempt made on Mrs. Logan's life."

George's head was spinning with unanswered questions. He found the two women in front of him made him light headed and rather nauseous. "How is that possible?" Rather than being relieved, he felt a prick of annoyance. "That would mean that she would have had to have been there the night of the parent/teacher meeting. Wouldn't Mrs. Logan have recognized her?"

"Maybe she was in disguise," Mrs. Johnson guessed.

"And how would she have managed to put the poison in my mother's purse?"

"Maybe someone else did it," Mrs. Johnson said.

George tried to look shocked, as though he hadn't thought of that theory before, as though he hadn't accused his own wife of such a thing.

"And maybe," Mrs. Johnson said, "the person who sent that threatening note to Mrs. Logan is not the person who tried to murder her."

"So," suddenly George was utterly exhausted, "the person who attempted to kill Mrs. Logan and the person who put the poison in my mother's purse and the person who sent the note, they're three different people."

"Shouldn't we tell Grace her sister is not dead?" Mrs. Hopwood asked suddenly.

"Who is Grace?" George asked.

"The entire thing makes no sense at all," George said. "And I suppose I shouldn't care. But if my mother did not die of natural causes, and someone killed her, then I want to find that killer and, so help me God, I'll kill her myself. Or him."

"Would the state consider an autopsy?" Mrs. Johnson asked.

"Probably not."

"I wonder how much they cost," Mrs. Johnson said.

"Would you consider chipping in for one?" George asked and he could tell by Mrs. Johnson's startled reaction that she did not consider this to be an option. Well, why should she chip in? Really, what difference did it make to her and the other teacher if the real killer was caught?

"I'm not feeling well," Mrs. Hopwood said suddenly. "Is there a ladies' room here?"

"You need a key," George reached in his desk and took out a key, attached to a large wooden board. "Go out to the waiting room, down the hall, first door on the left."

George decided then and there that he wanted to know more about Clara Edwards. He leaned over to his computer and told Mrs. Johnson that he wanted to Google her name. Mrs. Johnson, who was clearly a bold woman, rose and went on the other side of the desk, and leaned over him. He could smell her perfume, a combination of musk and roses.

"Here it is," he said as he clicked on the picture of an older woman, with a pinched, drawn face. "She looks rather old-fashioned."

"No," Mrs. Johnson scolded him, "that's not the right Clara Edwards. This Clara Edwards is a character on *The Andy Griffith Show.* Look." She bent down even further and her two ample breasts brushed against George's face.

The door flew open and there stood a furious Marsha. They had barely spoken since he had accused her of framing his mother, so he was shocked to see her standing there.

"So she's the woman you're having the affair with, a woman old enough to be your mother!"

Mrs. Johnson sprang to attention.

"Marsha, please!"

"I knew it. I knew there was a reason why you accused me of trying to murder Mrs. Logan! So you can be with her!"

"What is she talking about?" Mrs. Johnson's voice quivered with anger. "Who is this woman?"

"I'm his wife. I bet he didn't tell you that he had a wife!"

"Marsha, you are being ridiculous. This woman, Amy Johnson, is just a teacher at St. Polycarp."

"Amelia Johnson."

"You see, I don't even know her first name."

"I think I should go." Mrs. Johnson was inching towards the door, trying to avoid contact with Marsha.

"That would be a good idea."

"She knew my mother. She is just trying to be helpful." Somehow George knew that his explanation was making things worse.

"We'll be in touch," Mrs. Johnson said as she scrambled out the door.

"I'm sure you will be," Marsha said tartly.

FIFTY-FOUR

MRS. JOHNSON BUMPED into Mrs. Hopwood in the hall and she quickly relayed what had just happened inside George's office.

Mrs. Hopwood's head was spinning, her stomach was on fire, and she was fighting to hold back vomit.

"Can you believe it?" Mrs. Johnson was clearly incensed. "And then she had the nerve to say that I was old enough to be his mother. I am surprised that she didn't mention my African American roots."

"I think I've been poisoned." Mrs. Hopwood struggled to get the words out.

Of course, Mrs. Johnson did not act surprised. In fact, Mrs. Hopwood noticed that she clenched her jaw, the way she always did when she was annoyed.

"Did you hear me? I think I've been poisoned."

"When?" Mrs. Johnson stabbed at the elevator button. "You didn't eat anything in his office."

"No, but you know how I never eat cafeteria food? Well, today they were serving grilled cheese sandwiches and I do like them and I asked Norma for one."

"And she poisoned you?"

The elevator doors slid open and, because there was an older man inside, Mrs. Hopwood thought she should whisper. "I noticed that there was some white powder on the bottom of the sandwich. I thought it might just be flour."

"But now you think it was arsenic."

The man had a smirk on his flat, white face.

"I only know that I'm not feeling well."

"Well, don't throw up in my car."

The elevator doors snapped open and the ladies proceeded through the lobby.

"Is it so impossible?" Mrs. Hopwood was not about to give up. "Two people are already dead, Bertha and Mrs. Arlington, and Mrs. Logan has been threatened. Why shouldn't someone come after me?"

"Because you're not that important." They had reached the car and Mrs. Johnson instructed Mrs. Hopwood not to put on her seatbelt. "The pressure might not be good for your stomach or my car seat."

Mrs. Hopwood wasn't convinced. "Maybe I know something that I don't think I know."

"You have been watching too many of those TCM movies again. But I do agree that you might have a good point."

Mrs. Johnson waited until they were settled and she had started the car before she elaborated. "Miss Turnipseed knows more than she is telling. I have a feeling that she knows that Miss Edwards is alive. She might even be hiding her in her own apartment."

"And why would she do that?"

"I haven't figured that part out yet." Mrs. Johnson made an abrupt stop at a yellow light.

"Don't do that," Mrs. Hopwood cautioned. "My stomach."

Mrs. Johnson sneered.

"Maybe you should take me to the ER."

"You'll be there for hours and you might catch a staph infection and you might die. You probably only have a mild case of indigestion. I think the cheese they use is moldy. Now, this is what I'm thinking."

Mrs. Hopwood rested her face against the glass on the window, which was nice and cool and made her feel a trifle bit better.

"I think you and I should invite Miss Turnipseed for a drink."

"Somehow she doesn't look like a woman who drinks."

"You'd be surprised. And don't lean against the window like that. The door handle on that side is shaky. Anyway, I think we should talk to Miss Turnipseed. We could take her out for a cup of tea. Tell her what we know and, more importantly, find out what she knows. What do you think?"

"I think," Mrs. Hopwood said, "that I'll be lucky if I make it home without vomiting."

FIFTY-FIVE

MISS TURNIPSEED WAS unpacking her tote bag when Mrs. Johnson stopped by the front desk. It was barely seven-thirty, and this woman looked as though she was on an urgent mission. It was too early for demands, especially when Miss Turnipseed was feeling so sleepy.

"How are you this morning?" Mrs. Johnson asked in an upbeat tone.

"I'm fine, thank you."

"Mrs. Hopwood and I would like you to meet us for coffee after work."

The statement caught Miss Turnipseed by surprise. She knew that it wasn't an idle invitation. And instantly she understood. "You want me to go to one of your homes, is that it?"

"Our homes? No, not at all. We could go to a local diner."

Miss Turnipseed pursed her lips. "I don't drink coffee."

"How about tea then? And a nice muffin? Or a piece of chocolate cake?"

They were going to suggest that she go to the bathroom and then they were going to plant evidence on her.

"We really need to speak to you, Miss Turnipseed." Mrs. Johnson eyed the empty office, belonging to Mrs. Logan, as though Mrs. Logan was going to suddenly materialize out of nowhere. "It's about your friend, Clara Edwards."

If she watched the two women very carefully, if she left a note on the desk in case something should happen to her—maybe it wouldn't be so bad. It was a long time since she had a bite to eat outside of her own kitchen which had turned frightening after the disappearance of Kit Kat—and the thought of a large piece of chocolate cake was tempting.

"I can't stay long," she told Mrs. Johnson, "and I won't go to the ladies' room."

Mrs. Johnson's brown forehead wrinkled. "We'll meet you outside at three-thirty."

ALTHOUGH MISS TURNIPSEED was slightly suspicious of the teachers' motives, she was rather looking forward to the excursion. While climbing down the stairs to the cafeteria to put her prune juice in the refrigerator, she thought of another reason why meeting the ladies would probably be a good idea. They might not only share information about Clara Edwards, but, if they were indeed guilty about placing the magazine at her desk and hiding the application papers, maybe she could wrestle the truth out of them.

She knew that Mrs. Johnson was smart—she wasn't sure about Mrs. Hopwood, but Miss Turnipseed was plenty smart herself. If she hadn't taken that wrong turn, so many years ago, she could have gone to college, maybe been a teacher herself. Or a nurse. It was possible that she could somehow trick them.

Or maybe they were trying to trick her. Maybe they found out about her past and they were now going to blackmail her.

Although it was a little late for that.

SHE ARRIVED AT the cafeteria, and the dining women hadn't come yet. She would be able to sneak some sugar and some bread for her morning toast. She tiptoed into the vast kitchen and stopped when she heard a sound. The sound of a cat. A sound she recognized as Kit Kat's.

Was she imagining things?

No, there it was again—a faint meow, coming from the walk-in pantry. Her heart beating hard and heavy, she touched the knob, praying it wasn't locked. It wasn't.

"What are you doing?"

Miss Turnipseed leaped and both women screamed. It was Norma, one of the lunch ladies behind her.

"I heard a cat in the pantry." Miss Turnipseed placed her hand over her heart

"A cat?" Norma threw off her coat and started to put on her apron.

"My cat is missing."

"Why would your cat be here?"

Miss Turnipseed thought any explanation would be too convoluted and lengthy, so instead she flung the door of the pantry open. Shelves and shelves of canned goods were lined up like soldiers off to the battle. But the floor was clear. There was no sign of a cat.

Except—there was an open window.

And cat hair on the floor.

Miss Turnipseed bent down and rubbed her hand over black cat hair.

"A cat has been inside here." She whirled around and faced Norma.

"Not here. Against city code. We wouldn't be able

to get money from the government, if we kept animals here."

"Cat hair." Miss Turnipseed stuck her hand in front
of Norma's startled face.

"That isn't cat hair. It's hair from Jane's old muskrat
coat. You're hearing things, Miss Turnipseed."

"I don't think so."

AND SHE DIDN'T think so. Somehow Kit Kat had gotten
out of her apartment and found its way to the school.
She waited until Norma was busy in the freezer and
then she sneaked out the back door and into the small
courtyard.

She called for the cat several times, but there was
no sign of Kit Kat.

It had started to rain, a light, cold October mist and
it hurt her so to think of her little cat, who had never
really been out of her apartment, suddenly in the middle of the city, hungry and confused.

He could have climbed the wall, but she couldn't.
She couldn't even see over the wall, so maybe Kit Kat
had gone to the neighboring apartment unit.

Or maybe it wasn't Kit Kat at all, but another black
cat.

Or maybe it was a rat.

Or nothing at all.

Miss Turnipseed looked up to see Mrs. Logan at the
window with a puzzled expression on her face. There
was no way to explain.

Instead she hurried back in and went upstairs. It was
crucial that she be there when the mail arrived. Maybe
it wouldn't be too late to hold the Corey Checks.

At least for a while.

FIFTY-SIX

MRS. JOHNSON CHOSE the restaurant, a diner not far from the school. The food was plentiful—if a little tasteless—and the price was cheap. She had the distinct feeling that she would be footing the entire bill.

Miss Turnipseed ordered a piece of chocolate cake with chocolate ice cream on top and a cup of peppermint tea. Mrs. Hopwood just ordered a small salad which Mrs. Johnson doubted she would eat, and Mrs. Johnson ordered a burger with well-done fries—which she was sure Mrs. Hopwood would dip into.

"So what is this about?" Miss Turnipseed was sitting straight as an arrow, with an anxious expression on her wrinkled face.

"Do you know that Mrs. Arlington passed on?" Mrs. Johnson asked.

"I heard that through the grapevine and I'm very sorry. But I didn't know the woman well."

"Her son thinks she was poisoned," Mrs. Hopwood said quickly.

Mrs. Johnson resented the interruption. If she was paying the restaurant bill, she felt she should do the interrogating.

"Poisoned?" Miss Turnipseed began to wring her hands, which told Mrs. Johnson that the statement made her anxious and put her immediately on guard.

"And the last person to visit her…" Mrs. Hopwood started.

Mrs. Johnson was too happy to finish, "was Clara Edwards."

Even with two dabs of very bright red rouge, Miss Turnipseed's face paled. "I don't understand. It could not have been Clara Edwards."

"And why is that?" Mrs. Hopwood leaned forward in an aggressive manner. "Because you know as a fact that she's dead?"

Mrs. Johnson had had enough. She swiftly kicked Mrs. Hopwood under the table in her bad knee. Mrs. Hopwood yowled.

"Are you insinuating that I killed Clara Edwards?" Miss Turnipseed dropped her tea onto the saucer.

They were creating a racket and several people turned their way, some in annoyance—some in curiosity.

"Of course not." Mrs. Johnson was determined to smooth this over. "It just means that Clara Edwards may be alive and may be responsible for some of the things that have been happening."

Miss Turnipseed dipped her fork into her chocolate cake. Her brows furrowed in thought.

Mrs. Hopwood looked over at Mrs. Johnson and then whispered, "Do you think that's a possibility?"

"Well."

"If you know something, you have to tell us," Mrs. Johnson said firmly, knowing that Miss Turnipseed did not have to do any such thing.

"It's just that strange things have been happening in my apartment. Someone has been moving things. And with my door locked, someone stole my cat. I heard a cat in the alley right outside the school. It might have been Kit Kat."

"Yes, well." It was important to Mrs. Johnson that she didn't sound dismissive.

"I saw that cat too," Mrs. Hopwood said slowly as she chopped up a tomato.

"When?"

Miss Turnipseed lunged forward with the fork in her hand, missing Mrs. Johnson's ear by inches.

"A few days ago."

"Are you sure?" Miss Turnipseed asked anxiously.

"Of course, I'm sure," Mrs. Hopwood said sullenly. "A black cat roaming right outside the school."

"Kit Kat! I hope he comes back! I went to the ASPCA to ask about him, but I didn't get past the desk. I couldn't bear to see those poor, deserted animals, locked in cages. But the man said that no black cat had been turned in. And here's another thing," Miss Turnipseed leaned back again, "Clara had a key to my apartment. Just in case I ever got locked out."

"One cat looks very much like another," Mrs. Johnson said, waving her hand. "Did you have a key to Clara's apartment?"

"Certainly not." Miss Turnipseed took a bite of her cake. "Anyway, the whole thing hardly makes sense. Why would Clara hide out all this time? Where would she go? And why would she suddenly take it in her mind to try and kill Mrs. Logan and then poison Mrs. Arlington, if indeed she was poisoned?"

"Maybe," Mrs. Hopwood said, "Mrs. Arlington knew something that she didn't know she knew. Something she suddenly remembered and then when she babbled, Clara Edwards was afraid."

"TCM again," Mrs. Johnson stuffed a French fry in her mouth. "Was Clara Edwards angry at Mrs. Logan?"

"Well, yes, she was." Miss Turnipseed seemed more relaxed now that she wasn't being accused. "She was quite upset when Mrs. Logan told her that she would not renew her contract."

"Did you see her at the parent/teacher evening?" Mrs. Hopwood asked.

It was a stupid question and, from Miss Turnipseed's raised eyebrows, Mrs. Johnson guessed that she thought so also. "Of course not, if I had seen her, I would have recognized her."

"Unless she was in disguise." Mrs. Hopwood stole a French fry from Mrs. Johnson.

"The whole thing is rather silly." Miss Turnipseed pursed her lips. "Why would Clara go to a meeting with the intention of killing Mrs. Logan? How would she even know she would have the opportunity? And she would have to have the opportunity to actually poison the brownie. She couldn't do that with other people hanging around. Of course," she scooped up the last of her chocolate frosting, "stranger things have happened."

Mrs. Hopwood grabbed another French fry. "It had to be someone who would have the opportunity to actually poison one brownie and then drop it off at Mrs. Logan's desk—someone like a cafeteria lady."

"But the cafeteria ladies barely knew Mrs. Logan." Mrs. Johnson pulled her dish away. "And anyone could have taken a brownie, sprinkled poison on it in one of the empty classrooms, before dropping it off at Mrs. Logan's desk."

"And the cafeteria ladies don't have a key to my

apartment," Miss Turnipseed said. "So they couldn't have stolen my cat."

Mrs. Johnson took a deep, exasperated breath. If they had to tie a missing cat to the murder of Bertha and Mrs. Arlington, then perhaps the killings would never be solved. And certainly not by them.

"At first I thought I was losing my mind," Miss Turnipseed said. "because things were disappearing left and right."

"Yes, the cat," Mrs. Johnson said.

"But now," Miss Turnipseed bit her lip thoughtfully, "I remember that Bertha complained that there were no more brownies left. I even mumbled something to Mrs. Arlington."

"Are you saying someone threw them away?" Mrs. Hopwood almost jumped out of her seat.

Miss Turnipseed shook her head. "Or put them someplace else."

"You really should tell that to the police," Mrs. Johnson said.

"I suppose so, but the less I have to do with them the better. And just so you know," Miss Turnipseed took a final bite out of her cake, "I would take a look at those young teachers. They're not as innocent as they may seem."

FIFTY-SEVEN

In spite of the chilly October weather, George Arlington was sweating.

He had charged four thousand, two hundred and eleven dollars on his Sears credit card and when Marsha found out, there would be hell to pay. He had apologized for accusing her, but things were still very tense at home. Well, maybe this would be the last straw. She would divorce him then, and he would have to start all over as a single guy.

Because God knows he wasn't going to get involved with another woman for a long time.

He had to do it, though. He had to find out how his mother died. The police weren't suspicious, although they were puzzled by the fact that a woman, who had vanished a year before, suddenly visited his mother. But they balked at conducting an autopsy on a seventy-eight year old lady with dementia, who was still a suspect in a murder.

So George arranged for a private autopsy, and he was on his way to meet the doctor at a neighborhood bar. Trying to figure out who would be paying for the drinks. George had already given this man a fortune. Did he have to buy him a whiskey too? It kept George from thinking about the more pressing problem.

Had someone killed his mother?

He opened the door of the saloon and slid inside. It

was dark and hard to see. It smelled of liquor and tobacco and leather and body odor. He squinted and then spotted a rotund man, sitting in a back booth, nursing a beer. George took a tentative step forward.

"Mr. Arlington?" The man made a stab at standing before he collapsed and leaned against the cushioned booth.

"Dr. Crosby?"

Dr. Crosby reached over to a ragged briefcase and mumbled, "I have the report right here."

"Of course, I'll read the report," George said, as he slid into the booth, "but I want to know in simple terms how my mother died."

"In simple terms her heart gave out."

George felt a pain across his chest, as though his own heart might give out.

"Of course, I have to tell you this. There are certain poisons that will cause a heart to just stop beating, especially in a woman that has prior problems and may be on medication."

"Did you test for any of them?" George asked breathlessly.

"No, I couldn't. I know what you see on television. Someone suspects that their aunt was murdered, an autopsy is performed and five minutes later a handsome coroner comes out and says that he found traces of strychnine in the stomach. But here's the truth. There are a hundred substances that can cause a heart to stop beating. And unless you know specifically what you're looking for, it is virtually impossible to test for all of them."

"So," George said, "we're at a dead end."

"I'm sorry. I told you when you hired me that it

was a long shot. And think of it this way, your mother most probably went from natural causes. There must be some comfort in that."

George was finding it hard to find comfort in anything.

Dr. Crosby threw down a twenty dollar bill. "Have a drink on me," he said. "So where do you want me to ship her body?"

George was thinking of the four thousand dollars he had already spent. "I guess I'll have to have her cremated."

"There's only one place that does that. Foskett's. You should give them a call tomorrow morning."

"Thank you, Doctor." George rose, shook his hand and watched as the doctor shuffled towards the front door.

He ordered a whiskey and ginger ale and then reached for his cell phone. There was only one person he could share this with.

Amelia Johnson.

He dialed and hoped she would answer. She did, picking up after the first ring.

He could hear crying in the background, so he knew that this wouldn't be a lengthy conversation.

"I just met with the coroner."

"Jeffrey James, if I have to tell you again to put down those oil paints…"

"Shall I call back?"

"No, no. I want to hear this."

"He said my mother's heart just gave out."

"There are poisons that can do that."

"I know. But the coroner said, without knowing what the poison was, it's just impossible to test for it."

"What about—Justin Joseph, go to your room right now. No now!" A huge wail compelled George to hold the phone several inches from his ear. "What about testing for the same poison that killed Bertha Butterworth? Fluoroacetate."

George felt his heart quicken. "How did they determine that was the poison?"

"Because of the half eaten brownie. And because it was found in your mother's purse."

"You're right," George said. "I never thought of that."

"I mean, the killer, if your mother was indeed murdered, probably wouldn't use two different poisons. I'd call the coroner back and ask him to run a blood test, or whatever they do. That's it! Now, you're going right to bed! Let me know how you make out."

The line went dead, just as George's drink was delivered. His first thought was that he might be throwing more money down the drain.

But if what he suspected was true and there was definite proof that his mother had been murdered, then maybe the county would pay.

And besides he owed it to his mother.

FIFTY-EIGHT

MRS. HOPWOOD DIDN'T sleep well at all, especially after Mrs. Johnson's phone call. George was going to demand another autopsy on his mother, this time, looking for a specific poison—the poison which killed Bertha Butterworth.

She finally fell asleep at four thirty. The alarm rang an hour and a half later. She rose in the icy apartment—management did not put on heat until the end of October. The thought of Montgomery lying there, cozy, under the comforter, snoring slightly, his mouth open, annoyed her.

She knew that her husband had been depressed since losing his job, and she wanted to be sympathetic. But she was depressed too. And she had to work.

At least for the time being.

She brewed her coffee and got dressed in the dark, careful that she was not mixing navy blue and black. Then she bundled up and headed for the bus station, where she saw Pearl standing there.

MRS. HOPWOOD WAS not the kind of woman who liked to make small talk in the morning. The most she could do is stroll over to Mrs. Johnson's room with a cup of coffee, sit in a student's chair and listen to Mrs. Johnson speak— and Mrs. Johnson never seemed at a loss for words.

So she was tempted to turn around and hide and,

maybe miss the next bus and wait for another. But surely she would be late, and she was already in enough trouble. Besides Pearl had already seen her and had given her a big wave.

Mrs. Hopwood trudged to the bus stop, gave a weak smile and murmured a good morning.

"Oh my, I never knew you took this bus," Pearl said as she smiled, exposing uneven yellow teeth. "Where do you live?"

"211 Pine Street."

"Oh, that is a nice neighborhood. I live on Sycamore, you know right by the river. It gets a little chilly come the winter, but I have beautiful views from my bedroom window."

Mrs. Hopwood mumbled "How nice" but she didn't think it was nice at all and was rather miffed that someone who worked in the school's cafeteria lived in a better section of town than she did.

"You're Mrs. Hooper, aren't you?"

"Hopwood."

"Oh sorry. I am so bad with names. How long have you been working at St. Polycarp?"

Yes, this woman was a chatty Kathy and Mrs. Hopwood didn't feel like carrying on the conversation. "Seven years," she said, hoping that Pearl would realize that she was answering in two words and not expanding the conversation.

"I like it there very much. The other school I worked at, St. Jude's…"

Mrs. Hopwood's pulse increased. "You worked at St. Jude's?"

"Yes, but, of course, it closed. Not enough enrollment. When I read about that poor cafeteria lady dying,

I called Mrs. Logan and asked her if there was an opening."

"So you have known Mrs. Logan for a while?" The bus was coming and Mrs. Hopwood stuck her hand into her jacket for the fare.

"For a couple of years, yes. I know Mrs. Logan can come off as a bit of a prude, but actually she can be quite nice. And after what happened to her..."

Mrs. Hopwood stepped onto the bus and followed Pearl to a two seater. "What happened to her?"

Pearl leaned forward, sliding her ample body closer. "Oh, her husband just up and left her for another woman. Poor thing I found her crying in her office."

"Who did he leave her for?"

"I think it was someone from Cozad."

"Did you know Clara Edwards?" Mrs. Hopwood persisted.

"Yes, of course. And God forgive me, I hope the woman didn't come to any harm, although I know there has been some talk about that. Clara was a nice person, very generous, very friendly. But she was also a rebel rouser."

"You mean she was a troublemaker?"

"Exactly," Pearl said firmly. "For instance Mrs. Logan didn't like to hire substitutes because she wanted to save the diocese money. So if a teacher was absent, she would ask other teachers to cover the missing teacher's class during prep time. Clara wasn't having any of that. She firmly objected and told other teachers that was against union rules. That teacher had to be paid, if they gave up their planning time. When Mrs. Logan asked that teachers not wear sleeveless blouses, and really I must say I agree with her about that, I mean, who wants to look at someone else's armpits? Anyway, Clara said that wasn't in the contract and teachers could dress how they please, even wearing sneakers."

"Is that why Mrs. Logan fired her?"

"She didn't fire her." Pearl tilted her head to the side. "She just said she wasn't going to renew her contract. I don't know much about her teaching ability, but I do know once when I went up to her classroom to drop off some gluten free bread, her students were reading and so was Clara. But Clara was reading one of those romance books. Oh, here is our stop!"

Mrs. Hopwood rose slowly dreading the day ahead. Her prep came at the very end of the day and she had lunch duty as well as recess duty.

"Isn't this nice?" Pearl said as they disembarked from the bus. "Maybe you and I can meet every day at the bus station and travel together. It's so much more pleasant that way. Don't you think?"

What Mrs. Hopwood was thinking was taking an earlier bus to school.

FIFTY-NINE

Miss Turnipseed went home immediately after she had met with Mrs. Johnson and Mrs. Hopwood. She was still suspicious of their motives, but they seemed harmless enough. And they had actually been helpful with information.

And they fed her.

So therefore she wasn't very hungry and decided that she would skip eating a bit of her store bought roasted chicken and her can of mixed vegetables. She would take to her bed and watch something light on television, perhaps a Hallmark Romance.

The moment she opened the door, she smelled it.

The cat.

She paused at the threshold and began to call Kit Kat's name and sure enough he jumped from above the bookcase onto the couch and then to the floor as he scrambled over to her and began to rub his fur against her pantyhose.

Miss Turnipseed was so shocked she dropped her tote where the bit of chocolate cake she had brought home in a doggy bag fell out. Kit Kat wasted no time and began to gobble the frosting. Miss Turnipseed knew that chocolate was bad for dogs, she wasn't sure about cats and, it happened so quickly, and she was so surprised, she found herself unable to move.

Maybe it wasn't Kit Kat at all. Maybe just someone who looked remarkably like her own cat. She thought of Mrs. Johnson's words, "One cat looks very much like another." But obviously Mrs. Johnson had never had a cat because the white spot over Kit Kat's eye confirmed his identity.

And it wasn't just that. It was the way he snuggled up to her and the way he gobbled up the tuna fish spiked with raisins. He knew the house and exactly where the litter box was.

While Miss Turnipseed was thrilled to have her little cat home, she was also very spooked. While it was possible that Kit Kat could have run out of the house, when she emptied the trash, it was not possible that he would have run back in without her seeing him.

Someone had been in her apartment.

Her suspicions were confirmed when she realized that her desk drawer had been open and her letters had been rearranged. Miss Turnipseed always kept her letters in a certain order, the most recent ones always went on top. These letters were scattered and she didn't do it.

The police had said there was no sign of a break-in, which meant that no one had picked the lock. Someone had managed to make a copy of her keys. That someone would have had to dip into her purse, which she always kept in the top desk drawer. Maybe when she was down in the dining room, or visiting a classroom, or ran across the street for tea, taking only her wallet.

Someone at St. Polycarp.

Immediately she put the chain on the door and placed a call to the school. Of course, she only reached the answering machine. She left the message that she would be a little late coming to school tomorrow.

She was going to change the locks in her apartment. Immediately.

Miss Turnipseed was waiting for the locksmith, when her phone rang. She picked it up without thinking. It was probably Mrs. Logan wanting to know how soon she would be in, and Miss Turnipseed had no idea.

It all depended on the locksmith and, as far as she knew, locksmiths could be very unreliable.

She answered the phone the way she always answered. "Hello, this is Teresa Turnipseed."

"Teresa?"

The voice sounded very familiar, even though it was slightly muffled. A shiver ran down Miss Turnipseed's arm, and she reached for her brown cardigan. "Who is this?"

"It's Clara."

"Clara?!"

"Clara Edwards."

"Oh, Clara. Where are you? Everyone has been looking for you for almost a year! Where have you been? Have you gotten in touch with Grace?"

"Teresa, I'm in trouble. I need your help."

Miss Turnipseed felt her stomach cramp. In her surprise to hear from her friend, she had quite forgotten that her friend was a suspect in a murder, maybe two murders. And as far as doing a favor for someone, Miss Turnipseed was not the kind of woman who liked to do favors. She felt that was just a way to make an enemy.

"I think you should go to the police," she advised. "They are looking for you and you can explain everything to them and they will help you. I can meet you at the precinct, if you want. We can ask for my cousin, Patrick. Actually, I am supposed to meet him next Thursday for dinner. We can go…"

"Bitch."

The line went dead.

Miss Turnipseed was shaking so much that she fumbled, putting the phone back in the cradle. Had Clara actually called her that horrible name? That was not the Clara she knew.

Maybe she never knew Clara at all.

Or maybe—maybe that wasn't Clara, just someone pretending to be her.

Immediately after the locksmith finished, Miss Turnipseed was going to the police.

And she would demand protection.

SIXTY

MRS. JOHNSON WAS busy teaching the beatitudes when her cell phone rang. She knew perfectly well the rules which Mrs. Logan enforced, but she kept her phone on anyway. After all, she was a mother with two young boys and a nanny, who was easily overwhelmed—although if the truth be told her twins could overwhelm Maria Von Trapp. When she looked down and saw that it was George Arlington on the other end of the line, she didn't hesitate.

"Have the results come in?" she asked eagerly.

"They have. And sure enough my mother was poisoned. They found traces of fluoroacetate in her stomach."

"Did you call the police?"

"Of course. They didn't have much to say, but why would they? If it wasn't for me, they wouldn't even know my mother was murdered."

Mrs. Johnson looked up to see Mrs. Logan staring at her on the threshold.

"I have to call you back," she said hurriedly to George and then disconnected her phone and threw it in her drawer. "Class, I am going to talk to Mrs. Logan for a few minutes in the hall. Please memorize the beatitudes because when I return, you will have a quiz on them."

There was a unilateral moan.

"And I don't want to hear a word," she threatened.

She scurried over to the door and closed it gently. "That was George Arlington," she said. "He had a private autopsy performed on his mother. The results just came in."

Mrs. Logan crossed her arms and stepped away.

"His mother was poisoned."

Mrs. Logan seemed to forget all about the broken cell phone rule. Instead she stared at Mrs. Johnson with an expression of disbelief. And then she sank down on one of the students' chairs, a chair which was kept in the hall for wayward pupils. "What do the police think?" Her voice was hoarse and raspy.

"I didn't get that far." Mrs. Johnson wanted to add, "before you made me hang-up" but it was apparent that Mrs. Logan was shaken enough, without Mrs. Johnson becoming adversary.

"We need to take this to my office." Mrs. Logan rose slowly, gripping the chair with her two hands.

Mrs. Johnson followed her through the reception area, noticing that Miss Turnipseed was not at her desk. She perched on the chair across from Mrs. Logan's desk.

Mrs. Logan slammed the door, before sinking into her own chair. She was obviously angry, but Mrs. Johnson was uncertain as to why.

"I know that you have teamed up with Mr. Arlington to try and solve the mystery of who tried to poison me."

"I am just trying to be helpful."

"I appreciate that. But there is no way you can imagine the terror I am feeling, the hell I am going through."

"Well, actually I can. When I was in Sicily…"

"I know all about what happened to you in Sicily. I

have done due diligence on you and Mrs. Hopwood. I even know what happened a few years ago, which was, unfortunately, another poisoning. The diocese is very upset about the state of affairs here. We will be lucky if they don't close the school mid-year."

"But we," Mrs. Johnson thought it would be prudent to include Mrs. Hopwood in the conversation, "had nothing to do with the poisoning. In fact Mrs. Hopwood and I actually stopped the murders. And as far as Sicily is concerned, if you know the circumstances…"

"You created those circumstances," Mrs. Logan interrupted.

Mrs. Johnson was at a loss for words.

"All right, let me make myself very clear. I don't want you or your friend," Mrs. Logan's mouth wrinkled as though she had just tasted a sour pickle, "investigating the attempt on my life. It is bad enough that I'm frightened to death, but coming here and having two Nancy Drews asking questions and coming up with wild, unsubstantiated theories is very distressing. Not to speak of wasting valuable class time. I can't tell you what to do once you leave the premises. But what I would advise is, if you think you have pertinent knowledge, tell it to the police and let them take it further. Do you understand?"

Mrs. Johnson understood but she didn't like it one bit.

She wondered what the union would say.

"Now I'm not going to write you up this time, but if I catch you on your cell phone again during class time, and religion none the less, then I have to put it in your file." Mrs. Logan paused momentarily. "I don't mean to sound unreasonable, but I'm trying very hard to keep to a normal routine, at least while I'm here at school. That's what's best for everyone, especially the students. You may go."

Mrs. Johnson felt her insides seething. Wasn't there some sort of a law against telling people what they could say, even on company time?

She rose slowly, opening the door, just as a very flustered Miss Turnipseed came crashing into the reception area, knocking the phone to the floor. Her tam was on crooked, her gray hair sticking out on the sides, her scarlet lipstick, staining her teeth.

Both Mrs. Johnson and Mrs. Logan stared at her.

"Clara Edwards is alive," she said. "She called me last night."

SIXTY-ONE

"IF IT WASN'T for my persistence, you wouldn't even know that my mother had been murdered." George was sitting in Detective Paneretto's office and staring at him.

"Well, that is true." Detective Paneretto had joined his hands together and placed them thoughtfully on his mouth.

"Therefore, I think you should pay for the autopsy."

The detective's eyebrows went up.

"I don't mean you personally, of course. I mean the police department."

"Well, I have nothing to do with that part of the force. You have a lawyer?"

"My mother had one."

"Perhaps he can sue and recoup the charges."

"$5,133.19."

Detective Hargrove shook his head. "Expensive to get murdered."

"What are you going to do about it?"

"The autopsy?"

"No, catching my mother's killer."

"We have an ABP on Clara Edwards. We have every reason to think she is alive and it's possible she is behind the attempted murder of Mrs. Logan and the murder of both your mother and Bertha Butterworth. And I've had your mother transferred to the morgue."

"Well, that's a start. What about the threatening letter?"

Detective Hargrove hesitated. "We don't think that's necessarily related."

"And the poison in my mother's handbag?"

Detective Paneretto shook his head.

"Not related?" George guessed.

"We simply don't know."

George stood. "So now that I'm officially the family of a victim, you will be in touch. Right?"

"Of course." Detective Paneretto rose also and extended a pudgy hand.

But George did not shake it. Instead he clenched his fists and walked out.

HE WAS GETTING into his car when his cell phone rang. A picture of a disgruntled Marsha appeared. He was tempted to ignore it but she would only call back. Probably when he was at work.

"Yeah?" He could hardly disguise the contempt in his voice.

"Where are you?"

"Why do you ask?"

"Because you're not at work. They called and wanted to know where you are."

"I'm running late. I just came from the police station. An autopsy was performed on my mother." No need to say that he was the one who ordered and paid for it. She would find that out soon enough. "She was poisoned, just like that cafeteria lady."

Marsha didn't answer. He was going to assume she was shocked.

"They think a woman by the name of Clara Edwards is responsible."

"Oh good. So does that mean that I'm no longer a suspect in your mind?"

"I already told you that you're not." He started the car and was struggling to get out of the narrow parking space. Using a cell phone while driving was against the law, and he was doing it right in front of the police station.

"I know," Marsha said suddenly.

"You know where Clara Edwards is?"

"I know you're having an affair with that African American teacher. Last night when you were sleeping, I looked at your cell phone. Her number was there, again and again."

"She is helping to solve my mother's murder."

"Did she tell you that she's married? And that she is the mother of two children? I Googled her. She's been involved in several murders. Did you know that?"

"No, I don't know anything about her. Our relation-ship is not intimate."

He hung up the phone, wishing he had said what was on his mind.

"Just like ours."

SIXTY-TWO

Mrs. Hopwood knew something was up. She saw Mrs. Logan sitting in a student chair and talking to Mrs. Johnson. Both women looked distressed. Mrs. Hopwood could only surmise that they were talking about her.

Was she to be fired today?

Could Mrs. Logan do such a thing?

Should she call the union?

She gave the class a writing assignment and stood at the door. She watched as the women walked down the stairs. And then she quickly sent Mrs. Johnson a text. What is going on?

Can't talk, was the response. Or I'll be fired.

Great. Mrs. Johnson was keeping things from her. Well, Mrs. Hopwood knew that it would be easy enough to wrestle the information out of her friend after school.

But as it turned out, she would have to wait longer than that.

Because Mrs. Logan passed around a note, saying that there would be a full faculty meeting at three o'clock.

Upon hearing this news, Mrs. Hopwood's chest tightened. Maybe the school was going to close, and they would all be out of work, Mrs. Johnson included. But maybe that wasn't so bad, although there would be a lot of competition for very few jobs. At least, though, Mrs.

Hopwood would not have to explain why she alone had been let go.

The thought of St. Polycarp closing, though, filled her with sorrow. She really loved the school, at least she had. But it was time to face facts. St. Polycarp wasn't what it used to be, when Father Felix was in charge and her second grade students adored her. Nothing remained the same, and maybe it was time to let go.

As they walked into the library, Mrs. Johnson whispered that she had no idea what the meeting was about.

But she didn't sit near Mrs. Hopwood. Instead Mrs. Hopwood sat next to Taylor, who sat next to Dylan and both young teachers were gabbing about state standards, ignoring her completely.

"I need everyone's attention." Mrs. Logan stood at the front of the room and clapped her hands.

The conversation lulled.

"I'm afraid I have some rather bad news."

"Is the school closing?" Addison rose in alarm.

"No, not yet. But the cafeteria is."

The three cafeteria ladies bellowed in unison.

"But I was just hired!"

"This is hardly fair."

"No one was actually poisoned in the cafeteria. Not with our food."

"Why don't you sue the catering company?"

"What am I supposed to do for a job?"

Mrs. Logan put her hands up in exasperation. "This is not my decision. This is coming from the superintendent. Most of the students are bringing their own lunch anyway. The parents don't feel comfortable having their children even eating our snacks. While the brownie didn't come from the cafeteria, no one knows who the murderer is."

"I do." It was Addison who spoke. "It was Clara Edwards. I remember how she always had a grudge against you, Mrs. Logan, and now she is finally seeking revenge."

"Clara Edwards?" Pearl questioned. "I thought she was dead."

"Was she murdered too?" Jane, the cafeteria lady, spoke up.

"We all want to solve this as soon as possible," Mrs. Logan ignored the question. "This is my first year here also, and I am devastated by the turn of events. I am sure everything will be straightened out. The police are on it."

"And if it's not?" Norma said.

"Will the school close?" Dylan wondered.

"Over my dead body," Mrs. Logan said as she headed towards the exit door.

And Mrs. Hopwood thought, *that's just what the murderer is hoping for.*

MRS. JOHNSON OFFERED Mrs. Hopwood a ride home, which she eagerly took. And before Mrs. Hopwood could ask a question, Mrs. Johnson launched into a lengthy explanation.

"Mrs. Arlington was murdered, poisoned with the same substance that killed Bertha Butterworth. I was talking to George, when Mrs. Logan caught me. When I told her what I learned, she became very upset, hostile almost. She told me that I was not to do anymore investigating and it could cost me my job. That's it."

"So you're just supposed to let it all go."

"Apparently."

"Why do you think?"

"Why do you think what?" Mrs. Johnson made a sharp turn, throwing Mrs. Hopwood against the seat.

"Why do you think she doesn't want you to investigate?"

"Well, did you see that? That bicycle rider almost hit the side of my car. They're lethal weapons and no one seems to care."

"I think that there is something in her past that someone wants to murder her for. Only she doesn't want anyone to know what it is. I was talking to Pearl…"

"Who?"

"The new cafeteria lady. You know what she told me?"

"The traffic is horrible on this street. I am going to have to let you off a few blocks from your house."

"She said that Mrs. Logan's husband ran off with another woman."

"How is that a surprise? Deborah told us that last month. Besides what does that have to do with Clara Edwards?"

"I'm not sure," Mrs. Hopwood said as Mrs. Johnson stopped in the middle of the street and then ordered her to get out. "But there's more than meets the eye. And I'm determined to find out what it is."

SIXTY-THREE

AFTER THE PHONE call from Clara, Miss Turnipseed decided that she was not going to visit the police precinct. She was nice and cozy in her house and she had no intention of getting on a bus and waiting for hours in a dirty, drafty room. Instead she called her cousin Patrick.

"Still looking for your cat?" he asked her.

"That mystery has been solved," Miss Turnipseed said quickly. "This is about something else entirely. I just received a phone call from Clara Edwards."

"Who?"

Maybe, Miss Turnipseed thought, *I should talk to someone else. Someone who is actively working the case.* Still this was a small town. You would think that Patrick would have heard about the entire sordid matter.

"She has been accused of poisoning a cafeteria lady, except everyone thinks she's dead. But she called me."

"Are you sure it wasn't some sort of trick? Did you recognize her voice?"

Miss Turnipseed was beginning to feel annoyed. Of course, Patrick was asking her the same questions that the police might. So she was honest. "It didn't sound like her but it was over a year since I spoke with her, so I couldn't say for sure."

"Well, I will pass it on to the appropriate people and someone will call you back."

"See that you do." Once the police had this information, then Miss Turnipseed would no longer be a suspect and maybe, just maybe she could get out of this pickle of a mess. She said nothing about dinner on the upcoming Thursday night.

"By the way, I have a quick question. One of the teachers asked me to ask you. Mrs. Logan is doing a Corey Check on all of the teachers. This teacher, in her youth, did something very stupid, so she has a record. Is there any way that record could be erased and won't show up in a Corey Check?"

"How old was she?"

"Nineteen."

"It wouldn't be sealed then. My best advice is for her to come clean and tell the principal. If it was a long time ago, it won't matter."

Everything matters to Mrs. Logan, Miss Turnipseed thought.

MISS TURNIPSEED DIDN'T care one bit about the cafeteria being closed and she didn't know why the teachers cared so much. It would be appear that it was safer for everyone.

Of course, she could understand the confusion and anger of the cafeteria ladies. They were going to be out of a job, especially Pearl, who had just left one school to come to St. Polycarp. Maybe St. Polycarp itself might close, and then Miss Turnipseed herself would be unemployed, which filled her with terror.

Well, if Mrs. Logan found out about her past, she would probably have to leave anyway.

So really why should she care what happened to St. Polycarp?

AFTER THE FACULTY MEETING, she bundled up in her coat, her scarf, and her wool hat. It was cold for the beginning of October. Something told her that it was going to be a long, bitter winter.

She was leaving the school, walking towards her apartment, when she heard footsteps behind her. It had been a dull, cloudy, gray day and it was growing dark. She whipped around and spotted a woman, in a long coat and a knitted hat, a woman who was struggling to catch up to her.

"Teresa, please stop."

Miss Turnipseed recognized the voice right away. It was Grace, Clara Edwards's sister.

"I need to talk to you. Can we go inside here?" She pointed to a small coffee shop across the street, the same one Miss Turnipseed had dined in with Mrs. Johnson and Mrs. Hopwood.

"I don't have any cash on me," Miss Turnipseed lied.

"I'll pay."

With visions of hot tea and sweet chocolate cake in her head, Miss Turnipseed led the way.

Once they were inside the restaurant, and both women had freed themselves from the bulky clothes, Grace started to talk. "I've been reading the papers and I think this whole thing has been a horrible mistake. I don't see how my sister could possibly be alive. She would have gotten in touch with me. I know it!"

"But she called me," Miss Turnipseed insisted.

"Did you recognize her voice? Do you know for sure it was she?"

Miss Turnipseed took a sip of her very hot tea before answering. Also, she was trying to think of whether or not it would be prudent to tell Grace about what Clara had called her.

It was inconsistent with Clara's character.

"It sounded like her," Miss Turnipseed frowned, when she noticed the small slice of cake the waiter had delivered. But at least it was an end piece, rich with frosting.

"Someone could have pretended to be her, when she visited Mrs. Arlington."

"But why?" Miss Turnipseed asked.

"The why is obvious. To blame both murders on my sister, who was probably killed herself."

Miss Turnipseed couldn't answer, because her mouth was crammed with cake.

"You ask why. Well, here's another why for you. Why would my sister try to kill Mrs. Logan?"

"She was about to be fired."

"So she disappears for a year and then breaks into Mrs. Logan's new school and tries to poison her with a brownie? My sister wasn't that imaginative. Do you really think Clara could do something like that?"

"I really didn't know your sister that well." Miss Turnipseed was savoring the frosting, swirling it around in her mouth. "But truly, I don't know what you want me to do about it. The entire thing is police business."

"You could tell the police that you are not certain that it was Clara's voice you heard on the phone. You can tell the police that you might have made a mistake and you can't think of one reason why she would try to kill Mrs. Logan."

Miss Turnipseed paused and slowly drank her tea. "What if they give me a lie detector test? I can't say with any certainty that it wasn't her."

The silence was thick as the waitress slapped down the bill.

The cake was gone, her tea was cold and Miss Turnipseed felt slightly nauseous. She was tired of talking. Her stomach was churning and she longed to be home, snuggled in her bed, watching television, with her little cat beside her.

And what if her cat wasn't there?

She wouldn't answer the phone.

"Teresa?"

"I hope you're right. I don't want to say I hope Clara is dead, because that sounds so heartless. I just hope that she had nothing to do with this entire matter. Next time I talk to the police, I will admit I'm doubtful." She stood up and grabbed her coat. "I hope you don't mind, but I have to get home to feed my cat."

She bounded out of the restaurant, careful not to linger, just in case Grace expected her to leave the tip. Of course, she had lied. She wasn't about to mention that she was unsure of Clara's guilt. Why should she get involved? At the very least, Clara had deceived everyone, making people think she was dead when she was very much alive.

She stopped suddenly.

Up ahead a woman walked— a woman with a gray coat and a gray hat—a woman with red hair.

And from the back Miss Turnipseed was certain that she was seeing Clara Edwards.

SIXTY-FOUR

MRS. JOHNSON COULD hardly concentrate on teaching her sons their math facts because so much was buzzing around in her head.

Mrs. Logan wanted her to stop investigating, and she had even threatened Mrs. Johnson with the loss of her job, if Mrs. Johnson continued to poke her nose where it didn't belong.

Which struck Mrs. Johnson as very peculiar.

If someone was trying to murder her, she would want all the help she could possibly get.

"No, Jeffrey James. Four and six is ten. Not nine."

As far as Mrs. Hopwood's suspicion about Miss Turnipseed, maybe she had a point. Maybe Mrs. Logan was about to find something out about Miss Turnipseed, something she hadn't known before.

"Justin Joseph, stop making fun of your brother. You didn't know what six and six were."

If the police were looking for Clara Edwards, then that meant they thought that Mrs. Hopwood was in the clear. Of course, it didn't explain a lot of things.

Who had sent that threatening letter?

Who had the opportunity to put the poison in Mrs. Arlington's handbag?

"No, it is not multiplication. Not really."

If only George had learned what Mrs. Arlington had seen—because she certainly knew something. That was why she had been killed.

"Why don't you two boys quiz each other?"

"She couldn't find the brownies."

"Who couldn't find the brownies?" Justin Joseph asked.

"I want a brownie!" Jeffrey James demanded.

"I'm just thinking out loud. But I'll give you both a cookie if you quiz each other and, in ten minutes, you both know your addition facts."

The way they were swapping exasperated looks, it was obvious that one cookie wouldn't do it. She bargained for two.

She couldn't find the brownies.

Who couldn't find the brownies?

Mrs. Logan?

Maybe Mrs. Arlington noticed that Mrs. Logan didn't have a brownie and took one and put it on her desk, not knowing that it was poisoned. Maybe the brownie was never meant for Mrs. Logan, and the entire thing was an accident and someone else was supposed to be murdered. Or maybe Mrs. Hopwood had a point. Maybe it was just random, someone who hated their school.

No, that didn't explain the threatening letter Mrs. Logan received.

And it didn't explain the poison in Mrs. Arlington's purse.

By the time, Mrs. Johnson retired, her boys knew their addition facts.

And she had a horrid headache

THE PHONE RANG at five forty-five in the morning, which Mrs. Johnson knew was not good news. Especially when she saw that it was Mrs. Hopwood.

"I'm not coming into work today," she said.

"Are you sick?"

"Yes, I am sick," Mrs. Hopwood said bitterly. "I am sick and tired of being disrespected by that principal. I just can't face it anymore."

Mrs. Johnson grabbed her terry cloth robe and headed for the kitchen. She had to keep her voice at a whisper, lest she wake her husband or worse, her twins.

"Well, maybe you do need a day off, just to stay in bed and watch television and eat bags of chips and cartons of ice cream." She was searching for the coffee and praying that they were not out of filters.

"I can't stay home. Montgomery is here, hanging around. He is on the computer and he says that he's looking for jobs, but I think he's on one of those gambling sites. I'm going to Starbucks with my Kindle. I'm going to stay there for a while and then head to the library and hide out there, read the scandal sheets and chew Juicy Fruit Gum."

"Just remember when you're doing that, I'll probably have to use my preps to cover your classes. What are you doing in Math?"

"Give them a multiplication test. That should take the whole period. I gotta go."

They were out of filters. Mrs. Johnson had meant to buy some at the grocery store but she hadn't been there for some time. Instead her after school activities consisted of visiting George Arlington and having tea and cake with Miss Turnipseed.

She would have to use a paper towel, which didn't work as well at all, and really made a mess.

It was time to get back to her own life, but somehow she had a feeling that wasn't going to happen anytime soon.

SIXTY-FIVE

GEORGE WAS STANDING in his mother's bedroom. He could still smell her familiar scent, the lilac perfume she always wore. Of course, it would be his job to clean out all of her belongings. Marsha had refused to do it, although she already had plans for the space. She would be separating the three girls, and Catherine couldn't wait to have her own room.

"Throw everything away," Marsha ordered, as though his mother never had anything worthwhile to save, anything of value at all.

Somewhere in the middle of all this debris, he was going to find his mother's jewelry. He remembered that she had possessed a few good pieces, a set of cultured pearls from his grandmother, a diamond and sapphire tennis bracelet from his father, and an emerald brooch she had bought for herself. He would save the pieces for his daughters.

Hell would freeze over before he'd give them to Marsha.

He hadn't realized that his mother collected so many shoes, most of them with little heels, t-straps, sling backs and peep toes, in garnish colors, like bright orange and parrot green. Some of them looked barely worn, still in plastic and stuffed with tissue paper. But when he touched them they were hard and rigid. And cheap.

Reluctantly he threw them in the black garbage bag.

And then there were the purses, all different shapes and sizes. He examined each one carefully, finding mostly crumpled tissues, worn down lipsticks, loose coins, cough drops and a half eaten mummified cookie. One had a twenty dollar bill in the zipper compartment, another ten dollars. There was an appointment card from a dentist dating back fourteen years.

But the handbag she used the most, the orange one, was still with the police, being held as material evidence. He had no hope of ever getting it back.

He checked the pockets of the clothes. Marsha was right. The dresses were old, dated and some of them stained beyond repair. His mother had gone into debt just to look pretty and fashionable and now—it was all trash.

And then the coats and the jackets, crammed in at the end of the closet. Immediately, he spotted her beige trench coat. She wore it often but she hadn't worn it when they arrested her. They just barged in the house…

He had to try and get that memory out of his mind.

I'll make it right for you, Mom, he vowed. *I promise you that*.

He took the coat out of the closet and pressed it to his face. It smelled of lilacs and peppermint and a little body odor. He reached into one pocket and pulled out a receipt from Dunkin Donuts and a dirty handkerchief. He dug deep into the other pocket and felt a crumpled, ripped piece of paper.

Unfolding it with sweaty hands, he expected it was going to be blank. But to his amazement, it was recent, dated just a few months ago. It was a warning from *Stash It Storage Company* to claim property. Evidently

there was a fire and this was a second warning, before
all items would either be sold at auction or disposed of.

His mother had something in storage? And she continued to pay for it? How? Without a check book? Well,
maybe she paid by the year and last year she was a
little more lucid.

Probably just old furniture, when she sold her house.
Still he couldn't just let it sit there, not without knowing what it was.

Hoping it wasn't too late, he dialed the number at the
bottom of the printed note. He thought his call would
go straight to voice mail, but instead was surprised
when a human being actually picked up the phone.

"Yeah?"

"Hello, my name is George Arlington."

"What do you want?"

"I'm calling in response to this note about the storage space."

"That ship sailed a long time ago, buddy. Look at
the date."

"I know that, and I apologize. But actually it's my
mother who had the storage space, and she had dementia. Even if you sent it to her, she probably didn't
know what it was."

"Well, what do you want me to do about that?"

The challenge caught George by surprise. "So," he
said quickly before the man could hang up, "maybe
you could just tell me what was in the storage space."

"You got to be kidding. You know how many notices I sent out? Two-thirds of the people didn't even
bother to respond. They rent storage space because they
think someday they're going to want their belongings.
The years go by, they've done without it, and they got

no place to put it. Half of them can't even remember what the hell they're storing. Then they die, and their kids are stuck with a bunch of junk."

"I know but it's important. Her name was Bernice Arlington."

"Arlington," the man repeated thoughtfully. "You know what? I don't think we had any Arlington here."

"Are you sure?"

"Pretty sure. I say that because we sent out the notices in alphabetic order and I vaguely remember starting with the Cs. Of course, I can't be sure. My brother did the actual mailing."

"Well, maybe I could talk to him."

"Not likely. He's dead."

"Oh."

"Someone bashed his head in with a lead pipe and stole his wallet. They got thirty-three dollars. I'm sorry but I really can't help you."

George was left with a dial tone.

His mother didn't have a storage space. So she must have picked up the note somewhere. Which wouldn't be peculiar—the years leading up to her death, she was always picking up things that weren't hers, coats from the senior center, mail for the neighbors, grocery bags about to be delivered to someone else.

What was odd was the tale about the man, who was hit over the head with a lead pipe.

Because in George's mind, maybe that was just one murder too many.

SIXTY-SIX

Mrs. Hopwood was snuggled in a corner, reading an Agatha Christie novel when Mrs. Johnson burst into the library.

"Why didn't you answer my texts?!" Her black eyes were popping.

"I shut my phone off. Alexander keeps texting me. I'm telling him to either go back to the dorm or come home. And I don't want to talk to Montgomery, who wants to know what's for dinner."

"Well, let's go."

"You have to wait until I check out this book."

"Well, hurry up. I'll be waiting in the car."

Mrs. Hopwood hadn't even thought to ask where they were going. She only hoped it was far, far away and that they would be gone for a long time.

"So what's up?" she asked the moment they got in the car.

"I got another call from George Arlington. I actually had to take it in the teachers' bathroom, so I wouldn't get caught, talking on my cell phone. He told me that he found a storage receipt in his mother's belongings. Evidently the storage place burnt down and some of the items were lost. They were giving customers a chance to collect their items or to collect the insurance."

"So we're going to the storage place?" Mrs. Hopwood was hoping that they were going to go someplace to eat. She was starving.

"No, I told you. The storage place burnt down. We're going to talk to the owner. I did some research on him and learned that he's the manager of a store. And you will never guess in a million years who the owner of that storage company was."

Mrs. Hopwood was feeling overheated and rather hungry. She didn't feel like guessing.

"Bertha Butterworth's husband!"

Mrs. Hopwood perked right up. "That's rather a," she hesitated, "a coincidence, isn't it?"

"I'll say. And get this! His brother was a co-owner and he was murdered."

"Murdered!"

"In an attempted robbery."

Mrs. Hopwood said the only thing she could think of. "Oh my! So we're going to ask Mr. Butterworth what Mrs. Arlington was storing? Why didn't George do that?"

"Mrs. Arlington wasn't storing anything in there. We have to find out who was."

Mrs. Hopwood's head was spinning. "Why do we care?"

"Because as George said to me, there just have been too many murders."

"I could murder someone myself," Mrs. Hopwood muttered as Mrs. Johnson pulled into a parking lot in front of a dollar store.

"What are we doing here?"

"I told you. We're going to talk to Bertha's husband."

"So let me get this straight. The owner of the storage company, who was Bertha's husband, is now the manager of a dollar store? All right," Mrs. Hopwood said reluctantly. "Maybe they'll have some peanut butter crackers in there."

MRS. JOHNSON MARCHED into the store and demanded to speak to the manager while Mrs. Hopwood trotted alongside and examined a small can of cashews.

A man, whom they vaguely recognized from the funeral, stood beside a display of rice crackers. "No refunds. Store credit only. It says right there on the sign." He pointed in the distance to a small, printed poster.

"We're not here about merchandise," Mrs. Johnson said in a self-satisfied tone. "Don't you recognize us?"

The man scratched his cheek and took a moment to look the teachers up and down.

"Speaking of merchandise," Mrs. Hopwood said quickly. "Do you have make-up pads?"

"Aisle 4."

"But I really need the unscented because I have sensitive skin."

"Never mind that," Mrs. Johnson poked her. "We're from St. Polycarp School. We are so sorry about your wife."

"That damn school is cursed. My wife got murdered in that school. You're lucky to be alive, if you're still working there."

"Actually, we're here about your storage unit."

"Yeah, well I don't own the company anymore."

"My aunt may have rented a space from you," Mrs. Johnson said.

"Ma'am, like I told the guy who called before you, those claims were settled months ago. You're too late."

"We don't want to file a claim. We just want to know if my aunt rented from you."

"How about long tail combs?" Mrs. Hopwood asked hopefully as Mrs. Johnson released an exasperated sigh, "You can't find them anywhere."

"Her name is Clara Edwards."

Mr. Butterworth stared into space and, for one moment, Mrs. Hopwood thought they had hit pay dirt. Then Mr. Butterworth asked, "Isn't she the woman who is going around poisoning people?"

"Our family doesn't think she's guilty," Mrs. Johnson said quickly.

But Mr. Butterworth had another issue. "She's your aunt? I saw a picture of her in the paper. She looks white."

Mrs. Johnson had a quick reply ready. "She's related by marriage. Did she rent something from you or not?"

"No, I would have remembered the name for sure. Sorry." He started to walk away.

Mrs. Hopwood was just about to ask him about gift bags when Mrs. Johnson demanded they leave. "I had a long day. I had two preps in which I had to watch your class. And then I had to watch the desk for Miss Turnipseed—"

Mr. Butterworth whipped around. "That's it," he said. "There was a Turnipseed."

Mrs. Hopwood grabbed a small can of cashews.

"I remember. An older lady, and a real pain in the neck." Mr. Butterworth wiped his own pale neck. "She missed the first notice about the storage units burning and then she went berserk. Screaming like a banshee at my brother. You would think the way she carried on that she thought we started the fire ourselves. Or that she was storing expensive art in there."

"Do you know what she was storing there?" Mrs. Johnson asked.

"Some old dusty appliances. And they weren't even damaged. I gotta go. I'm late with the payroll."

Mrs. Johnson and Mrs. Hopwood stared at each other.

"I'm buying these," Mrs. Hopwood said as she stuck a can of cashews in Mrs. Johnson's face.

"Don't be surprised if they break your teeth."

THE MOMENT THEY got in the car, Mrs. Hopwood offered Mrs. Johnson cashews, which she declined.

"I can't figure this out," she said. "This has something to do with the storage unit, but what?"

But Mrs. Hopwood had thought about it, as she waited in line. "What if," she said, "what if Miss Turnipseed was storing something very valuable in there, maybe something stolen. She was waiting until things calmed down in order to sell it. We should do some research about robberies that occurred during that time. And what if Clara Edwards somehow found out and blackmailed her? And what if Miss Turnipseed refused to pay and instead decided to murder her? After all, we only have Miss Turnipseed's word that Clara Edwards is still alive."

"You've been reading too many Agatha Christie mysteries, besides, your theory doesn't explain at all why Mrs. Logan would be a target," Mrs. Johnson said as she made a sharp turn and the dollar cashews were flung on the floor.

LATER THAT NIGHT, with Montgomery snoring beside her, it hit Mrs. Hopwood, like that baseball which was flung at her chest during one of Alexander's games.

Because she suddenly remembered something she had seen.

And what she had seen told her exactly who the killer was.

SIXTY-SEVEN

"MR. ARLINGTON?"

"Yes?"

"This is Pamela Atkins from the Honeyspot Psychiatric Hospital."

George felt his muscles quiver and then he wondered why. His mother was already dead. What else could they tell him? "How can I help you?" he asked as he cleared his throat.

"When your mother checked in, she had a few personal items. We, of course, kept them for her. I wondered if you wanted to claim them now."

George was immediately suspicious. "What sort of things?"

"Well, there is the blue rain coat she wore when she entered and a little hat. I went into the pockets and there was a pair of pearls. I can't be sure but they looked expensive. And she had fifty dollars on her as well."

"I'll be there." George's mouth had gone dry.

"You have to go to the fourth floor and check in at the office. You can pick up the death certificate there and settle her bill."

"Her bill? My mother was on Medicare."

"I know, but Medicare only covers eighty percent."

"The government put her there. I would have kept my mother at home!"

"I understand, but really, Mr. Arlington, I'm just the receptionist."

George hung up the phone angrily. There was no doubt that his mother had gotten the short end of the stick. But at least they were honest enough to return her jewelry.

IT TOOK GEORGE forty-five minutes to find the right office and then he had to wait an additional fifteen minutes to get help. He was presented with a bill for $393.17. When he protested that his mother was placed there by state order, he got a similar response, which consisted of a phone number.

For one moment the woman behind the desk, who had a pointed chin and a strip of light brown hair above her lip, was reluctant to hand over his mother's belongings. Then she looked into the plastic bag, shrugged her shoulders— George was guessing it was paltry— and almost threw the bag at him.

He rode down the elevator, holding the bag against his chest. It was the last remains of his mother and somehow he didn't want to look at it at home, with Marsha hovering over him. So he sat in the lobby, way in the corner, ignoring the few people roaming the room aimlessly.

He opened the bag slowly, taking deep breaths to calm himself. He recognized his mother's dress. At one time it had been bright pink—his mother's favorite color—but the dress had faded to almost white. There were stains underneath the arms and a slight rip at the waist. They even gave him his mother's underwear.

They had put the pearls and the money in a separate envelope and it was all there. Of course, there was a possibility that there had been more, but he would never be able to prove that. And really what did it matter?

And then there was the blue coat. He was sure the pockets were empty but just in case, he dug his hand deep inside and came out with a dirty napkin.

The napkin was engraved with the words, St. Polycarp School.

And stained with the remnants of what looked like a brownie.

SIXTY-EIGHT

MRS. JOHNSON WAS enjoying her heavily buttered bagel when the door burst open and Mrs. Hopwood stormed in.

"Addison is the murderer," she announced.

Mrs. Johnson yawned and took another bite of her bagel. A poppy seed was caught in her back tooth and now she was going to have to floss. She glanced at the clock. "I'm exhausted. The twins kept me up all night. They were convinced that the bogey man was hiding in their closet. I wanted to tell them not to worry. The real bogey man is right here at St. Polycarp."

"Did you hear what I said?" Mrs. Hopwood leaned over in an aggressive manner.

"Addison is the murderer." Mrs. Johnson's coffee was lukewarm. She liked it piping hot. Well, she would have to drink it anyway.

"She was having an affair with George Arlington."

Mrs. Johnson was suddenly wide awake. "What brought you to that conclusion?" she asked thickly, as she savored the last bite of her bagel.

"When I was at a faculty meeting with Addison, her cell phone rang. She didn't answer it, but I saw who was calling her. Someone from Featherston Investments."

"George?" Mrs. Johnson said breathlessly.

"Remember that man, who was staring at me from outside the window, and I thought he was spooky. Well, that was George. Only it wasn't me, he was looking at, but Addison just below me."

"I'm still not connecting the dots," Mrs. Johnson said. "Are you saying Addison and George Arlington were having an affair?"

"I am. Remember what Marsha said to George when we were in his office? She knew he was having an affair. She thought it was with you, which, of course is crazy. It was with Addison. They must have met at the other school, when Mrs. Arlington was haunting Mrs. Logan."

"But why would Addison want to kill Mrs. Logan?"

"Probably because if Mrs. Logan found out about it, she would fire Addison lickety-spilt. Because of her own history, she took a very dim view of girls who had affairs with married men."

"And the purse?" Mrs. Johnson rose slowly as she heard heavy footsteps outside the door.

"When you found Mrs. Arlington's purse in your classroom, where did you bring it?"

"I told you, I brought it to the office. I handed it to Miss Turnipseed." Mrs. Johnson stopped as a chill went down her back. "Addison was there."

"Need I say more!"

"But Clara Edwards is alive," Mrs. Johnson argued.

"Is she? Remember Addison knew Clara Edwards. They both taught at the same school. She could have easily disguised herself with a wig and glasses to visit Mrs. Arlington. She could have phoned Miss Turnipseed."

Mrs. Johnson saw David Springer's fat face in the glass on the door. "What about the storage unit?"

"I don't think that figures in at all. It's just what they call it, a red herring."

"I doubt that. I think it all ties in some way, although I'm not sure how, since it involves Miss Turnipseed," Mrs. Johnson said thoughtfully. But first she had to teach the causes of the Civil War.

AT FOUR O'CLOCK promptly Mrs. Johnson grabbed Mrs. Hopwood at the front door. She wanted to talk more about Mrs. Hopwood's theory, but instead they ran straight into Norma, who was heading for the school.

"We were dismissed so suddenly," she said, "that I left several of my things down in the dining room, a coffee mug from my grandson and my water bottle, which I bought in Niagara Falls."

"We miss you ladies," Mrs. Johnson said, which was really the truth. There was something about the cafeteria ladies, which was very comforting.

A smile broke out on Norma's round face and she patted her dyed shoe polish black hair. "I will tell you who I miss. I miss Bertha, although before she died I think something was bothering her. Trouble at home, I suppose, maybe to do with her husband."

"Well, she had that horrible tragedy in her family," Mrs. Hopwood, whose hand was on the door of the car, spoke, "Her brother-in-law murdered like that."

"It was terrible," Norma shook her frizzy curls. "I remember when it happened. She was devastated. Such a senseless act. I don't know what the world is coming to."

Mrs. Johnson shook her head and muttered, "Terrible."

"Well, I have a theory of my own about Bertha's

death," Norma said proudly. "Maybe the poisoning wasn't meant for Mrs. Logan, maybe it wasn't deliberate at all. Maybe it was just a random act, you know, like a serial killer, who has something against the sugar in baked goods."

"Well, it's an idea," Mrs. Johnson said reluctantly, "but it doesn't explain why Mrs. Logan got a threatening note or the murder of Mrs. Arlington."

"Oh." It was as if the light went out of Norma's eyes. "I hadn't thought of that."

"Well, good luck to you." Mrs. Johnson took out her car keys.

"There is something else." Norma's head cocked to the side.

"Something else?" Mrs. Hopwood repeated.

"I mean it's probably of no importance. But the day Bertha died, I overheard Mrs. Logan arguing with one of those new teachers."

"Which one?" Mrs. Hopwood asked breathlessly.

"Addison."

SIXTY-NINE

Miss Turnipseed was late coming to school on Wednesday morning. In spite of changing the locks, she still could not rid herself of the thought that someone had been in her apartment. All the rearranged things were small, and perhaps someone else might not notice.

But then again someone else didn't know two murder victims.

Or maybe three—if you counted Clara Edwards, who may or may not still be alive.

So when the alarm clock went on at 6:00, she turned over for just one moment and then jumped out of bed, when she saw that forty-five minutes had lapsed.

She immediately called Mrs. Logan to tell her that she was running late, a task which she dreaded. Luckily, her call went straight to voice mail. After so many years, of being so reliable, Miss Turnipseed knew that she was being irresponsible. And Mrs. Logan was not one to tolerate lax workers.

She dressed in a hurry, managed to gulp a cup of tea and half a slice of toast, fed Kit Kat and then waited fifteen minutes for a bus. When she walked into the office, Addison was sitting in her chair.

Addison was sitting in her chair and rifling through her drawers.

Miss Turnipseed stood in front of Addison for several minutes before Addison noticed her. Clearing her throat, her face reddening, Addison slammed the bottom drawer.

"Maybe I can help you." Miss Turnipseed could not keep the coldness out of her tone. "Were you looking for something?"

"I need some Scotch tape."

"You can check in the supply closet."

Addison didn't bother answering her, which didn't surprise Miss Turnipseed. These young teachers had no respect whatsoever for age.

The question was what else were they capable of?

SHE FOUND MRS. JOHNSON at the copy machine.

Miss Turnipseed pounced from behind and whispered in her ear. "She was searching through my desk."

Mrs. Johnson was clearly startled. She dropped all of her papers, whipped around, hitting Miss Turnipseed in the chest.

"I'm sorry I didn't mean to scare you."

Right now Mrs. Johnson looked scary. Her cocoa skin had turned a darker shade and her black eyes were popping. "What do you want?" she growled.

"I found Addison searching through my desk." Miss Turnipseed had to whisper because the second grade was right across the hall from the copy machine and she was afraid that Addison would hear. Even through a closed door.

And, of course, there was her best friend, Dylan, who might come prancing down the hall at any moment, leading her fourth graders.

"So what?" Mrs. Johnson bent down rather awkwardly to gather her papers. She began to breathe heavily as she held onto the machine while rising. "Maybe Addison was looking for something."

"Or maybe she wanted to place something in there, like she might have done before. Remember she knew Clara Edwards too. And just so you know, they didn't get along."

Mrs. Johnson didn't say anything for a moment, as she fiddled with the copy machine. Then suddenly she asked, "How did Addison get along with Mrs. Logan?"

"On the surface, fine," Miss Turnipseed had to admit. "Until recently. All I know is a few days ago, after school finished, she was in Mrs. Logan's office for a long time. And then she came out, crying."

"Let me ask you a question," Mrs. Johnson said suddenly. "Have you ever rented a storage unit?"

"A what?"

"A storage unit."

Miss Turnipseed thought that was a very peculiar question. She tilted her head and asked Mrs. Johnson if she was looking for a recommendation.

"No, nothing like that."

"I've never had anything to store." Miss Turnipseed could not keep the sadness out of her voice.

"Just wondering," Mrs. Johnson said in an airy manner and she gathered her papers.

"St. Polycarp. Can I help you?"

"This is Sister Maria Constance, the superintendent." Miss Turnipseed knew exactly who she was. "I need to speak to Mrs. Logan."

"Please hold on, Sister."

Mrs. Logan was on the phone discussing subtraction regrouping with an anxious parent, so Miss Turnipseed wrote her a note and slid it across the desk. Mrs. Logan put a rapid end to the conversation.

"Hello, Sister. What can I do for you?" And then she motioned for Miss Turnipseed to close the door on her way out, which Miss Turnipseed did with some reluctance.

A moment later Mrs. Logan came flying out of her office, grabbed her coat from the coat rack and announced that she was going to an emergency meeting at the diocese. "I should be back in about an hour," she told Miss Turnipseed.

Miss Turnipseed felt the usual buoyancy, when the boss was away, but seconds later her elation turned to panic. What if the diocese had received the Corey Check? What if the meeting was about her? What if she was about to get fired?

AFTER TAKING SEVERAL messages for Mrs. Logan and distributing the mail into the teachers' boxes—Mrs. Hopwood's box was particularly troublesome, loaded with dated catalogs and magazines and even a handwritten note from a parent—Miss Turnipseed returned to her desk.

It was getting close to dismissal time but she still had to drop the messages and the mail onto Mrs. Logan's desk. She walked into the room, overcome by the musky scent, holding her breath, as the smell filled her nostrils.

Then she noticed that one of the drawers of the file cabinet was open. And not just any drawer. The one that Mrs. Logan always kept locked.

Considering everything that had happened in the

past, Miss Turnipseed would definitely be better off in the dark.

But her curiosity outweighed her common sense, and she found herself closing the office door, and then very carefully and very quietly opening the forbidden file drawer.

In the back of color coded files she discovered Mrs. Logan's luncheon container. The folders themselves were neatly arranged in alphabetic order and Miss Turnipseed was surprised that Mrs. Logan had kept files on all of the teachers who taught at St. Jude's.

Of course, it would be reasonable that Dylan's, Addison's and Taylor's would be there, but she couldn't think for the life of her, why Mrs. Logan had kept Clara Edwards's.

Miss Turnipseed removed Clara's file and decided to have a peek. She fully expected to see teachers' observations and employee contracts—emergency information.

Instead she found something completely different.

And suddenly she was very afraid.

SEVENTY

Mrs. Hopwood was in the middle of explaining the difference between the nominative and the objective cases in grammar when Mrs. Johnson came marching into her room.

Mrs. Hopwood shoved her into the hall and cautioned her that they shouldn't be fraternizing during teaching time.

"Mrs. Logan left the building. And why are you teaching cases in English? No one cares about those anymore."

"I do. It's the only way to learn how to speak correctly."

Mrs. Johnson shook her head. "Miss Turnipseed cornered me near the copy machine. She told me that she caught Addison going through her desk. And that Addison came out of Mrs. Logan's office, crying a few days ago."

"So I was right!" Mrs. Hopwood was keeping her eye on her classroom. Not that it did much good. The students were already out of their seats.

"I was thinking about what you said." Mrs. Johnson's voice dropped down an octave. "Remember when Bertha stopped and told someone that she looked familiar? It could have been Miss Turnipseed, but Addison was standing right there. Remember she was looking for bulletin board paper? Addison even told Bertha that Bertha didn't look familiar. It all ties in."

"What can we do now?" Mrs. Hopwood was feeling rather grumpy. Her stomach hurt and she was coming down with a headache. "Can we go to the police? We don't have any proof. And the last time I was there, when I was taking the lie detector test, I accused Miss Turnipseed."

"Speaking of Miss Turnipseed," Mrs. Johnson was edging towards her classroom. "She cornered me by the copy machine. I asked her about the storage unit. She denied ever having one. And, quite frankly, she doesn't look like the sort of woman who would let her belongings out of her sight for five minutes. She also told me that she caught Addison looking through her drawers."

"That's enough!" Mrs. Johnson bellowed as she stepped into Mrs. Hopwood's classroom. "Anyone caught out of his seat will stay after school with me! Is that understood?!" The students scrambled back to their places.

Mrs. Hopwood knew that it was an empty threat. Mrs. Johnson hated to stay after school.

Nevertheless, a hush fell over the class.

"Remember this too," Mrs. Johnson went back to her mumbling. "Addison might have been afraid that Mrs. Arlington would remember seeing her with George, and somehow the affair would leak out. So for that reason, she put the blame on George's mother."

Mrs. Hopwood was just about to say that all made sense, when she saw Addison parading down the hall.

And the way that Addison was glowering at them, Mrs. Hopwood thought that Addison might just be thinking about committing another murder.

Mrs. Hopwood was forced to endure lunch without Mrs. Johnson, since Mrs. Johnson was doing the dreaded lunch duty. She was alone in the teachers' room, trying to enjoy her dry turkey sandwich on a hard roll when Addison walked in.

Mrs. Hopwood immediately took out her phone to check her e-mail, but out of the corner of her eye, she watched as Addison unwrapped her lunch. A green salad dotted with feta cheese was accompanied by whole wheat bread sticks, a diced apple with a slice of cheese and a can of flavored orange seltzer.

"So," Addison broke her breadstick, "are you and your friend still investigating?"

Mrs. Hopwood thought it best to play dumb. "I'm sorry. What did you say?"

"Everyone knows that you and Amelia Johnson are poking your noses where they don't belong."

"Well, first of all," Mrs. Hopwood was giving up on her sandwich and starting on her Oreos, "there was some talk about me sending that threatening letter to Mrs. Logan, just because the words were cut out of my magazine. And poor Mrs. Johnson had the misfortune of being under suspicion, because she handled Mrs. Arlington's handbag, in which someone planted poison."

"No one planted poison in that handbag." Addison stabbed at her lettuce. "I don't care what people say. Mrs. Arlington just wasn't in her right mind. And Mrs. Logan was so nice to her, that's the thing. On the night of the parent/teacher conference she escorted Mrs. Arlington out so gently. Even though Mrs. Arlington was ranting and raving about what a horrible person Mrs. Logan is. Mrs. Logan even hugged her good-bye. Little did she know that Mrs. Arlington was planning to poison her."

"Well," Mrs. Hopwood decided she'd rather be in the classroom, "if what you're saying is true, then maybe Mrs. Arlington didn't have a motive for hurting Mrs. Logan. Someone else must be guilty." Mrs. Hopwood looked around and saw a group of eighth graders marching through the hall. They looked very formidable, so she decided to take a chance. "Are you having some problems with Mrs. Logan?"

Addison dropped her fork and narrowed her eyes. "What are you implying?"

"Well, a few people have heard you arguing with her."

"I suppose you mean that insufferable Miss Turnipseed. Well, everyone should mind their own damn business!" She popped out of her seat.

"Except your business is with George Arlington, isn't it?"

Under her expensive golden brown make-up, Addison's face turned a funny shade of gray. "That was over a long time ago," she said in a low voice.

"But there was a question about how much you would do to keep it a secret."

Addison pointed a pale pink manicured finger at Mrs. Hopwood, who leaned back. "If you're thinking that I was involved in the murder, think again. I wasn't the one with the poison in my handbag. And I have a rock solid alibi for the night Mrs. Arlington was murdered. I was at a TRX class at my gym. Anyone can alibi me."

Mrs. Hopwood couldn't think of an answer.

"And just so you know, Miss Busy Body, Mr

Logan knows about the affair." Addison flashed a fake smile. "I don't know how she found out, maybe she saw us together. She wasn't happy, but there isn't much she can do about it. She can hardly fire me, just because she doesn't like my moral code."

Addison hurled her lunch in the nearby trash can. "Besides, she can never deny that I'm a very good teacher, which is more than I can say for you!"

And then she marched out of the room.

SEVENTY-ONE

When Mrs. Johnson was through with recess duty—and after almost getting hit in the head with a basketball—she went to the empty teachers' room and called George Arlington.

He answered right away.

"How are you feeling?" she asked out of sheer politeness.

"I'm hanging in there."

From his tone Mrs. Johnson knew that he was lying. Well, after all, his mother had just been accused of murder, then she died, then it turned out that she herself might very well be the victim of murder.

So how should he feel?

"I just want you to know that Mrs. Hopwood and I are still looking into several possibilities. At first we thought maybe Miss Turnipseed was the guilty party, but now we're looking at one of the teachers."

"Don't!" It came out like an order.

"Don't accuse a teacher? We know about you and Addison."

"It's over," George said flatly. "And Addison would never do anything like that. She just isn't capable. But really, don't accuse anyone." Mrs. Johnson could hear him breathing hard over the phone. "The hospital called to tell me to pick up some of my mother's belongings."

"Did you find more storage papers?"

"I wish. I pulled out a dirty napkin from her trench coat."

"I don't understand."

"It was stained with chocolate."

Mrs. Johnson felt as if her heart had left her chest and was now pounding in her head. "That doesn't mean that it was a brownie."

"The napkin had the school's name imprinted on it."

For a moment Mrs. Johnson was at a loss for words. "What are you saying?"

"I wouldn't say this to another living soul, not even to my wife—especially to my wife. But I think my mother did it."

"Who killed her?" Mrs. Johnson fired back at him.

"Who knows? Maybe she killed herself."

Mrs. Johnson was quiet. And then an idea occurred to her. "If your mother did it, then she must have had an accomplice. Someone who sent the letter for instance, someone who pretended to be Clara Edwards."

"I don't know." George paused. "I'm just tired. I want this all to go away."

"But it's not going to go away," Mrs. Johnson said, "until we know for sure what happened."

George hung up the phone without saying a word.

Mrs. Johnson chewed her salami and cheese sandwich very slowly.

Too many coincidences, she thought.

She washed down her lunch with a cold root beer and then proceeded down to second grade. She was going to take a picture of Addison.

"SHE DIDN'T DO IT," Mrs. Hopwood said as she climbed into the car. "I had a long talk with Addison in the teachers' room and she has a rock solid alibi for the night Mrs. Arlington was murdered."

"Well, maybe," Mrs. Johnson fished in her black handbag for her car keys, "she didn't kill Mrs. Arlington but that doesn't mean she isn't guilty of the attempt on Mrs. Logan's life."

"Mrs. Logan knows about the affair Addison had with George. Addison says she could never get fired over that and she's right."

"Well, maybe she found out after she tried to kill her. I can't believe you confronted Addison." Mrs. Johnson pulled out a small bag of cheese doodles, two broken crayons and a blue mitten. "That could have been dangerous. I talked to George. He told me he found a napkin stained with what looked like a brownie in his mother's coat pocket."

"That stain could have been anything." Mrs. Hopwood frowned.

"Not on a napkin with St. Polycarp's name inscribed. I took a picture of Addison. I was going to go back to the dollar store and ask Mr. Butterworth if he recognized her. Maybe she pretended to be Miss Turnipseed, when she rented the storage space."

"Why would she do that? Just bring me home," Mrs. Hopwood said. "I'm feeling very piqued."

SEVENTY-TWO

IT CAME TO Mrs. Hopwood in the middle of the night, like the electric shock she suffered, when she held her blow dryer too close to the ceramic rollers.

It was the only possibility that made any sense at all.

Her heart beating heavy, she wanted to call Mrs. Johnson. But it was two twenty and if she woke Mrs. Johnson and the twin boys woke as well, the police wouldn't have to look very far when investigating her own murder.

So instead she sent Mrs. Johnson a text.

Know without a doubt who the killer is. I even know the motive. Meet me at Paddington's. Seven-fifteen.

Her mind racing, she found it difficult to return to sleep so she stayed up until the alarm clock rang.

MRS. HOPWOOD ORDERED a cheese Danish and a coffee and she waited for Mrs. Johnson, who arrived ten minutes late, looking bleary and irritated.

"This better be good." She plopped down in the booth and made a space for her school bag. "I didn't have a good night's sleep."

"You haven't had a good night's sleep since the twins were born."

Mrs. Johnson didn't bother to deny it. "So what is this about?"

"Remember when we were standing near the office and Bertha said—you look familiar?"

"Yes, and we thought she was talking to Addison."

"No, you thought she was talking to Addison. I thought she was talking to Miss Turnipseed. But none of us considered a third possibility."

"Which is? I'll have a hot tea with lemon and a piece of apple pie." Mrs. Johnson handed the waitress her menu.

"For breakfast?" Mrs. Hopwood took a sip of her coffee.

"Don't you dare judge me."

"All right. The third possibility is that she was talking to Mrs. Logan."

"All right. So Bertha had seen Mrs. Logan before. What does that prove?"

"I think Bertha saw Mrs. Logan, when she rented that storage unit."

"Thank you," Mrs. Johnson said to the waitress and she dropped the cup on the table. Mrs. Johnson mumbled that the tea looked cold. "Mrs. Logan didn't rent that storage unit. Miss Turnipseed did."

"Or someone pretending to be Miss Turnipseed did. I don't think that Mr. Butterworth asked for ID when he rented the storage unit."

"This tea *is* cold. Why can't people be competent? I'm going to have to ask her to heat it up in the microwave. Why would Mrs. Logan give Miss Turnipseed's name instead of her own?"

"Because of what she was storing."

"It's too early in the morning." Mrs. Johnson flagged the waitress and complained about the tea, just as the waitress plopped down her apple pie.

"Everyone assumed that the brownie was meant for Mrs. Logan."

"Do you think I should have some cheddar cheese on top?"

Mrs. Hopwood didn't care about the cheddar. "There was one person who knew that Mrs. Logan would never eat that brownie. That was Mrs. Logan herself."

"Maybe it's too early in the morning but are you suggesting that Mrs. Logan is the murderer?"

"That's exactly what I'm suggesting. She was smart enough to make herself look like a victim."

"Are you sure that this all adds up?" Mrs. Johnson broke off a piece of her pie.

"It's the only thing that does add up. In fact everything adds up. Let's go back to the beginning." Mrs. Hopwood tore off a piece of her Danish and took her time to savor it. To savor the Danish and to savor the moment when she would explain how she solved the crime. "When you returned Mrs. Arlington's purse to the office, you gave it to Miss Turnipseed, and I am betting everything I own, which isn't much, she handed it right over to Mrs. Logan. Mrs. Logan returned it to Mr. Arlington. For all we know, Mrs. Logan might even have invited Mrs. Arlington to the parent/teacher conference.

"Addison made a point of telling me how gentle and kind Mrs. Logan was to Mrs. Arlington the night in question. She even hugged Mrs. Arlington. Now we both know that Mrs. Logan is hardly a hugger, but she might have used that moment to put the napkin in Mrs. Arlington's rain coat."

"Addison might have suggested that, just to take blame off herself."

"How does that admission do that?"

Mrs. Johnson was too busy sipping her steaming tea, to answer that question. Instead she asked one of her own. "What does this have to do with Clara Edwards?"

"Do you remember what Pearl told me? She said that Mrs. Logan's husband ran away with a woman from Cozad. Do you know where Cozad is?"

"No, I teach world geography." Mrs. Johnson dug into the apple pie.

"It's in Nebraska."

Mrs. Hopwood gave Mrs. Johnson a chance to think about that as the waitress slapped down the check. "And if you remember, Grace said that she and Clara were from Nebraska."

"So," Mrs. Johnson said, "what exactly are you trying to say?"

"Just this." Mrs. Hopwood reached for her wallet and took out five dollars. "I think that Mrs. Logan killed Clara Edwards and maybe her husband."

"And Bertha?" Mrs. Johnson examined the bill.

"She saw Mrs. Logan, talking to her brother-in-law, just before her brother-in-law was murdered. And suddenly she remembered."

"And her brother-in-law knew that Mrs. Logan was a killer?"

"Think about it."

"We don't have much time to think. We're going to be late. All I have is a ten."

"Then take my five." Mrs. Hopwood stood up. "The storage place burnt down and everything that wasn't burned had to be moved. Including Mrs. Logan's items, which consisted of…"

Mrs. Johnson bit her lip thoughtfully. "A freezer."

"And maybe Bertha's brother-in-law had a pee

in that freezer and just happened to see the bodies of Clara Edwards and Mr. Logan. That's why he was murdered."

Mrs. Johnson grinned from ear to ear, but Mrs. Hopwood was thinking the least she could have said was, "Good work." Instead she asked Mrs. Hopwood, "So how do we prove this?"

"There is only one way," Mrs. Hopwood said. "We have to find that freezer."

SEVENTY-THREE

Mrs. Johnson spent the rest of the afternoon, calling storage units, and then helping her twins write their most vivid memories. Since they were six years old, this should have been an easy assignment. How many vivid memories could they have?

But because they were six years old and couldn't spell and were just learning to print, the assignment proved rather difficult—for Mrs. Johnson. So while she was dictating how to spell the word "beautiful" she wrote a text to Mrs. Hopwood.

Called all the storage units within fifty miles. Pretended to be Mrs. Logan first and then called back, disguised my voice and said I was Clara Edwards. Finally I tried Miss Turnipseed. It didn't matter. They had no records under any of those names.

It could be under any name. Besides, even if we found out where Mrs. Logan was storing the freezer, it doesn't mean we could gain access to it. We would have to break into the unit and then who is to say that the freezer isn't padlocked?

It could be in her garage.

You want to break into her garage?

Just saying....

"I spelled beautiful for you two times! Use another word. Pretty."

Maybe we could trick her.

Mrs. Johnson didn't think that was a good idea.

Mrs. Logan isn't stupid. Besides, that's dangerous. A woman who killed five people

Five people?

Her husband, Clara Edwards, the storage man, Bertha and Mrs. Arlington.

I forgot about the storage man.

How could you? If she hadn't killed the storage man, she wouldn't have had to kill Bertha, and then if she hadn't killed Bertha, she wouldn't have had to kill Mrs. Arlington, by pretending to be Clara Edwards.

Mrs. Hopwood reminded Mrs. Johnson that was her theory in the first place. Then she asked Mrs. Johnson the dreaded question.

Where do we go from here?

And Mrs. Johnson gave her the usual answer.

Not sure. The police won't believe us. I will think on it tonight and let you know tomorrow.

Mrs. Johnson put away her cell phone when she had to spell pretty again. The paragraphs were so badly written she made her sons write them over. She had to listen to the twins' complaining, so for the moment she forgot all about Mrs. Logan.

Mrs. Johnson was a little nervous going to school on the following morning. Now that she was convinced that Mrs. Logan was a serial killer, she knew no one was safe. Well, maybe not no one—but certainly not Mrs. Hopwood or herself, who were brazenly trying to solve the mystery of Bertha Butterworth's death.

If Mrs. Logan thought for one moment that they knew she was a killer, then there would be more victims.

So with a text, she cautioned Mrs. Hopwood to stay away from Mrs. Logan and do nothing to incite her.

Mrs. Johnson made an effort to avoid Mrs. Logan herself and, until one thirty, she was able to do just that. That was until one o'clock when Mrs. Logan came into her room, looking flustered and slightly bewildered.

"I need for you to cover the front desk from now until two, while your children are in music."

Mrs. Johnson wasn't happy about this change of plans. She was hoping to run across the street to the corner deli and pick up a coffee and a turkey sandwich.

"I don't know if you're aware of it, because you haven't been around all day."

"I was teaching." Mrs. Johnson couldn't keep the sarcasm out of her tone. But then she saw the way that Mrs.

Logan glared at her and she added with a hard smile, "I meant to drop by the office to pick up my mail."

"Miss Turnipseed did not come in today."

Probably scared to death, Mrs. Johnson thought, but aloud she said, "Is she sick?"

"I really don't know. But I just found something out, which is most disturbing. Remember I said I was going to run a Corey Check on all of the staff?"

Mrs. Johnson was afraid of where this conversation might be leading.

"I just got the results. It seems that Miss Turnipseed is a convicted felon. She actually served time in a penitentiary. Of course, I called the police right away. They already know. They already know and yet they had no qualms about letting her work side by side with me. And to think I trusted that woman with my life!"

Mrs. Johnson could barely find her voice. "What was the crime?"

Mrs. Logan's answer was a scowl. "I'd rather not say. But it's a good thing, she's not here because when she does come in, I'm going to ask her to pack her bags! I'll expect you downstairs in five minutes."

Mrs. Johnson knew that something had to be done. And soon.

She just didn't know what it was.

Mrs. Johnson took her spelling tests to correct, while she manned the desk, and then she shot a brief text to Mrs. Hopwood.

Miss Turnipseed did not turn up for work today. According to Mrs. Logan, she has a criminal history. So now I don't know what to think.

Mrs. Logan might suspect that we know the truth and now she is lying, trying to throw suspicion off of herself. For all we know Miss Turnipseed could be as dead as a doornail. We really should tell the police.

Still thinking about the freezer. Just be careful.

Mrs. Johnson could send no more texts, because Mrs. Logan opened her office door and had the nerve to ask Mrs. Johnson to type up the minutes from the last principal's meeting. Still typing with one finger, it took Mrs. Johnson nearly half an hour to finish one page.

And she was constantly being interrupted by the phone.

Until the phone call was for her.

"Mrs. Johnson, we tried to reach you on your cell. This is Mr. Stephenson, the principal."

Mrs. Johnson's stomach lurched. "I know who you are."

"Well, take a deep breath. I don't want to alarm you."

"I'm already alarmed."

"Jeffrey James fell off the monkey bars and he's in the hospital. It's all good but he's going to need stitches. Is it possible for you to come to Mercy Hospital?"

"I'm on my way."

Mrs. Logan was on the phone and Mrs. Johnson had no qualms about interrupting her. "My son is in the hospital. I have to go. I'm sorry."

A flash of annoyance flickered across Mrs. Logan's face, but that was just too bad. She could watch the front desk.

Mrs. Johnson hurried back to her classroom, gathered her coat. Before tossing her cell into her briefcase, she sent one last text to Mrs. Hopwood.

Had to go. Jeffrey James is in the ER getting stitches. Do nothing to incite Mrs. Logan.

Will call you tonight and we'll decide where to go from here.

By THE TIME Mrs. Johnson had got to the hospital, her husband had arrived and Jeffrey James had been stitched up. Justin Joseph was the one wailing and the parents had to console both boys by buying them candy bars.

While they were chewing in the back seat of the car, Mrs. Johnson got a text from Mrs. Hopwood.

Forget what we thought about Mrs. Logan. It's not true. Mrs. Logan deserves better from you and I.

Something about that text made Mrs. Johnson uneasy, although she couldn't quite say what. And her uneasiness grew when she saw the plain white envelope under her door.

"Aren't you going to open it?" her husband asked.

"It could be a bomb. Well, maybe not. It's too flat."

"Probably a notice from the landlord. Did you pay the rent?"

She had, just a wee bit late.

With a quickened pulse, Mrs. Johnson tore open the envelope.

And what she saw made her shiver.

SEVENTY-FOUR

MRS. HOPWOOD WAS texting Mrs. Johnson, who was still in the emergency room, when she heard the distinct footsteps of Mrs. Logan coming down the hall. Quickly, she buried her phone under her lesson plan book and began writing the homework assignment on the blackboard.

"Where are your children?" Mrs. Logan marched into the empty classroom.

"They're getting weighed at the nurse's office. They should be back any minute."

"I need someone to sit at the front desk during dismissal time. I can dismiss your children."

It wasn't negotiable. Mrs. Hopwood knew that. She also wasn't comfortable having Mrs. Logan in her classroom, when she wasn't there. She would probably grill the students, and then later use their answers for ammunition. But what choice did she have?

So she trudged to the front desk and answered the phones and sent the first grade student, who had vomited to the nurse and told Dylan that she had no idea how to put toner in the copy machine. Nor did she care.

When Mrs. Logan returned, Mrs. Hopwood said that she had to leave because she had a doctor's appointment. Which, of course, was a lie. But the way things were going, she might just need a doctor soon.

She went back to the classroom, cleared her desk, looked around and wondered what Mrs. Logan discovered. Nothing seemed out of place, so she dashed out of the school as soon as possible.

She was on the bus, when she decided to call Montgomery. He had a job interview and she was anxious to learn what happened. She reached into her handbag to pull out her cell.

It wasn't there.

She rummaged through the used tissues and the mint candies and the sticks of gum and the grocery receipts before she remembered. She had buried it between the pages of her lesson plan book, when Mrs. Logan entered her classroom.

But somehow she didn't remember seeing it, when she had put her lesson plan book in the drawer. Maybe it was there and she didn't notice it. One thing was for sure. She needed to get it back. What if it slipped on the floor and somehow got lost? She couldn't rest until she found it.

She got off at the next stop and waited for another bus. But it was cold and had started to rain, so she decided to walk. And walk she did, quickly. She arrived at the school, just at about four o'clock and let herself in with the key Father Felix had given her so long ago.

The school was so quiet, it was almost eerie. That made sense. Miss Turnipseed, who had recently fallen under suspicion, was strangely absent. There was no sign of the janitor.

Mrs. Hopwood, who was not about to relinquish her theory about Mrs. Logan, could only hope that she had left for the day.

Mrs. Hopwood crept up the stairs, holding her

breath and tiptoed into her room. It was neater than she had ever seen it. She was guessing that Mrs. Logan made the children clean before they left. Mrs. Hopwood opened her door and took out her plan book.

No phone.

She looked in her other drawers and then on the floor. Maybe she should call it. Somehow, though, the thought of that made her stomach flutter.

And when she looked up, she saw Mrs. Logan, standing by the door, smirking.

Before Mrs. Hopwood could utter a word, Mrs. Logan held up her cell phone. "Looking for this?"

Mrs. Hopwood shrank back as Mrs. Logan came towards her with a demonic glint in her tiny eyes. "I know we're not supposed to use our cell phones during class," her throat felt as though a cotton ball had lodged in it, "but my husband had a job interview and I needed to know how he was doing."

"But it wasn't your husband you were texting, was it?"

Mrs. Hopwood's mind was whirling. How had Mrs. Logan managed to see all of her texts? What about the password?

And, as though Mrs. Logan could read her mind, Mrs. Logan blurted out, "I found your cell phone the moment you walked out the door. There wasn't enough time for it to lock."

And then Mrs. Hopwood knew she was dead.

"So you think I'm a serial killer?"

"You know how imaginative I am. It was just a theory and really we have no proof. If you do something to me…"

"Imaginative and rather flighty. If you should disappear…"

Mrs. Hopwood had backed into the windows, rigid and trembling, but still she held her ground. "Too many people have disappeared. Clara Edwards, Miss Turnipseed…"

"I have no idea where Miss Turnipseed is. I tried to tell your friend that she's a criminal."

Mrs. Hopwood decided right then and there that it would be best to play along. So digging deep, and trying to be the actress she thought she would become, when she was ten years old, she forged ahead. "Yes, I see that now. Miss Turnipseed tried to kill you, because she didn't want you to find out about her past. She killed Mrs. Arlington because poor Mrs. Arlington saw her sprinkle the poison on the brownie. And Clara Edwards? Who knows where she is and who cares?"

"Yes, that sounds good." Only Mrs. Hopwood had not been convincing, because she heard the doubt in Mrs. Logan's voice and saw the way her posture had stiffened. "Except for that freezer. You keep mentioning that freezer."

"Mrs. Johnson suspects Miss Turnipseed. I think it could be Addison. It could be anyone, really—"

It wasn't working. Mrs. Logan was looking at her with an intense, fevered stare and an animalistic growl erupted from her throat.

Her mind spinning, Mrs. Hopwood didn't know whether to argue, to plead, to fight back or to cry out. Yet all she could do was tremble, when she saw Mrs. Logan come towards her holding a piece of taut wire.

Mrs. Hopwood wasn't going to go down without a

fight. Desperately, she looked around her classroom for something she could use as a weapon—the big statue of the Blessed Mother. Somehow it seemed sacrilegious, but her life was on the line. She would just have to hope that Mary would forgive her.

Yet how could she reach it? She slid over slowly, but Mrs. Logan was fast and managed to grab her.

Before Mrs. Hopwood could utter a scream, she heard the sound of sirens and someone banging on the school's front door. Then she did scream—a blood curdling yell that startled Mrs. Logan enough to drop the wire and speed out of the room.

Mrs. Hopwood was too traumatized to move, even when she heard policemen outside.

Then she heard the sweetest sound of all. Mrs. Johnson's voice as she raced up the stairs.

"Are you all right?" she asked breathlessly, as she leaped into the classroom.

"How did you know?" Mrs. Hopwood croaked.

"Miss Turnipseed sent me a copy of Clara Edwards ID in overnight mail. She found it in Mrs. Logan's file. Mrs. Logan used it to pretend that she was Clara, when she visited Mrs. Arlington. There is no way she would have Clara's license if she hadn't murdered her."

"But how did you know I was here?" Mrs. Hopwood's voice was raspy, as though the wire *had* been strung along her throat.

"I didn't. But I knew that Mrs. Logan had your cell phone. She sent me a text. She said, Mrs. Logan deserves better from you and I.

Mrs. Hopwood managed to nod.

"I knew it couldn't be from you. I've listened to you

for years talk about how pronouns following preposi-
tions take the objective case, so it should have been you
and me. I knew you would never make that mistake."

Mrs. Hopwood slid down to the floor and fainted.

SEVENTY-FIVE

Mrs. Johnson was feeling warm and comfy. Maybe it was the two glasses of red wine, or maybe it was because her stomach was full of steak and baked potatoes and hot bread or maybe it was because of the company.

George Arlington had insisted on taking her and Mrs. Hopwood and Miss Turnipseed to dinner and he picked the most expensive restaurant in town. The only fly in the ointment was Marsha Arlington, who insisted on coming along to keep her eye on George, because she was not convinced that he and Mrs. Johnson were not having some sort of dalliance.

Mrs. Johnson already had one husband and she had no desire whatsoever to get another.

"I want to make a toast," George Arlington held his scotch glass up high, "to catching murderers and the three best detectives I've ever known."

"You have never known any detectives," his wife reminded him.

George ignored her, as Mrs. Johnson raised up her wineglass and Miss Turnipseed, her sherry glass, and Mrs. Hopwood, her water glass. "Congratulations for solving the mystery," he said to Mrs. Hopwood.

"We both solved it," Mrs. Johnson was quick to add.

"So let me understand this," Miss Turnipseed said. "Mrs. Logan rented the storage space in my name."

"She didn't want anyone to connect her to the bodies, just in case they should be discovered," Mrs. Hopwood said. "And she tried to drive you crazy by hiding things, by taking your cat, by entering your house. She made a copy of your keys, so if you figured out what was going wrong, no one would believe you. She did the same thing to Clara. She admitted to stealing the note in Grace's shopping cart, because she heard Clara telling Mr. Logan over the phone that the letter said that if anything happened to her, the police should look at Mrs. Logan."

"Bertha recognized her, talking to her brother-in-law before he was robbed, and she was afraid that Bertha would remember," Mrs. Johnson said.

"And Mrs. Arlington?" Miss Turnipseed asked.

"The perfect patsy," Mrs. Hopwood said quickly. "Mrs. Logan knew that she would come to the school about her little boy, put the poison in the poor woman's handbag, invited her to the parent/teacher conference and then dressed up as Clara Edwards, using Clara's ID to murder her."

Miss Turnipseed shook her head. "I was afraid to return to school, once I discovered Clara's ID in her files. Well, thank God, it's over." Miss Turnipseed took a deep, satisfied breath and turned towards Mrs. Johnson. "Anything you need, well, I'll be your new secretary and I will be happy to serve you."

"You must be thrilled that they appointed you interim principal." George smiled.

Mrs. Johnson didn't miss the flash of jealousy coming from Mrs. Hopwood, but surely she was being unreasonable. Her husband had just gotten another job, a better one, and Alex had moved back to the dorm. So she should be overjoyed. Her job was secure. And really, Mrs. Hopwood was a better teacher than she realized.

"You know," she said to Mrs. Hopwood, "I think one of the reasons that Mrs. Logan took an instant dislike to you was because she knew that you would never let her get away with murder. You're too smart for that."

"Well, they got a warrant to search her garage," George said as he bit into his cheesecake. "And they found the bodies of Clara Edwards and Mr. Logan."

"What is it about St. Polycarp that invites murderers?" Mrs. Hopwood stole a bite of Mrs. Johnson's key lime pie.

"That's a negative comment." Mrs. Johnson scooted her pie away. "And we can't have any of that at the new St. Polycarp School. It looks as though the trouble has finally ended."

"Don't bet on it," Mrs. Hopwood replied.

* * * * *

ABOUT THE AUTHOR

MARIANNA HEUSLER is the author of eight novels including two prior St. Polycarp mysteries, *Murder at St. Polycarp* and *Cappuccino at the Crypt*. She is also the author of hundreds of published short stories and her mini mysteries have frequently been featured in *Woman's World*.

A retired teacher, she has taught at all grade levels in Catholic schools and also taught third grade in a private all girls' school on the Upper East Side of Manhattan.

Marianna lives in New York City with her husband, Joel, her son, Maximilian, and her little dog, Dolce. She spends her free time writing, working out, and volunteering for the Red Cross.

You can learn more about Marianna by clicking onto *www.mariannamystery.com* or by following her fashion blog at mariannaheusler.typepad.com.

Get 2 Free Books,
Plus 2 Free Gifts—
just for trying the Reader Service!

Get 2 Free Books,
Plus 2 Free Gifts—
just for trying the Reader Service!

H HARLEQUIN®
ROMANTIC suspense

Get 2 Free Books,
Plus 2 Free Gifts—
just for trying the
Reader Service!

LIS17R